When the Moon Winks

A Novel

Hope Andersen

ISBN: 978-1-7338973-3-4

Andersen. Hope
When the Moon Winks

Edited by: Linda Kleinschmidt and Alisha Bulkley

Warren publishing

Published by Warren Publishing
Charlotte, NC
www.warrenpublishing.net
Printed in the United States

For my daughters, Haldis and Kylie, with all my love.

"When the Moon Winks *is surprising and unpredictable, always funny and entertaining. Helen wrestles with challenges and becomes a whole woman, traveling from sadness to joy, learning to be open to her life. And yes, the resolution will warm your heart—it is true to life with more than one hilarious bump in the road.*"

—HAZEL DAWKINS, AUTHOR OF THE
DR. YOKO MYSTERY, *EYE WITNESS*

"When the Moon Winks *is a story that will make you laugh, shake your head at Helen, and reflect on your own choices … and leave you watching for the moon to wink.*"

—NANCY LIPETRIE, AUTHOR OF
THE WOODED PATH AND *ACROSS THE LAKE*

"*I really enjoyed Hope Andersen's new novel,* When the Moon Winks. *The significance of the title is so powerful, and I am a total sucker for happy endings! I related in so many ways to Helen's struggle to find a man, realizing she had to learn to find love and sanctuary in herself first. I loved that part of her story as well.*"

—KATY PATTERSON

"*I found* When the Moon Winks *to be a fun surprise. It is a great rainy day or beach read!*"

—CARRIE GEISLER

Acknowledgments

I want to thank my sister, Lucinda, for suggesting an idea to me that eventually led to this book. I want to thank, too, my sisters Sarah, Ursula, and Felicity, as well as Donna Milligan, who read the earliest draft and encouraged me to persevere. I most especially want to express my gratitude to my editor, Linda Kleinschmidt, for her thorough and insightful work that led to many improvements. In addition, I'd like to thank Thom Hayes, founder and CEO of 3 Llama Press, for his support and encouragement, and for putting me in touch with Warren Publishing. Mindy Kuhn and Amy Ashby at Warren Publishing have been delightful to work with. I am so appreciative of their talent, professionalism, and generosity. I would also like to thank Mitchell Community College for their assistance in promoting *When the Moon Winks*. Finally, my deepest thanks go out to my family who have stood by me while I labored over this book. Nicholas, Haldis, and Kylie, you are wonderful. Thom, my darling husband, you are greater still.

When The Moon Winks

Chapter 1

Helen Ferry watched as the waiter poured champagne into her crystal flute. She looked across the table at Frank, and for a moment felt pity for her husband. He wasn't drinking, hadn't for years, and celebrations like this one—their thirtieth wedding anniversary—had become rather lopsided. She generally drank a little too much while he sat glowering over his steak and mashed potatoes, making little train tracks in the white mush with his fork and picking the red onion out of his salad. *Where had the carefree Frank gone?* Helen wondered and sipped more of her bubbly champagne.

In truth, Frank had never been carefree and bubbly. He had always been too serious for words. Ever since she'd known him, he had surrounded himself with death. He drove ambulances in college, volunteered for the Peace Corps in war torn Africa, and then opened a mortuary.

"So, tell me what you are thinking, dearest," Helen blurted out, trying to change the chatter going on in her mind. She moved the vase of multi-colored summer roses to the side. They were now an unnecessary obstruction.

"Not much. Work."

"All work, no play makes Frank a dull boy," Helen whispered, and she reached over the table and took his hand in hers. He then quickly withdrew his hand from hers and excused himself to go to the men's room.

Helen watched Frank almost race across the room, and she felt her stomach tense. There was something wrong, something she couldn't quite get a handle on. It was probably the wine, she thought. *Is champagne actually called wine?*

He returned from the men's room. In her eyes, he was calmer, less gloomy. She felt relief.

"Did I tell you? I've gotten a new contract on a series. *The Sexual Politics of Shakespeare's Italian Plays.* They want me to do a tour with it, this time in the wine country in Italy. Won't that be delicious? We can have such a good time!"

Frank lifted his fork methodically to his lips, and between bites he kept cutting his steak into tiny strips, his mind absent from her.

"Oh, that's right. I forgot. You don't eat pasta and you don't drink wine," she remarked a bit annoyed.

All Helen wanted, all she ever really wanted, was appreciation for all she had accomplished. Never getting it from Frank, she turned into a solo warrior, overcoming obstacles, shattering glass ceilings, soldiering her way to the top of her career. Now here she stood, waving a victory flag, feeling hollow and empty as she stared across the table at her spouse.

Frank reached out and took both of her hands into his, this time looking at her with an intensity that sent goose bumps up her bare arms, in a nice way. Indeed, Helen felt the promise of something good ahead. Affection and adoration were around the bend, she thought. She felt herself getting warm with desire. She gazed at him provocatively, determined to seduce him. It had been too long. Frank might not have been much, but he was hers. If she had to, Helen could always close her eyes and dream he was someone else.

But they finished their entrées in silence, passed on dessert, and made their way home.

Chapter 2

The next morning, Helen woke from dreams of oceans, beaches, and frosty drinks to the chill air of their bedroom. They had turned off the air conditioning after a long stretch of late summer heat and had left the windows open to a forecast of cooler temperatures. The cool air felt divine, Helen thought, and she hugged her pillow tightly to her chest. The perfect beginning to a perfect Saturday. At dinner the night before, Frank had promised her a surprise. This dear, solid, slightly boring Frank, who had stuck by her all these years, had a surprise. She imagined he would go the traditional route and give her ropes of pearls, all milky and luminescent. She would wear them with her little black dress as they went out to dinner, again, and he ate the same things he always ate, again. Filet mignon. Mashed potatoes. Salad.

God! Life with Frank was so boring and predictable. She should have known, but how could she have known when she first met him as an undergraduate? He sat behind her every day in Astronomy 101, a little goofy and severe in his shiny black shoes and uniform, taking copious notes, but never saying a word. Meanwhile, she felt his eyes boring holes in her peasant blouse during each class. He may not have been the most attractive guy, but he was pleasant-looking enough with his duck-down hair and piercing blue eyes. Besides, she had recently been burned by Webb Richards, her high school sweetheart, so, after weeks of gentle flirtation she went ahead and made the play.

"How are you liking this class?" she asked him as they stood outside one cold fall night tracking constellations, which was difficult because of the full moon.

"It's all right. Just getting a requirement out of the way." It was then Helen noticed the shiny gold caduceus pin on the collar of his jacket.

"Are you pre-med?" she asked, holding him suddenly in higher regard.

"Yes," he responded proudly.

"Wow." She hugged her notebook closer to her chest. "I'm impressed. That's a lot of work."

"And you?"

"English," she answered sheepishly. "I know, lame. Right? But I'm going on for my PhD and then to teaching at a university," she added quickly.

"Impressive," he said, and he held out his hand. "I'm Frank Court."

"Helen Ferry." Helen took his hand in hers. His skin was cool and smooth. A surgeon's hands, she thought.

"I'd like to take you to dinner sometime," he asked almost coyly. Helen looked up at the moon, not yet sure if she really wanted to go out with this goofy guy. But then, the moon winked, or seemed to wink, right at her.

"Did you see that?" she exclaimed.

"What?"

"The moon. It just winked. I swear it did! Look at it."

"All I see are craters."

And that's how Frank came into her life.

Chapter 3

Now, at sixty, she had everything. They had everything—the daughter, the house, the careers, each other—everything except their wild, youthful romps through the fields on days when the sun was full and shiny.

That could all change, Helen thought, and she wiped a tear from her cheek. *I can be spontaneous again.* With that she ripped off her pajamas and started downstairs. Then, as she left the bedroom, she caught sight of herself in the full-length mirror. She gazed at her tall, still thinnish body with only a few wrinkles and sags, and only a few strands of grey in her copper colored hair. She did still look good for a woman her age. Didn't the other professors at the college and even some of her students flirt with her, appreciate how attractive she was?

But she didn't want someone else to want her. She wanted Frank, the man with whom she had spent thirty years of her life, to want her, desire her, scoop her up in his arms and love her. She wanted the breathless energy that fueled them when they fell in love. The coolness of the room and the passion of that thought combined and she found herself suddenly covered in goose bumps.

"Oh shit," she said, and grabbing a soft fleece robe from the back of the door, she went downstairs.

"Frank," she called out. There was no response, only the ticking of the grandfather clock in the living room and the coffee percolating in the Cuisinart. She walked into the kitchen. No one was there. She looked out the window at the driveway. His car was gone.

Odd, she thought to herself and turned around. That's when she noticed the most beautiful flowers she had ever seen. A magnificent bouquet of roses, Peruvian lilies, hydrangeas, golden rod, winter berry, and more. Not just the red roses he usually bought her, but a real gathering of flowers that joined to make a glorious bouquet.

"Oh, Frank," Helen whispered and opened the card at the foot of the vase. As she read the message, her shoulders tensed, and her stomach crunched. She realized then that there would be no milky pearls, no carefree jaunt to Italy. Tears filled her eyes....

"I have to tell you, I'm through. I have found a more stimulating life elsewhere. She makes me feel alive the way you used to, but haven't for a long time. My only concern is Gracie, how she'll handle the divorce..."

She let the card fall, pulled her robe together, ran to the sink, and threw up. Several times. Then she stood up, dabbed her eyes with a wet towel. She filled the empty coffee cup standing by the sink with water, rinsed her mouth, and spat it out.

"Trading me in, are you? You son of a bitch. What a cliché that is!"

Helen, who had grown out of touch with her feelings after too many years of emotional celibacy, gripped the edges of the stainless-steel sink and focused on the Japanese maple in the middle of the yard. Frank and Grace had given it to her as a gift on her fiftieth birthday. Now ten years later, it wasn't all that much bigger. But its leaves were turning a purple crimson, the color of healthy blood.

She didn't want to kill Frank as much as scold him, she told herself, when really, she was raging and crumpling inside all at the same time. How dare he ruin this glorious Saturday with its abundant sunshine and soft, cool breeze? How dare he dismantle their sturdy life, take apart the confidence she thought they shared, and set fire to her trust?

Life, which before was a placid stream of daily routines and simple chores, had suddenly become raging whitewater. Helen didn't know how to navigate the churning waters, so she dragged herself to the shore to lie down on the muddy banks of logic where she could think this through.

Chapter 4

Questions flooded her brain. Who was this other woman? Was she even a woman, or was she a girl? A man? Was she beautiful? Exotic? Stunning? How long had they been seeing each other? All those nights when Frank had stayed late at work, was he lying so he could secretly screw her in some cheap hotel? It wouldn't be an expensive hotel of course. Frank was a frugal man. Yet, she thought as she looked toward the dining room at the flowers, he bought me these expensive flowers. Or did he? Did she? Did she tell him what would most appease my shattered heart?

Sick with that thought of Frank's lover advising him on how to break the news, Helen marched from the kitchen to the dining room, yanked the flowers out of their vase, and, back in the kitchen, shoved the flowers headfirst into the garbage. And then, for good measure, she took the grounds from the coffeemaker and tossed them on top of the flowers.

Then she poured the remaining coffee, after filling her cup, over the flowers. She watched the lilies melt like wax, then sat down on one of the hard wooden chairs that came with the set she and Frank had bought when they were first married. She wept. It was then that she noticed the papers that he'd left for her, a thick parcel flagged with bright stickies. She felt the bile rise in her like sour milk and she raced to the kitchen sink once more.

In the living room, the clock tolled the quarter hour. 9:15 a.m., and life as she knew it had ended; she put her head back down on the table and wept some more.

By 10 a.m., she wasn't sad; she was pissed. She stormed back upstairs to her bedroom, where she passed the full-length mirror again, caught a glimpse of her swollen eyes, frizzy hair, and mottled cheeks. She decided to take a shower. A very hot shower. Hot enough to cauterize the wounds that Frank had left behind. Then she thought, maybe he'll have a change of heart. Maybe he'll come back. Still, he wouldn't have mentioned divorce if he had intended to do that. Even if he did, she wouldn't have him. Not after what he had put her through. Correction: was putting her through.

As she turned off the water and stepped out on the plush mat, she asked herself, *how could I not have seen this coming?* She wrapped herself in a thick terry towel, then wiped the steam away from the mirror over the sink. *You didn't see because you didn't want to see. You're in denial.*

When she really thought about it, she'd been in denial for a very long time. Frank's long hours at work and weekends spent on business. What mortician needed to spend so many hours with the grieving and the dead? Those days when he came home smelling of perfume he gave her the excuse that the family members had been hugging him. What a crock of shit that was! All along it was her. Her! Who was she? Was it some grieving widow he'd met while providing his services?

Was it someone at work he had never told her about? It couldn't be that one with the boobs ... or could it?

Helen yanked at her hair with a brush, thought about applying makeup, and then decided not to. She didn't want anything coming between her and reality. If Frank did come through that door, she wanted him to see just what a mess he'd made of her life. On second thought, she said to herself, I should make myself look fantastic so he will be sorry he ever even thought of leaving me. She quickly applied foundation, blush, eyeliner, a hint of shadow, and lipstick and emerged looking as radiant as she had felt just two hours earlier.

She pulled on a pair of jeans that hugged her butt nicely and buttoned up the softest eggplant colored chenille blouse she could find, leaving the first two buttons undone to allow just a bit of cleavage to show. Then she wiggled her feet into a pair of comfortable brown leather moccasins, and headed toward the stairs. She stopped long enough to push some silver bangles up her left arm and remove her wedding band and engagement ring. She lay them in a little bowl she had bought on a trip to Italy long ago.

Back in the kitchen, she opened the fridge and saw two bottles of her favorite wine. Frank had remembered. "You bastard," she said aloud. "How can you be so sweet and yet so cruel?" But she pulled the bottles out and took them and a wine glass out onto the patio. "What's a yardarm anyway?" she said as the grandfather clock in the living room chimed half past the hour.

She let the door slam behind her.

Helen sat on the patio at their small, round table surrounded by a magnificent garden. All her life she had loved flowers, but it wasn't until Grace was grown that she'd had time to devote to her passion. Now a decade later, she could truly enjoy the fruits of her labor. She sat very still and inventoried the plants around her, at least what was left of the spectacular display shining earlier in the summer. There were still some blossoms left—purple asters and golden black-eyed Susans, leggy cleome that looked like something from a science fiction movie, white phlox, and white hydrangea that mounded like a smoky cloud, and late red knockout roses that blasted color so bright you could almost hear it. The winterberry was brilliant and shiny. And the white anemone didn't look too bad either.

"Why am I doing this?" she asked herself. "Taking stock of the garden. It's my life that needs attending to." She opened a bottle of wine, poured herself a full glass, and chugged it. She filled the glass again. She started to glance over the papers Frank had left for her. She had barely gotten to "irreconcilable differences" when she heard someone call.

Chapter 5

"Drinking alone? May I join you?" Gloria Stiles, her backyard neighbor, stood at the one spot in the fence not concealed by rosebushes. A sixty-four-year-old divorcee who had made out well in the settlement, she dressed and acted twenty years younger. Today she was wearing leopard-print leggings and a black scoop-necked tunic, pulled together by a chunky chain belt and a mass of gold bangles to match, all of which, given her impossibly high gold sandals, set off her svelte figure extremely well. *Too bad,* a slowly inebriating Helen thought, *she has the face of an aging coon hound.*

"Certainly," Helen replied. "Why not?"

"Where's Frank?" Gloria inquired, helping herself to a dose of wine in her own over-sized glass.

"Don't know. Don't care," Helen took another swig from her much smaller cup.

"Little tiff?" Gloria probed, as she always did. Her "curiosity" caused her to be known as the community gossip, a title she wore like a rhinestone crown.

Helen had known Gloria for a quarter of a century. They had been back door neighbors for twenty-five years. At first, Gloria, snob that she was, avoided Helen and Frank. "They may have bought into the neighborhood," she told whoever would listen, "but they don't have two pennies to rub together. They simply don't belong." For many years they didn't, and they were ostracized by Gloria and her affluent friends.

Then, celebrity happened. An exercise that Helen used with her students at Yale, pairing unlikely Shakespearian characters with famous women—King Lear and Hillary Clinton; Lady Macbeth and Gloria Steinem—and putting them at the dinner table together, where all sorts of things aside from conversation occurred, was picked up by the Yale Rep, caught a famous alumna's attention, and became an Off-Broadway sensation. *Couples in Conflict* became all the rage. Suddenly, Gloria and her fleet had nothing but good to say about Helen, who was now appearing on talk shows and sporadically popping up on the covers of magazines.

The years went by. Helen's career flourished, while Frank's maintained a steady growth, and Sal, Gloria's husband, received promotion after promotion at his investment banking firm. Only Gloria stagnated, selling women's apparel at Bamberger's until it became Macy's and she quit. She watched Helen bring a beautiful baby girl into the world, but suffered three miscarriages herself, failed the real estate exam six times, and endured the humiliation of Sal's affair and divorce, all the while drinking herself "to Bolivia!" as she joked, halfheartedly.

Gloria always knocked on Helen's back door, and when Helen was there, she answered, but too frequently she was out of state or overseas. With or without Helen, Gloria kept herself buoyant by gossiping about everyone, people she knew, people she had never met, people living or dead. Partly out of guilt, Helen listened but didn't partake. She was now one of the few friends who actually indulged Gloria in her lamentations.

Now it was Helen's turn, but she was not one to share her misery. Besides, she felt ashamed, so she just replied with a grunt.

"BIG tiff! And on your anniversary! Tell me all about it," Gloria wheedled, taking a cautious sip from her glass. "You know you'll feel better if you talk about it. It's a proven fact."

"Sometimes you are so full of bullshit," Helen spat back.

Gloria sat upright in her chair. "And mad too! Now I know you need to talk about it." Gloria leaned forward and took her friend's hands into her own. "C'mon Helen. You can tell me. What did he do? Leave you for a younger woman?"

Helen burst into tears, and her head fell forward on the table with a clunk.

"Ouch," whispered Gloria. "That bastard! Doesn't he realize how wonderful you are? What a catch? I mean, look at you! You're beautiful and accomplished. You have a prestigious job at a prestigious university. You've published books. You've traveled the world…"

"Stop! It's precisely for those reasons that he left me. He wants someone, he says, who needs him. Who makes him feel like a man," Helen now moaned miserably, knowing that she had indeed put career ahead of all else, but only because he had ignored her. It was a vicious catch-22 with no winners, only the bodies left behind.

"You didn't make him feel like a man?" Gloria asked, her right eyebrow arched precariously.

"Evidently not. I guess I was too independent or something," Helen confessed, fully aware that she was at least partially responsible for their marriage's demise. Though really, she had just been trying to contribute, to pay for Gracie's private school, to pay off their mortgage, and to also indulge them in a nice vacation every once in a while.

"Why wouldn't he be happy that you were making a good living?" Gloria asked, baffled.

"I don't know, and I don't care. Well, I do actually care, but I can't afford to care," Helen tried to explain.

"I've got you," Gloria refilled her glass halfway, then slapped the bottle to see where the rest of the wine had gone.

The two women sat in silence and drank, as the bees hummed in the flowers and an occasional car drove by with a whoosh of wheels. The sun shone down through the trees and made small stars in their glasses, which Gloria then reached over to refill. Helen covered hers with her hand.

"No more for me. Thanks." She felt slightly woozy and sick to her stomach. She questioned whether her current course of action, getting shitfaced, was the best choice under the circumstances.

"What, are you a lightweight? This situation deserves a good drunk!" Gloria encouraged her friend.

"Thanks, but no. I need to make a plan instead."

"A plan? So soon? Are you done grieving already? I like that!" Gloria exclaimed, swilling her overfull wine glass and spilling it on her blouse. "Oops! See what you made me do?" she laughed.

Just then a Mayflower moving truck pulled up in front of the house across the street, followed by a black Range Rover.

"Oh goody!" Gloria exclaimed. "It must be the new neighbors! Let's go check them out!"

"You go. I'm going to sit here and brood some more."

"Suit yourself." Gloria sashayed to the corner, drink in hand.

Helen sat and tried to think, but only more thoughts about Frank and their thirty years together buzzed in her brain like the bees in her garden. She wondered where she had gone wrong. What might she have done differently? She believed she had been a good wife, a good mother. Hadn't she provided the stability in the family, the security while Frank worked his way up slowly, oh so slowly, in the mortuary business? She had indulged his morbid fascination with the dead because she loved him. She had defended him to her colleagues and her friends. She had even put up with being called Morticia by those who mocked her and her loyalty. Misguided loyalty, as it turned out.

Then she thought about Grace. What would Grace say? She adored her father. He had been the one who was there for her throughout the troubled times. Always. Grace would probably blame her.

This thinking is getting me nowhere. She got up from the table and went inside to make some coffee.

As the coffee brewed, Helen wandered aimlessly around the kitchen. It was a big kitchen with lots of airy space and a fireplace at the end by the sturdy wooden table they had bought so many years ago. Big glass windows looked out onto their yard. The deep purple clematis were climbing up the wall even this late in the season, and her bright-red knockout roses still adorned the two tall bushes that Frank had planted for her on their twentieth anniversary. She might have to leave this house. There were so many memories here, and she didn't know if she could bear the hurt. But no! I will stay here! I won't let him rob me of my life, damn it! I didn't do anything wrong.

As Helen leafed through the catalogs and bills on the table, she saw an envelope that caught her eye. It was an announcement of her fortieth High School Class Reunion, cleverly subtitled "All Grown Up." If this was grown up, she'd like her youth back, please, although remembering the angst and torment of her early years made her long not to be young, or younger, but rather to be some other. To be someone who didn't attract disaster when it came to romance. In other areas of her life, she was quite successful and content, but in the men department, she found herself miserably deficient and depressed. The coffee buzzer signaled the coffee was ready. She stuffed the reunion announcement in her pocket, fixed a cup of coffee, and went back outside.

Sitting alone in the garden with the breeze blowing the leaves on the Japanese maple and the bees humming in the last flowers, Helen thought that maybe this wasn't such a bad thing. She and Frank had been struggling for years, he in his solid, staid undertaker ways struggling to appreciate her more creative, intellectual side. The quintessential *Couple in Conflict*. They coexisted, but they never connected. Just that once, and then there was Grace. Not that they didn't have sex; they did. Long ago. But it was all very one-sided of late. Not like the passion they had once enjoyed. She had thought that was just the result of aging or at least she had attributed it to that. But now she thought differently. Sex could be stimulating well into your eighties if you really loved someone. And that fire could still burn brightly if you were with the right person. Frank was not the right person. For her at least. He had evidently thought the same, so he had gone out and found someone who ignited his desire. *So, what does she have that I don't have? Youth? Beauty? A limber body? A tantalizing tongue?*

Helen took a gulp of coffee and tried again to regain her composure even though there was no one around to see the tears slowly sliding down her cheeks.

"Damn you," she said while wiping the tears away.

Just then Gloria came sashaying down the driveway with a tall, tanned, extremely attractive man on her arm. Helen wondered if he was from UPS but there was no brown uniform, no box. "Look what I brought you!" Gloria chirped. "Just kidding. He's spoken for. Helen, this is Lou. Lou, this is Helen."

Helen stood to shake hands with the glorious Lou. When she did, the paper in her back pocket fell on the ground. She bent over to pick it up and so did he.

"Let me get that for you," he offered.

"That's fine. I've got it." As they bent down, their heads almost collided, and their hands touched.

"What is that? A lottery ticket?" Gloria asked bending in to see what all the fuss was about. Lou backed away, and Helen stood up triumphant with the paper in her hand.

"It's nothing," she said. "Just an announcement of my fortieth high-school homecoming."

Lou looked amazed. "That would make you, what? Six when you graduated from high school?"

"You're sweet." Helen blushed even though she had heard the same line before.

"He's a flatterer," Gloria chimed in. "He tried it on me. It worked."

Lou grinned. "Ladies, I am generally a very good judge of age. Now you, Helen, I'd put in your late forties, at most early fifties."

"Close," Helen smiled.

"Well," Lou continued, "if you go to that reunion, I guarantee you'll be the best-looking woman there."

Helen looked down at the sheet, folded it and put it back in her pocket. "I don't think I'll be going," she said quietly.

"Why not!" Gloria exclaimed. "You never know who you'll see there. You could find the love of your life!"

"Frank was the love of my life."

"Oh horseshit!" Gloria yelled. "He never was. You just stayed stuck together because you were both too busy or lazy or scared to get divorced. This breakup is the best thing that could have ever happened to you."

"Well, I can't go to that reunion alone. That would be so embarrassing."

"Why don't you take Captain America here?" Gloria asked, waving her glass in the direction of Lou, who just stood there, arms crossed, like Mr. Clean. "You'd make a handsome couple."

"Gloria! You can't just volunteer this man. He has a wife!" Helen cried, now embarrassed by Gloria's forwardness, and she was not entirely sure she wanted to be left alone with such an attractive man. The thought crossed her mind that getting even with such a specimen might have disastrous, but also pleasant, results.

Lou grinned his spectacular grin. "Not exactly. I don't think my partner would feel threatened by you. No offense, but you're not my type."

Helen thought for a moment, and then she caught on. "I see, I think," Helen replied, blushing. "You know lots of my friends and colleagues are gay."

"Yeah, we're everywhere!" Lou laughed loudly.

"That's not what I meant," stammered Helen.

"Relax." Lou put his arm around her shoulder. "We'll go. We'll have a good time. You'll make all the other women jealous because you're so smokin' hot. Who knows, maybe you'll find someone new."

Helen thought about the proposal for exactly five seconds. "All right! I'll do it. You know, there are three men I'd really like to look up. Hopefully they'll be there."

"Atta girl!" Gloria effused. "Let's celebrate! Now where is that wine? C'mon Lou. Sit down and tell us all about yourself. I'm dying to hear your story."

Whatever Lou said was lost on Helen. She could see his lips moving, she watched Gloria react in peals of laughter or disbelief, but Helen was lost in her own thoughts.

Where was Frank now? Was he rolling around in bed with some bimbo who had stolen his heart and who appealed to his aging male vanity? She thought of that scene in *Love Actually* where the wife catches on that her husband is cheating on her. Joni Mitchell is singing in the background, "It's love's illusions I recall. I really don't know love at all."

Maybe I should just go to the reunion and find some zipless fuck, as Erica Jong would say, to help ease my pain. No, if I go, I'll look up my old friends—Alan, Micah, and Webb. Any one of them would have been a better spouse than Frank. She had lost touch with them years ago, and she wondered what they were now doing. She would go to the reunion, and if God saw fit, she would run into them, or at least one of them. If the spark was still there, she would lure him into bed and maybe assuage her broken heart.

If only it was that easy, she thought. But she knew better. *It would take more than one night of wild sex to patch up the pieces of my life.* But still, she was willing to give it a try. Helen finally smiled, returning her attention to the conversation.

"You girls aren't the only ones with secrets," Lou offered, winking at Helen.

"You're certainly right about that. Now Lou, about this reunion. Are you really willing to go?" She had rolled the idea over in her mind and had decided to follow some advice she had heard years ago: Don't get mad, get even. She would get even, no matter what the cost.

"I wouldn't miss it for the world. When is it, and where?"

"A month from today actually, only about two hours from here, in the northwest corner of the state." Just thinking of her old school brought back a wave of memories, a cross between nausea and bliss, like eating too much Christmas candy.

"Perfect," he smiled at her.

"Seeing as you are my new best friend, how would you and your partner, and of course you too, Gloria, like to come to dinner at my place tonight? I'm really in the mood for some good curry!"

Chapter 6

Helen peeled the onion for the curry and then chopped it into small chunks. As she did, her eyes began to tear up. She was glad for the excuse and let herself succumb to a genuine cry. She might not have found Frank to be the most stimulating companion, but they did have a history and a life together. It was hard not to feel devastated by the loss of all that, no matter how hard she tried to quell her feelings.

The ache in her chest told her she'd better simply let go. As she tossed the onion into the heated skillet, her tears hit the pan, and the hot oil popped and hissed. Frank had never liked her curry. He always said it was too spicy and hot with too many unusual flavors he didn't know. To him, it just tasted dirty and was a dish only the poor ate. He preferred grilled food with no seasonings, no sauces. Then you knew what you were getting. Chicken with a few green beans and a dollop of mashed potatoes (hold the garlic) was his idea of a feast. Well, those days of bland meals and lonely nights were gone.

Helen wiped the tears from her eyes. She'd had enough of the maudlin memories. This Thanksgiving she was going to roast a turkey with oyster and chestnut stuffing and heaps of Brussels sprouts, parsnips, and leeks. She'd prepare the beet and applesauce puree she had eaten at Gloria's one year, and her potatoes would teem with the forbidden garlic. She would prepare a festival of the senses, and if she had to eat it alone, so be it. She'd sit alone and drink wine and eat until her stomach was fat and hard and stuffed with gratitude for her own life.

She actually was grateful that the long charade was over. She was grateful that she could eat any smelly concoction she wanted to eat. She was grateful there would be no more black socks in the laundry. She was grateful, ironically, that Frank had found someone to love because he certainly had stopped loving her years ago. When he planted the roses, he had said, "These will keep you company in your old age." Not us. Not ours. You. Yours. But without him. It now occurred to Helen that they had never made love again after that moment. That was truly the beginning of the end.

Who was this woman? Was she plain and staid like Frank? Did she eat corn flakes and skim milk, no sugar, like he did? It suddenly was very important that she know who this woman was. As Helen took the large chopping knife in hand, she had a thought: "I'll follow him," she said aloud. "I'll follow him and sit outside her house until she comes out." *How difficult can that be? Just stay two cars back like in the movies and wear a dark hat and sunglasses and borrow Gloria's car. He'll never know I am following him.* "That's it!" She yelled aloud to no one but herself. "That's what I'll do!"

Gloria had been sleeping off her wine on the couch. She sat straight upright.

"What? What is it? Is there a fire?" she called out confused.

"No, no, it's nothing. Go back to sleep. I just had a brainstorm."

"It better be good," Gloria mumbled from underneath a pillow.

"What?"

"The curry. It better taste good," was Gloria's muffled reply.

"The curry will be wonderful."

Once again, the house was still and quiet. Gloria snored ever so slightly, blowing air through parted lips. Helen added the chicken cubes to the skillet and sautéed them with the onion. She tossed several handfuls of frozen green peas into the mixture and showered the concoction with curry powder, cumin, cinnamon, and turmeric. The aroma of the dish wafted strong, almost bitter, up into the room.

Just as she turned the flame down to a simmer, the phone rang. *What if it's him? What should I say?* She turned over several pithy remarks in her head—Frank who? Frankly, mister, I don't give a damn. You be Frank; I'll be Ernest. The phone kept ringing with the dings and dongs that reminded her of Easter when she was a girl. "He is Risen! Hallelujah!" Only this time there was no cause for celebration.

"Answer the damn thing, will you?" Gloria growled from the sofa and pulled the pillow tightly over her ears.

Helen tentatively reached for the phone and saw that the caller was not Frank, but Grace. She quickly answered.

"Gracie?"

"God, Mom, where are you? Why didn't you pick up?"

Helen didn't know what to say. She didn't want to lie to her daughter, but could she really tell her the truth? Grace was far away in Indonesia. What if she fell apart at the news? There would be nothing that Helen could do to console her only child. Correction. Their only child.

"Mom, say something. What's the matter? Is Daddy ok?"

"He's fine. We're both fine," Helen lied bravely.

"You're lying, Mom. I can tell. I didn't live twenty-one years with you for nothing. What happened? Did Dad have a stroke? A heart attack?"

"Your father has never been better," Helen said through gritted teeth.

"Then it's you. What's going on, Mom? Are you okay?"

"Of course," Helen responded quickly, though why that was any of her daughter's business she didn't know.

"Do you have breast cancer? A brain tumor? Cirrhosis of the liver?"

"Why would you say that?" Helen felt affronted. "Do you think I'm an alcoholic?"

"No, Mom, I was just teasing to get the truth out of you."

"Well, I'm in perfect health, thank you. How are you?"

"I'm okay, I guess."

"So now who's the liar? I didn't live with you for twenty-one years for nothing either."

"Touché."

"So?" Helen prodded, glad that the spotlight was finally off her.

"Truth is, I hate this place. I hate Indonesia. It's too busy and smelly and expensive. I haven't been able to breathe for weeks. I hate teaching these people. I don't want to sound racist, but they all look the same. They grin and nod and always try to touch my hair. They are all rich and spoiled. I am homesick."

Helen racked her brain to think of just the right thing to say to her daughter, but she was exhausted and preoccupied with her own problems. She wanted to tell Grace to buck up, live with her choices, be a big girl, but all that came out was a feeble, "Surely something good must have happened while you've been there."

"Of course, Mom. I met the most amazing guy. You'll love him. He's handsome and funny, but the trouble is, he travels a lot. Indonesia isn't even his home base. He's going back to the States for the holidays."

The holidays? Helen suddenly realized. *I'd forgotten about Grace.*

"I hate the idea of being here for Thanksgiving, and when I think about Christmas, I just dissolve. I miss you and Daddy. I want to come home."

Helen thought seriously before delivering her next words. "It won't be the same this time, Grace."

"What do you mean?"

"You're not a little girl anymore," Helen responded.

"I don't want presents, if that's what you think. I just want us to be a family."

"That's it, Grace. We aren't anymore."

"What are you saying?"

Helen took a quick breath in and blew it out slowly. How do you tell your child, your only child, that life as she knew it is over?

"Daddy's moved out. He asked me for a divorce."

"What," Grace's voice was at first just a whisper. "WHAT?" She then yelled. "Why didn't you stop him? What did you do? Did you have an affair with someone for God's sake? I know Dad's not the most stimulating man, but did you have to do that?"

Helen could feel herself beginning to burn from all the accusations, the assumptions. She tried to restrain herself, protect her daughter from any disillusionment about her father, whom she knew her daughter adored, but then she thought, *why should I protect his reputation? It's mine that's being attacked.* With a blast of courage and integrity, she hollered the truth.

"It's your father who's the philanderer, Grace. Not me. He'd been seeing this woman for some time, and he finally had the balls to tell me."

"You're kidding. How could he? Didn't you know something was up? Why didn't you do something?"

"This mess is not about me, Grace. It's about your father. He's the one wearing the black hat."

"I can't believe you're not even defending him. Fight for him. It's like you don't care."

"He made his choice years ago. I can't afford to care anymore."

Grace's sweet voice became more strident. "You can afford to care, Mom," she began. "It's that you're choosing not to, just like you chose not to be available to either of us for all those years so you could further your career. It's no wonder this has happened." Grace then persisted brutally, "Dad left you for another woman because maybe she'll give him the attention he deserves! The attention you didn't give him!"

The phone went dead. Grace was gone. Helen stood in the kitchen, the curry bubbling and tears streaming down her cheeks. This time no onion precipitated the flow. She had lost both of them, and she hadn't even done anything wrong. Or had she? She had strived to be the best in her field, and she had achieved success and notoriety. But her family hated her, rejected her because she was not the wife and mother they wanted her to be. It wasn't fair that a man at the pinnacle of his career was held in high regard by his friends, doted on by his wife and kids, but she was being punished. She turned the curry to low, pulled her apron over her head and let it fall to the ground. She poured herself a glass of wine. To hell with resolve, she thought. But before she even had a chance to lift the glass, the phone rang again. It was Grace.

"I'm sorry. I shouldn't have said all that," she said as Helen answered the phone.

This conversation was more reasonable; things were always more reasonable after taking a breath. Grace apologized for being bitchy and mean. It was the surprise that had ambushed her, and the sadness that her family had become like so many others—broken, shattered, un-whole. She had hoped for so much more. She, too, was afraid of the change.

What would it mean for the holidays, for every day? Helen wanted to tell her that she felt the same. Instead, she turned to the platitudes that she thought might ease the blow a bit. "Maybe it's for the best," "I just want your father to be happy," and, "A little change might do me good, too." Still Helen knew in her heart that this change was enormous, and she was frightened by what the future might hold. Successful as she was, and as financially solvent as she could wish for, she wondered how she would weather life doing it all alone. Frank may not have been stimulating, but he knew about cars and taxes and plumbing. His foot massages were to die for, and in so many ways, he looked out for her. He was her handyman, and now he was gone. To take care of another woman.

"I'll bet she's young. And beautiful," Gracie said, breaking into Helen's thoughts.

"Why do you say that?"

"Because look at you. You're gorgeous and smart and successful. He wouldn't settle for anything less."

"Thank you, I think. But I don't really care."

"Have you seen her?"

"I don't think I care to."

"Why don't you follow Dad and go get a look? You can borrow Gloria's enormous sunglasses and wear that floppy straw hat we got you for gardening." Helen smiled. Her only daughter had picked up on her fantasy too and was running with it.

"Maybe I'll borrow Lou's car. Is a Range Rover a car or a truck?"

"Who is Lou?"

"Our new neighbor. He's taking me to my reunion."

"Dating already? I'm disappointed in you, Mom. You're behaving just like Dad. I guess I can't visit anyone this Christmas because you'll both be shacking up with new loves."

"Lou is gay and very attached to his partner. And I, for one, intend to stay single. You're welcome to come at Christmas. I'd love to have the company."

"What? Don't you need me now? I hate this place, Mom. And admit it, you could use a little support."

"I don't want you to throw your life away to help poor old Ma."

"The way I see it, it'll be a big party. Let the good times roll!"

"You'll have to get a full-time job of course. And contribute to the household."

"Done."

Helen was swept by a sudden sense of panic. She didn't want Grace back for the holidays. She especially didn't want her back right now. She wanted to piece her shattered life together slowly and without interruptions, to be accountable only to herself. She knew Grace would probably throw a fit, probably never speak to her again, but she had to do what she had to do. Only she couldn't. It was too selfish. Her daughter needed her, so she had to respond.

"Mom? Are you still there?" Grace asked quietly.

"Yes, Sweetheart, I'm here. I'm thinking, well, it's hard for me to say this, but I don't think you coming home now would be a good thing. I think I need a bit of time to pick the shards up off the floor and clean the house. If you know what I mean."

"I understand, and, I can't come home right now anyway. I'm sorry. I have some commitments, and I need to keep them," Gracie said. "So, unless you really need me.... Then I could be on a plane in a heartbeat of course."

Helen pumped the air with her fist, smiling, and looked up at the ceiling. *Wherever you are, whatever you are, thank you.* Then, she cooed in the phone, "You've gotta do what you've gotta do. I really admire your dedication and your maturity, but it's not a trait you inherited from either of your parents."

"Don't sell yourself short, Mom. Hey, I've got another call. I love you. I'll call soon! Bye."

And then she was gone.

Helen went back to her cooking, but now the smells just made her gag. If Grace was homesick, so was she for a family that stayed together with loyalty and fidelity, happiness and love. She'd never had any of that in her marriage, which made her miss it even more. Now that the farce of her union with Frank was done, she was left with nothing. A big empty house, a bottle of Chardonnay, and herself on a bright fall day. What about winter and Thanksgiving and Christmas? Who would hang the star? Her tears fell again into the pot, and the pot hissed back.

Chapter 7

Gloria walked into the kitchen, wrapped up in a blue fleece blanket, and rubbed Helen's back.

"Cheer up, gal. We've all been through it, or something similar anyway. You'll have a new man in your life in no time."

"I don't want a new man, but I do want a new man. I can't live with them and I can't live without them. What do I do?"

"Do nothing or go buy some new clothes. Get an expensive haircut. Schedule weekly spa treatments," Gloria responded.

"How is that going to help? All it's going to do is take care of the outside. What about the inside? It's inside that hurts so bad!"

"If you take care of the outsides, the insides will take care of themselves."

"Says who?"

"The Bible," Gloria declared a bit too solemnly.

"What?" Helen yelled back, grasping her hair in her hands. "What Bible?"

"This Bible," Gloria said, and she pulled a fat issue of *Cosmopolitan* magazine out of her purse. Helen couldn't help but burst into laughter. "You laugh," Gloria said a bit indignantly, "but before your divorce is final, I bet I'm sitting in the cat bird's seat with a wealthy corporate retiree, dashing through the snow in his red Corvette all the way to Tiffany's."

Helen just shook her head. "Unbelievable! Unbelievable!"

"Not at all. What we believe will come true, comes true. It's the law of the universe, and I, for one, do not intend to break it any time soon." With that, she slung her huge handbag over her shoulder, rearranged her "girls" so the bag appropriately curved, and clattered out of the house on now wobbly legs, a glass of wine still in her hand.

"Dear God," Helen prayed silently to whatever was out there. "Please don't let that ever be me." Somewhere, she thought she heard God laughing.

Chapter 8

A month later, Helen found herself regretting that she had ever agreed to return to the school at which she had led such a troubled youth. She dreaded running into the boys and girls (now men and women) who had known her back when she boozed and drugged and sexed her way through her life. She was very different now. Would they notice the difference or only see her through their own jaded older eyes? Besides, she wasn't over Frank. She had thought she would be by now. She had thought thirty days would be enough to at least erase the habit of him, but as the days grew shorter and the space between them wider, she only felt a deepening sadness that she could not overcome with bravado. She missed him. She missed him at home. She missed him when she traveled. She would miss him here, too.

"Get over it!" a critical voice blasted in her head. "He's with someone else now and loving it. You are finished. You're done." She finally resolved that she might as well have fun at this stupid reunion, although she still regretted agreeing to go.

As she crossed the bridge over the Housatonic and turned onto the campus, Helen gasped. First, at the beauty of the mountain, dappled in light, and orange and yellow and scarlet maples, and then the pines and mountain laurel, all still shiny and thick from the recent rain. She looked up on the mountain and there it was—The Rock now painted in this year's class colors, mocha and teal.

Helen remembered sneaking up the mountain with thirty of her classmates to paint The Rock at the end of their Junior year, all slightly inebriated from the booze provided by a couple of naughty boys. She remembered catching her denim bell bottoms on the brambles and slicing open the palm of her hand on a thin, sharp rock. And then there was the pot. Lots of pot. It was amazing they got the rock painted at all. Really it was just a handful of sober Classics majors who did the job, painting the massive rock cherry pink and apple green, decorating the stone with a gaggle of paisleys, large and small, and a bold '72 at the top. Those who weren't passed out or mesmerized by the artwork made their way back down the mountain, through the spider webs draped from tree to tree, the soft, moist grass and the sharp needles and stones. The sun was blazing by the time they reached ground level, and they were all starving, so they raided the kitchen to the school dietician's dismay. However, the truth was that Miss Clifton smiled as much as she shook her head and passed out plates heaped with bacon and eggs and sweet sticky cinnamon rolls. "You are just kids," she declared with an air of sadness. She had never married and had no children of her own.

Helen gasped again, this time with disgust, when she looked down on the meadow that ran alongside the river.

Well, once a meadow anyway. Now, impersonal concrete buildings surrounded by a sea of macadam had taken over the spot where they had once played Frisbee and enjoyed impromptu concerts in the grass.

"I hate change," Helen said as she pulled into the parking lot across from the monstrosity that was deemed to be progress. "Why did I come anyway?"

Lou pulled up beside her in his black Range Rover. They had decided to take separate vehicles because he had some business in the city on Monday. Besides, Helen wanted to be alone with her thoughts for a while.

"Pretty place," Lou said, getting out of his car.

"It is," Helen agreed. "Except for that mess. It's new and hideous."

"Well, given I have no idea what it looked like before, I think it looks just fine."

"Let's check in," Helen said, grabbing her bag. Lou tried to take it, but she insisted.

"We'll look more authentic if you let me be a gentleman," Lou said softly.

"Oh, all right!" Helen thrust the bag at him.

"Where to next?" Lou asked. Helen pointed to a quaint, white Colonial across the street. Set against the colored mountains, its whiteness shimmered in the sunlight. The cobblestone path leading to the front door was bordered with blue ageratum and grey dusty miller.

"Let me guess," Lou said, "school colors?" Helen nodded and smiled for the first time since they had arrived.

They entered the building which boldly announced "Admissions" on a gold plaque. The hallway was quiet and cold, and their footsteps echoed against the bare wood floors, but they could hear the bubbling of conversation, and laughter rising like a filled helium balloon. They made their way down the hall to the music stand that had a sign pointing right. All of a sudden two young people, an African American boy in madras pants and a pink polo shirt and an Asian girl in a lilac Lily Pulitzer print dress and sweater set with a strand of pearls around her neck, swooped down on them. They were giggling and out of breath.

"Oh," exhaled the happy boy. "When did you get here? We're so sorry. We should have greeted you."

"I'm Annabeth," said the girl, sticking out her hand. "It's a pleasure to meet you."

Helen took the girl's hand. "Helen Ferry. You may have me under Helen Court, but I go by my maiden name. Ferry. Class of '72. This is my friend, Lou."

"'72? Girl, you look good!" exclaimed the boy. "Oh, sorry, Ms. Ferry. I'm Trevor."

Lou looked at Helen and winked. "Told you so!"

"Let's get checked in, shall we?" said Helen, taking charge.

"Of course," Annabeth and Trevor chirped. "Right this way."

Helen and Lou sat across from the young pair at a big mahogany desk, but she found it hard to concentrate on the myriad of questions they were asking about her life and work over the past forty years. They knew, of course, that she was somewhat of a celebrity, a status that had earned her the right to one of the better rooms in the dorm, with big windows looking out over the river and a small fireplace that actually worked, complete with kindling and some wood.

"It's actually a faculty apartment," Trevor explained, "but we thought you might be more comfortable there."

"I really don't require special treatment," Helen protested.

"Oh, but you do!" Annabeth exclaimed. "You're kind of a role model."

"Dear God," Helen muttered under her breath. Lou, sitting in the chair next to her, stifled a laugh.

"Is there anything else we can help you with?" the two young people asked enthusiastically.

"There is one thing. I wonder if you have an Alan Roache registered yet? Micah Johnson? Webb Richards? I was hoping to reconnect with all of them."

"Let me see." Trevor pushed his black-framed glasses up on the bridge of his nose and perused his list several times looking for the three names. "I'm sorry, but they don't seem to be here. But that doesn't mean they're not coming. We have late registrants all the time. In fact, we arranged accommodations for twenty-five to fifty extra people because…"

"Thank you," Helen said cutting him off. "I'll keep my fingers crossed that they show up." Both Trevor and Annabeth also crossed their fingers on both hands tightly and smiled wild, strained smiles.

"Yes. Well then," Helen said, rising from her chair, "I think we'll be off."

With their room assignments in hand and their luggage taken care of by their new young friends, Helen turned to Lou.

"Not a word," she cautioned him fiercely. "Now, do you want to see our rooms or would you like a tour first?"

"I am at your pleasure," Lou nodded agreeably.

"Good. I'd like to stretch my legs after the long drive so let's take a tour. But I warn you, I may fall into a reverie, and if so, you'll have to knock me back to my senses."

"My pleasure."

"Say that again, and I'll knock you senseless!" Helen smiled.

"I think not. I am a big burly man, and you're just a slight damsel," Lou teased.

"That's crap," Helen sparred back.

"Do they say crap here? Isn't it crapola?"

"Hey, are you mocking my *alma mater*?"

"Yes, but only in jest. This is a beautiful campus. I wish I'd been fortunate enough to go to a school like this one."

"Where did you go?"

"Not important. Say, what's that building over there?" Lou pointed up the path toward the right.

Helen looked over at the massive stone structure set against the mountain, a hub for the several covered walkways with open windows that fanned out like the spokes on a wheel. Heavy ivy climbed up the walls, around the pillars, and into the doorways. Moss sprawled against the tiles on the roof. The building seemed solid underneath the massive intrusion of green as though nothing could shake it from its firm, traditional resolve.

"It's the chapel," Helen told Lou. "It didn't used to be this decrepit," she added sadly.

"Decrepit! I'd hardly call that decrepit," Lou said. "Look at it. It's magnificent! If it didn't sound so corny, I'd call it the Green Giant!"

"Corny indeed," Helen laughed.

"What about the Green Machine?"

"Isn't that some kind of vegetable smoothie?"

"Well what is green associated with anyway?" Lou asked, as the two walked closer to the church. Its red doors flashed like an ominous eye that dared anyone to make any references to Smaug. "I have it!" he piped up.

"What?" Helen asked in grim anticipation.

"The Green Monster!" he shouted, thoroughly pleased with himself.

"Really?" Helen looked incredulously at Lou. "It's already taken. Fenway Park."

"You're right. You have to excuse me though, being from California and all."

"How about we just call it the Chapel and leave it at that." She started off on the path with Lou striding beside her.

"Looks even bigger the closer you get," he commented. "Why call it a chapel? Isn't it a church?"

Helen didn't have an answer, so she just said glibly, "Size isn't everything, but I guess you being a man, even a gay man, you wouldn't know that."

"Oh, dear lady," Lou smiled. "You are so wrong on so many counts."

The chapel was cool inside and smelled of incense. When they opened the doors, organ music spilled out into the open air.

"Damn," Helen swore under her breath.

"I've never cared for organ music either," Lou whispered to her.

"It's not that," Helen replied. "I just thought I'd be able to take you inside here and show you where my friend Webb and I used to get loaded on communion wine."

Lou looked at Helen, his eyes open wide. "Seriously, isn't that like a capital offense both in the church and in the school?"

"Absolutely. That and smoking pot in the dorm rooms and swimming naked in the swimming pool. But that never kept us from doing both. In fact, it was the push. Didn't you ever break any rules in high school?"

"Honestly? I was so scared someone would find out I was a queer, I lived life on the straight and narrow. Well, not straight. I just made sure no one would be able to get me for anything."

Helen patted his arm. "Your secret is safe with me here."

Lou smiled, leaned over, and whispered in her ear, "And yours with me."

"Oh, my buddy," Helen laughed, "you don't know the half of it. By the time we're done here, you'll have so much stuff on me that I'll have to kill you." Lou looked alarmed. "Just kidding. Let's go to the auditorium. This place is depressing me."

"Why depressing?"

"It's reminding me of how boring and tedious my life has become. Makes me feel old," Helen smiled wistfully.

"Growing up isn't easy," Lou added. "But it beats the alternative. So, tell me what happened in the auditorium?

Helen leaned over and whispered in his ear. "Many years ago, I met a boy named Webb. We were cast as Titania and Nick Bottom in *A Midsummer's Night Dream.* He was smart. handsome, rebellious, every girl's fantasy, so I was on cloud nine.

When I read ahead in the script and saw that we would kiss, however, I panicked. What if I didn't do it right? But when the time came, and our lips met, and he gently entered my mouth with his tongue, I thought I might explode. Of course, more developed, and the next thing I knew we were meeting in the prop room backstage every afternoon for weeks. There was a red silk daybed, the kind you might see a Rodin model resting on, and a massive gilt mirror. Webb liked to position us, so he could watch me. He made the word 'undulating' into an aphrodisiac. That's all he'd say. I could taste him at that word. So that's why I like the auditorium. I had a lot of hours of pleasure there."

As she told Lou her story, his face blushed bright red, and he pushed her away. "Good God, woman, you were a regular slut! I'm not sure whether I should be appalled, embarrassed, or excited."

"Those were the days," Helen sighed. "Actually, I'm a little appalled now too, but I do hope Webb or Micah or Alan or all three will actually show. Then I can pick up where I left off. I'm hornier than a Texas steer. Not that Frank and I ever had sex in the last ten years. We didn't. But now I am single, and I am ready to jump in the ring again."

"There are ways you can take care of yourself," Lou suggested a bit too politely.

"I've done that little silver bullet thing, and it's not the same," Helen pouted. "I want a man, a real live man with all his attachments. Too bad you're not straight. I could take you from here to Chicago." Helen's hand covered her mouth. "Oh, my! What am I saying? I'm so sorry. Let's go back."

"Not to worry," Lou put his arm around Helen's shoulder. "But just so you know, if I was straight, you'd be just my type."

Chapter 9

Lou and Helen walked in silence back toward the dorms and their rooms. The quad was starting to fill up with people rolling their carry-ons. The air was thick with the crackling hum of conversation as friends who hadn't seen one another in a long time greeted each other with high fives and hefty embraces.

Looking straight ahead, his arm no longer wrapped around Helen, Lou asked sincerely, "Is it just the sex you want, Helen, or is it something more?"

"No," Helen said, "The sex would be okay. I want that, but I also want someone to give me a high five every time I walk in the door. I want them to be glad to see me when I come out of the bathroom and love the fact that I walk in at night. I want someone to love me. I want to be adored."

"I guess that's what we all want," Lou said quietly. "Maybe you'll find it tonight. With your friends. At the dance."

"I hope so," Helen wished softly.

"Tell me what you're wearing," Lou said, taking her hand and swinging it to and fro.

Helen laughed. "I'm not going to tell you," she teased. "You'll have to wait and see."

❀

That evening, when Helen came down the stairs in the dorm, she took not just Lou's breath away, but she took a number of other men's breath away, as well. She simply dazzled in a Grecian style white gown made of light, soft fabric that clung to her lithe, tanned body, accentuating all the right curves in the right places. Her long copper-colored hair was piled high on her head, woven in an exquisite pattern and held in place with tiny pins that sported sparkling crystals at their ends. On her arm was a serpentine silver cuff that ran from her wrist to her elbow and in her ears were slender shafts of silver that shone like bolts of lightning. There was no necklace to distract from her cleavage, but she wore silver sandals like the goddess Athena might have worn.

"They may kill you, you know," Lou declared, as he reached out and took her hand.

"Who?" Helen asked innocently.

"Any of the other women at this shindig. You're going to make all of them feel fat and ugly and old. You really do look dazzling. Absolutely perfect."

"Thank you, Lou. I'm so nervous about seeing the boys. I hope they'll think I'm dazzling too."

The two walked into the auditorium that was set up for the dance that night. Helen looked around. The decorations seemed the same as any at any other reunion in any other high school in the land. The walls were papered in blue crepe, and giant disco balls twirled overhead spewing out dots of light around the darkened room. A net of silver and blue balloons loomed in the corner, waiting to cascade down on the dancers' heads. On the stage, the DJ, who appeared to be channeling Elton John, cried out songs and twirled the disks.

Helen looked gracefully around the room, all the while clutching Lou's arm. When she saw nothing, she let go of Lou. "I am going to circulate." Lou simply nodded and went to retrieve some refreshments.

All night Helen anticipated the arrival of one, if not all three, of her friends. Trapped in the occasional conversation or dance with a stranger, she seemed attentive, but truthfully, she was preoccupied, disappointed, and pissed off. She was a beautiful woman, a Cinderella with whom everyone wanted to dance. But she was waiting for her prince, and he, they, were nowhere to be found. At midnight, when the balloons floated down, the women cried, and the men stomped on the balloons, setting off what sounded like gunshots in the night, Helen turned to Lou.

"I'm ready. Let's go." They left the hall. Helen was feeling sad and angry, angry that she had wasted so much time and money on something that she had nothing to show for now.

The next morning, they were standing by their cars preparing to go their separate ways, Lou to the city and Helen back home. Lou leaned against his car and crossed his arms.

"It wasn't exactly nothing you got out of this little jaunt. Look, we got to know each other a little better…"

"True," Helen conceded.

"And you got to know that you can have any man you want, especially the way you looked last night," Lou continued.

"But I don't want any man. I want one of those three men," she cried out.

"Then go find them!" Lou tossed back. "In this day and age, you ought to be able to figure out where they are. Look them up. Call them, and say hello!"

"But what if they don't remember me? Or worse yet, what if they do, and they don't want to see me?" Helen whined.

"You'll never know unless you try, Helen. You'll never know unless you try." The two were silent for a few minutes. Helen was thinking and thinking hard.

"I'll do it!" she burst out. "I'll find where they are, and I'll do it. I don't know when. I don't know how I'll fit it into my schedule, but I'll do it! I'll do it!" She walked over to Lou and wrapped her arms around him and gave him a big hug. "Thank you so much," she whispered.

"You know, for a woman who's got so much going for her, you sure don't have a lot of self-confidence. Always remember, no matter who you end up with, you've got to love yourself first. You'll never feel love from anyone else unless you love yourself first." He opened the door to the Range Rover and got inside. He said, "See you back home," as he drove away.

Helen stood there for a moment, watching Lou go, hugging herself tightly around the waist, and pondering all that he had just said. *Love herself first?* Not. She wanted a man. And she knew just which one she would contact first. The sweetest of them all, the one least likely to break her heart, as she had his so many years before—Alan Roache, Mr. Peace Corps himself.

As she remembered, she realized that of the three friends, he was probably most like Frank.

Chapter 10

The semester passed, bringing midterms and the dull stretch in November that all teachers dread when life in the classroom seems as drab as the landscape outside, all browns and greys and cold, relentless rain. It seemed forever until Thanksgiving break, which she did not spend cooking up a savory feast as she had bravely intended. She couldn't bring herself to do it without someone to cook for. Frank was gone. Grace was far away, and Uncle Ted, her only remaining relative, at the age of ninety-two, had been admitted to a nursing home in Vermont. She had spent many Thanksgivings at his house. He was a self-made millionaire who lived alone on 250 acres with his dogs, horses, chickens, and sheep. Those visits were some of her best memories. He had taught her how to tap the maple trees in winter and to eat snowballs drizzled with maple syrup in thick pottery bowls. She remembered cross-country skiing on the miles of trails he cleared through his woods, later taking saunas in the little shed he had built in the backyard, and rolling in the snow after too many mint juleps. She also remembered sitting in front of the fireplace in silence, a comfortable silence, not needing to speak at all, just feasting on leftovers and feeling truly loved.

Uncle Ted had been there for her throughout all her youth. When his sister, her mother, died, and Helen's father had become sullen and mean, Uncle Ted was there. He invited her to stay with him for the summers, teaching her how to grow vegetables, take care of ponies, and identify trees. He was the one who had arranged to send her to boarding school, the best and finest in the state, where he had also gone in his youth as a scholarship child. As he achieved success, he gave back to the school that had given him his start. The boathouse bore his name, as did the scholarship that funded a deserving student every four years.

Helen was proud of her uncle's legacy. But now he was in a nursing home, ravaged by Alzheimer's. He no longer knew who she was. Sometimes she wondered if she knew who she was either. She sat on Thanksgiving Day at the table with Lou and Ron and a handful of their friends, making small talk and feeling emptier and sadder with every breath. She wondered if she would ever feel happy again. Her only hope lay in the knowledge that once school let out on the fifteenth of December, she would travel to visit Alan in Chicago and then Micah in Charlotte and finally Webb in Cambridge. She was looking for a Happy New Year and hoped that she would find it somehow.

Chapter 11

On the twentieth of December, Helen stood silently in her suite at the Ritz Carlton in Chicago, looking out over Lake Michigan. It was dark, and all she could see from the living room window were the skyscrapers lit up for the night and the deep, black space beyond. Whether that was the lake or the sky she was not sure. But from her bedroom window she saw a whole different scene. The lights of the Magnificent Mile sparkled like thousands of diamonds through the falling snow. Everywhere there were lights, a torrent of lights from the cars streaming down the street to trees wrapped in strands of white, blue, gold, and red, or blanketed in green. The view was indeed magnificent, maybe more so because given this splash, this explosion of light, there was also no sound, only the quiet hum of the heater in her room and the beating of her heart that she heard within.

She wondered how magnificent she would feel when she looked up Alan the next day. Was she wrong to have made this trip? To have pursued this course of action? *But no, Alan's a nice guy. He was always so sweet. He'll appreciate the surprise.* Better to begin here, in this Christmas fairyland, where she had a shot at her dreams coming true. She readied herself for sleep, settling into the most comfortable bed in the world, a bed she hoped to share with Alan tomorrow, and said aloud into the darkness, "Too bad Frank, you're missing all this for that bimbo bitch. Amen, and good night."

Things did not go as she had hoped the next day. Helen played her role, dressing herself in a black and gold dotted cashmere dress and over-the-knee black leather boots. Then she donned her heavy black coat and muffled herself in a black cashmere scarf, a hat and gloves, and oversized sunglasses. She slinked down the street like Spy vs. Spy and arrived at Alan's building as anonymously as a movie star, bringing even more attention to herself by trying to be so concealed.

Alan's office, a spacious unit on the twenty-third floor of a twenty-four story structure, was done in angles and metal and charcoal grey. The receptionist, a lanky young woman with a severe haircut and pitch-black hair, wore a sleeveless grey A-line dress. The only color was a jolt of hot pink from the chunky necklace around her neck and the slash of pink on her lips that made them seem fat, as if the woman had just been punched. No plants. No magazines. No music. No Alan. Helen waited for hours sitting on a rigid steel chair until her back could take it no longer and she finally left, discouraged, and hot.

The second day was no better. Helen thought if she arrived before lunch, she might catch a glimpse of him on his way out to eat. But lunchtime came and went. She thought about taking drastic measures and leaving him an anonymous note, but that was not something she wanted to do. It was better to meet him face to face. As Helen rose to leave, the receptionist gave her a smirk which held some weird message that Helen could not read. She went back to the Ritz and swam in the wonderful pool, floating on her back and watching the snowflakes come down on the skylights above her. Tonight, she would order room service. Lobster bisque, Chicago's famous deep-dish pizza, and a piece of raspberry drizzled cheesecake. Tomorrow she would shop for bigger clothes and presents. It was, after all, Christmas.

The following morning, she questioned her fantastic plan as she stood in front of the most gigantic, resplendent Christmas tree in Bloomingdale's. Who do I shop for? she thought. There's Grace, of course, but she's far away. She'd never get anything by Christmas. And truly, what did Helen know of Grace now, her wants, her needs, her desires? Whenever Helen asked her, Grace always replied, "Nothing," which of course really meant "everything." All the things she never had. Helen was no fool. She could read between the lines. But she'd pick her up a snow globe just the same, as she had wherever she had traveled ever since Grace was young. And a glass ornament. And something silly like stretchy putty or a clown nose, something to make her laugh. She loved it when Grace laughed, the way her nose wrinkled and her high-pitched little trill burst out. Helen sighed. What was she doing here? Shopping. For Frank? Frank was gone. He evidently had what he wanted. "Don't go there," Helen told herself. "That's done." Lou and Ron? Something from Pottery Barn maybe, and for Gloria, a bit of unique bling. That was her list, unless she counted dentists and doctors and therapists. But that seemed too sad and desperate, like scraping a bowl with a spatula to capture the last remnants of something sweet.

Helen had been standing there nursing all her depressing thoughts when she heard a voice behind her.

"Beautiful." She knew that voice. It had been years, but the deep timbre of Alan's bass still made her flip-flop inside.

"Alan?" Helen turned and saw Alan in a camel hair cashmere coat, fedora, and expensive shoes. He was scrutinizing the Bloomingdale's tree. *What were the chances,* Helen thought, *of us meeting here?* Practically nonexistent. "Have you been following me?"

"You've been following me," he said, rather matter-of-factly, pressing his hands together and putting them to his lips. She looked at him, now startled.

"I beg your pardon?"

"Don't lie, Helen. It's not attractive," Alan remarked. "What is it you want?"

"How did you know? How did you know it was me?" She thought she had concealed herself very well, hiding behind bulky coats and scarves and hats, and wearing Gloria's sunglasses to hide her eyes. "It was the sunglasses, wasn't it?" She sat abruptly down on a leather ottoman in front of the tree, to keep herself from buckling at the knees.

Alan smiled. "Yeah. Pretty much nobody wears sunglasses in Chicago in the winter, at least not on overcast days. That, and you haven't changed at all." He took out a handful of photographs from his inside pocket that showed Helen sitting in his waiting room in her disguise, eating at several different restaurants, and swimming in the hotel pool, rising from the hotel pool, and drying herself off in an oversized white towel. The last one was Helen in her kimono robe, putting on makeup in the hotel bathroom.

"Where did you get these?" she hissed and tried to snatch them. But Alan was too fast. He had swooped them back into his coat before she could blink an eye.

"Like I said, you haven't changed," he then grinned.

"Well, you certainly have," Helen growled. "What happened to that fair-haired youth who had dreams of changing the world? The Peace Corps volunteer? The boy who nursed sick birds and squirrels and people too, I might add. The love child?"

"Oh, I'm changing the world all right. Just maybe not into that better place we all dreamed of back then. I'm rich, I'm successful, I'm famous," he grinned again, pointing to a double-decker bus that had stopped in front of the window. On its side was an enormous image of Alan in a liver-colored suit, standing with his shoulders back and arms crossed against his chest. Beside it was a large slogan, "No secret's safe with me." And his number.

"I've seen it," Helen said curtly. "Hardly something to be proud of."

"Come on, Helen. Leave your tedious job teaching Shakespeare to students who don't give a damn. Leave that cheating mortician who never appreciated you enough."

"You have been following me," Helen cried out.

Alan sat down on the ottoman beside her, his hands interlaced across his chest. "It's what I do," he smiled, smugly.

"What exactly do you do anyway? Are you a private eye?"

"No, no, no," Alan stated emphatically. "Nothing as tawdry as that. I'm an information broker. I acquire and sell information."

"You're a blackmailer and a cheat! I wouldn't be surprised if you've become a Republican."

Alan laughed. "It's a little more sophisticated than that."

"Tell me."

"I don't want to bore you."

"You won't bore me. I'm fascinated." Helen crossed her arms over her chest, as much to keep herself from trembling as to feign the confidence she didn't feel at all.

"Actually, it's top-secret stuff. If I told you, I'd have to kill you," Alan said with a big grin.

"Why does everybody always say that?" Helen sighed.

"In this case, my dear, it's true," Alan said, now very serious.

"What about if you use me as an example?" Helen asked. "What would you do with my information and how would you get it?"

"Oh, that's easy," Alan replied, putting strong interlaced hands behind his head. "None of your accounts are secure, and you share your information all over the Internet. You use the same two passwords for everything, and you never lock your computer, your phone, or any door behind you. You are living in a fantasy world where everyone is safe and secure…."

"What about the photographs?" Helen interrupted, now nervously.

"That's easy. Just have someone follow you."

"Into my hotel room?" Helen squeaked.

Alan raised his hands up into the air. "I had to make a point, didn't I?"

Helen took a deep breath. "You hack into people's private lives to benefit yourself."

"Pretty much," Alan admitted. "But what I'm telling you is confidential. Of course, everyone knows that's what I really do."

"And then you sell all that information to corporations or bad people, and you make a bundle."

"Yes," Alan responded very matter-of-factly.

"Have you no scruples?"

"Not many," he admitted.

"What happened to you anyway, Alan? You used to be such a nice guy."

"You know what happened, Helen? Girls like you happened, girls who always chose the richer, handsomer, more popular guy. I decided to become that guy. I can have any woman I want, go anywhere I want, and do anything I want now."

"But are you happy?"

"You're damned right I'm happy. A lot happier than you are with that cheating mortician and your oh so boring life, right down to your cheesy little ringtone. House in the suburbs, Volvo sedan, one child. Face it, Helen, your life sucks. It's the same stuff, day in, day out. All work, no play. Only the pretense of being a Shakespeare scholar."

"Pretense? I am a Shakes…"

"Yeah, yeah. All that and fifty cents will get you a cup of coffee."

"How dare you!" Helen rose to her full height, now indignant.

"Sit down. I'm not done. The truth is, I could use a broad like you in my organization. Someone with class to wow my clients. You've still got it. You're trim, fit, but also mature. What do you say?" Alan grinned at her. "You in? Or are you out?"

Helen sat back down on the small ottoman near the window, considering everything for a moment. Alan unbuttoned his coat to reveal a red vest with bright brass buttons and a shoulder holster with a sizable gun. What a scary asshole he had turned out to be. Helen took her lipstick from her pocketbook and a small mirror. She applied the lipstick carefully, checked herself out, and put the lipstick away. Alan was mesmerized. She pulled on her cashmere gloves slowly, one at a time, and glanced up at him with a coy smile. When she was done, she leaned back and looked him square in the eye for what seemed like a very long time.

"You're in!" Alan declared eagerly.

Helen rose, and turning to Alan she said sweetly, "Go fuck yourself," and walked away.

"You're making a big mistake," he called out to her.

Helen just kept on walking, her heart pounding in her chest like a bass drum. The cold air blasted her face, as she passed through the doors, but she inhaled deeply, able to breathe again. When she got around the corner, she leaned against the building, took several deep breaths, and wiped the tears from her eyes. "Pretense!" she thought to herself. "How dare he? My life is not a fraud."

Bells! Helen heard bells, church bells ringing, nearby. She looked around and realized they were coming from her pocketbook. It was her phone with that "cheesy little ringtone" that Alan despised. She picked up the phone and saw it was Grace.

"Gracie!" she cried. "What a surprise!"

"You're surprised? What about me? I fly all the way from Indonesia to surprise you for Christmas and when I get here, I find the house locked up tighter than a drum without so much as a shred of tinsel or a piece of fruitcake to be found anywhere."

"You flew from Indonesia? Why didn't you tell me you were coming?" Helen walked down the street to find somewhere she could get in from the cold.

"It was my Christmas present to you. I thought because of Dad and all, and this being your first Christmas alone, you could use some support," Grace explained angrily.

Helen closed her eyes and tight tears popped out and bounced off her black cashmere coat.

"That was darling of you," she said, "but I made other plans."

"Obviously."

"I'll come home straight away, and we'll celebrate the holidays together."

But she regretted the words as soon as she said them. She was on a mission, and she really didn't want anyone or anything to get in the way. She had been someone's wife and mother long enough. Now she was ready to beat her own drum or dance to her own music or do that thing that women do when they finally come to their senses and realize that this is their only chance at life, perhaps their last chance.

"Mom? Are you there?" Grace asked a bit more quietly. "Where are you?"

"Chicago," Helen replied and watched her steamy breath blow from her mouth like Aeolus, the Greek god of the wind. She really needed to find someplace to warm up before she turned into a popsicle. She then giggled, shivering.

"Are you okay, Mom? Do you even have friends in Chicago?" Grace asked, now concerned.

"Not anymore," Helen said with too much determination, and she strode toward the Barnes & Noble bookstore whose yellow lights and bright colors beckoned her. "Look Gracie, it's really sweet that you flew all the way out here, but..." Helen entered the bookstore to the tinkling of bells.

"Are you saying now you don't want to see me?" Grace exploded in anger.

"No! no! no!" Helen replied quickly. "Not at all. Of course, I want to see you. I can't wait to see you! It's just that I don't want to be at home. Not this year. You can understand that, can't you, sweetheart?" Helen's imploring words let her hope her daughter would in fact understand.

"Of course," Grace replied quietly. Helen nestled herself into the back corner of the book shelves where she could have some privacy as she talked. Looking around she noticed she was in the self-help section and surrounded with titles like *How to Stop Worrying and Start Living, Women Who Think Too Much* and *Switch! How to Change Things When Change is Hard.* There are no coincidences in life, she suddenly thought to herself.

"I'm flying to Charlotte, North Carolina, tomorrow to visit an old friend from high school. How about I get you a ticket, and we meet there?" Helen asked.

"Christmas in North Carolina!" Grace whined. "There won't be any snow."

"Probably not," Helen agreed.

"And we won't have any stockings or trifle or anything," Grace continued.

"That's true."

"But we will have each other, I guess, and that's what really matters," Grace said wisely.

Helen breathed a big sigh of relief. Disaster averted. Reason reigned. "That's my girl," she cooed to her daughter.

"Who is this person anyway," Grace asked. "Are we staying at their house? They'll probably have a tree," Grace chirped a bit hopefully.

"It's a guy. His name is Micah, and we are not staying at his house. We'll be staying at an Airbnb."

"A guy? Is he married? Divorced? Does he have kids?"

"Your guess is as good as mine," Helen laughed. She was anxious to get off the phone and end the barrage of questions. "I just know he was the quintessential jock in high school. He could play anything—football, baseball, tennis, track."

"Mother, does he even know you're coming?" Grace now asked seriously.

"Of course, he knows I'm coming!" Helen said a little too emphatically. "Do you think I'd just appear on his doorstep? He's invited us for Christmas Eve dinner."

"You? You mean he's invited you," Grace said, clarifying the situation.

"Well, I'm sure he'll be delighted to meet you, too."

"Are you sure? I mean what if you two want to be alone…"

Helen laughed, though secretly she was hoping that scenario would be so. "If I do want to be alone with him," she told her daughter, "I'll give you money for the movies and a key to the car."

Chapter 12

The Charlotte Airport was crowded during the holidays, more so than usual, but not more than Helen had expected. The terminal was a web of lines, passengers checking in or out, waiting on delayed flights, hoping to be home or somewhere else for Christmas.

Helen waited for her bag in the baggage claim. She was wearing a bright red hat with a sprig of ivy on it, so Grace could spot her easily. The problem was that there was group of elderly women, probably just a few years older than she was, all sporting red hats and purple dresses. She'd heard of these women, the Red Hat Society, from Gloria, who had expressed her disapproval of them. "Just a bunch of lightweights," she'd said. "If I join a Society, it will be called something like Wild Things or Sexy Sisters, and we'll wear leopard-print leggings and gold high heels and sit on the back of a Harley, the motor vibrating between our legs. To hell with the hat! We'll have golden tiaras to keep our hair in place!" Helen chuckled at her memory and of the image.

She missed Gloria and Lou and Ron. She wondered if what she was doing was the right thing

"Stay with the group now, Honey," said a fat woman in a purple tent dress that covered her like a … well, a tent. The woman wore heart-shaped red sunglasses and a red velvet hat that resembled a puddle. *Dear God, please preserve me from all of this.*

"I'm not with your group," she said sweetly. "I am just waiting for my luggage, and my daughter. But I understand the confusion, so I'll just lose the hat." She took off her hat and shook out her copper hair. "But you know, it is Christmas," Helen addressed the woman, "and many people choose to wear red other than your group."

Then Helen walked away. She felt as if she were swimming in a school of fish, as the huge mass of people swarmed through the baggage area, toting colorful roll-ons and carrying bags full of gifts. She kept her eye on the clunking silver conveyor that tossed the suitcases around like flotsam, until she saw her paisley case arriving. Just as she reached for it, something in her back snapped, like a broken violin string. From behind her, a hand reached out, swept the case up, and guided her away from the crowd. Now crouched over in pain, she looked up and saw the most handsome face she had ever seen.

"Easy now," the stranger said, "I'm just going to apply a little pressure here." He touched her on her back, and like magic, she could stand upright again. She looked into the blue eyes set in a chiseled face. It was topped by masses of dark, curly hair and the same sensuous lips that Jim Morrison had sported in the sixties. This fellow was, alas, young, maybe in his thirties. Certainly, too young for her. Probably.

"Thank you so much," she said graciously, resting her hand on her back. "I don't know what happened. Something pulled…"

"I see it all the time," he said kindly, handing her a card. It was a very simple message, just his information centered on the grey card with a white line at the border. Nicholas Kingsford, Chiropractor. She looked at him, skeptically, wondering whether he would now give her a bill.

"In case you were wondering, I don't stake out airports looking for clients. In fact, I was on the same flight as you, and I happened to be reading this," he said digging a book out of his satchel, "when I saw you. I wonder, would you autograph it for me?"

He held out a copy of her first book, *Tempest in a Teapot: A Friendly Guide to Shakespeare's Greatest Play*.

"Good Lord! Where did you find this?" Helen blustered.

"The Internet is a wonderful resource. And I'm a fan."

Helen took out her pen and prepared to sign the book. "Is it Dr. Kingsford or just Nicholas?" she asked.

"Nicholas will do," he said, and he smiled.

"Well, Nicholas," Helen said as she wrote the inscription, "as one fan to another, I think Shakespeare is absolutely the bomb."

"You," Nicholas interrupted. "I'm a fan of you."

Helen stopped what she was doing and looked him square in the face. "A fan of me? Are you sure? No one's a fan of me!"

"I am," Nicholas said now enthusiastically. "When I saw you on that plane, I followed you. I've wanted to meet you for a long time."

"Oh dear," Helen said a bit sadly.

"Have I said something to upset you?" Nicholas asked, now concerned.

"No, no. I'm flattered. It's just that now I suddenly feel so very old," she confessed.

"Nothing could be further from the truth," Nicholas grinned. "I'm sure we will meet again, Helen Ferry." Then he winked at her and was gone.

Helen stood there for a moment, wondering if all that had just happened really had happened. "Whatever," Helen mused softly to herself. "That was totally weird." Helen scoured the crowds for any sign of her mystery man and saw Grace, sweet little Grace. She was lugging an enormous tote, with another fat bag slung over her shoulder.

"Gracie!" Helen called out, waving furiously. Grace smiled and came trudging through the crowds like a snowplow.

"Do you think you brought enough stuff?" Helen chided.

"It's a long story. I'll tell you later. Here, can you take this one?" she said, handing her mother the shoulder bag. "Thanks. Who was the hottie, Mom? You picking up guys in the airport now?"

"Of course not. He was a gentleman and a fan," Helen stated a bit too confidently.

"A fan?" Grace questioned, now suspicious.

"A fan of me," Helen said.

"Oh please! Really?" Grace exclaimed, and then she saw her mother was serious.

"It was nice. Nobody's been a fan of me for a really long time."

"What about me? I'm your fan. Don't I count?" Grace asked a bit petulantly.

"Of course, you count. You're my number one fan. I don't know what I'd do without you," Helen whispered and brushed her lips across Grace's silky blonde hair.

"Did he ask you out?" Gracie asked as they moved toward the exit doors. Helen could already feel the cool air spilling in from outside.

"He gave me his card," Helen replied and handed it to her daughter.

"It says here he's a chiropractor in a town called White Oaks."

"Really? That's where Micah lives!"

"I just wonder how a chiropractor becomes a fan of Shakespeare," Grace asked critically as they passed through the double doors out onto the less crowded platform. There they located the rental car zone and entered another line. "What have you been up to, Mom?"

"Don't be small-minded, Grace. People have all sorts of interests. Anyway, he's a fan of me."

"RRrrawgghhh! My mom, the cougar! I never would have guessed," Grace laughed.

Helen joined her, and they stood in the biting wind and waited for the shuttle bus to take them to the rental car station.

Helen and Grace finally found their way through the labyrinthian airport and out onto I-77. Helen looked over to find Grace staring at her, a look so probing and sincere it took her breath away.

"What is it?" she asked in a gasping tone. "What are you looking at?"

"You. I'm looking at you. You seem different. Did you color your hair? Get a face lift?"

"Don't be ridiculous. Well, maybe I did cover up the grey, but that was weeks ago now."

"Well, whatever you did, you seem calmer. Stronger. I was upset at first about the divorce, but I can see now you are getting better. You're feeling better about yourself."

Helen kept her eyes on the road in front of her, choosing carefully what to say next.

"I do feel better. More relaxed. More confident. I'm doing stuff I never knew I could do before. Handling bills. Fixing faucets. Switching out lights. That sort of thing. Someone wise once told me 'there's no point staying somewhere that makes you feel less than yourself.' But I also miss our life together as a family because we did have some good times. And you were the center of most of them. You were the glue that held us together so long."

"If I hadn't gone to Indonesia, you and Dad would still be together." Grace started to cry.

"You had to go to Indonesia. We needed you to go to Indonesia, so we could learn, face the truth about who we were as a couple."

They drove silently for a while, and the silence rang in their ears not like Christmas bells, but more of a dull humming like a fluorescent light in an interrogation room.

"How long had he been having an affair with Stephanie?" Grace suddenly blurted out.

"How did you know about that?" Helen was astonished at the words that had just come out of Grace's mouth.

Gloria. She blamed Gloria. But there was no blaming Gloria now because she had driven off with the bald man in the red Corvette and was living the good life somewhere in California where they'd appreciate her animal print leggings and colorful speech. *I will never forgive Stephanie. Stephanie—the name makes me gag even to think of it. Stephanie. Staphylococcus. Infection. Germ. She looked so innocent, so sweet from the outside with her elfin, gymnast's body and her pixie hair. But if you looked again, there were those boobs. Gigantic was not big enough to describe them.*

Helen was sure that Frank had helped finance that transformation from Olga Corbett to Mae West. He had used their savings, he told her, to buy into a timeshare which never materialized because, as he later explained, it was all a sham. "Easy come, easy go," he said, and he smiled. And then smiled again as he hugged Stephanie and her new acquisitions at the funeral for Judge Winthrop, who probably had suffered another heart attack in his coffin when he caught a whiff of the bimbo bitch in her black mini dress and too high heels. She was teetering like she was tipsy because her new bosoms were so pendulous that they literally knocked her off her feet.

Helen felt it then, the beginning of the end, but she couldn't believe it, admit it, accept it because the idea had seemed so ludicrous. *To lose a marriage over a set of silicone breasts? Whatever did he see, whatever did they all see in them?* But then she woke up and looked at herself more critically. Helen might have envied the other woman, but she didn't. She actually pitied Stephanie all her trips to the plastic surgeon, her grueling hours spent brutalizing her body into its double-zero size, her deprivation, and the bitchiness that came with it. Stephanie imagined she was beautiful with her fake boobs and her fake face and lips, her fake hair color and her fake laugh. But in truth, she was just a "hot mess." *And Frank was welcome to all of it.*

"Mom! Mom, are you listening to me?" Grace's voice broke into Helen's thoughts. "I said it doesn't matter."

Then, there was silence again. Helen was crying. Grace reached over and touched her mother's arm.

"I'm sorry, Mom. I shouldn't have asked. It's not my business."

"No, it's all right," Helen wiped her eyes with her hands and then took the sleeve of her coat and wiped her snotty nose.

"Mom!!!" Grace cried. "Really!!"

"I know," Helen grinned, looking over at her daughter. "That would have driven your father wild. That's why I do it. Because I can. I can fart. I can belch. I can go around the house with no bra and makeup. But she can't. She's all done up like a doll. Tights abs and tits and face. Tight, tight, tight all the time." Helen pounded on the steering wheel.

"Mom," Grace cautioned again.

"How long was he seeing her?" Helen said through tight gritted teeth. "For years. Maybe seven. Maybe more. And it was all happening right under my nose. Stupid me!"

Grace put her hand on her mother's arm again.

"But now he's gone, Mom, and you can move on," she said quietly.

"That's what I'm trying to do, baby. That's what I'm trying to do. Move on."

Chapter 13

Helen had made their reservations at an Airbnb in the old part of White Oaks. Driving down the back roads from I-77 to the home, she was astounded by the beauty of the countryside. The rolling hills and winding roads were bordered by pastures filled with black and brown and white cows or golden-mane horses and miniature goats. A giant tractor, its wheels and body coated in mud, inched slowly along ahead of them. She would have happily inched along with it, but Grace insisted she pass. Even when she reached the more populated areas, the houses were modest with wide, welcoming porches and large, sheltering trees. The Airbnb was a simple one-story brick ranch with a front porch held up by four white columns, all wound like barber's poles with thick red velvet ribbon. Strings of icicle lights hung from the lip of the roof, and a lush wreath of pine cones, berries, and greens decorated the front door.

Grace and Helen parked their little rental car on the gravel driveway and entered through the tall gate. Inside the gate was a pool, crystal clear and burbling happily beside a deck. A pergola, also adorned with lights, was off to one side. Flanking the steps to the back door were live twin Christmas trees covered with miniature white lights and tiny red bows.

Helen stood there, her hand poised, ready to ring the bell. But she couldn't move. She wondered if it had all been a big mistake, coming to a stranger's house for Christmas. What if they didn't like her? What if their hostess was judgmental or prying or mean?

"Mom? What are you waiting for?" Grace asked impatiently.

"It's just that…" Helen realized she sounded pretty feeble.

"Oh, for Christ's sake," Grace huffed and pushed the bell. They heard the distant tinkle of bells and a voice calling "coming" faintly. Then the door swung open and out stepped a cheery, plump woman, probably in her seventies or eighties, Helen guessed.

"Happy Holidays! Come in, Helen, is it? And this must be Grace. I'm Sylvia, your host. Please do come in."

The house smelled of cinnamon and pine and all the things a house should smell of at Christmas. Grace closed her eyes and breathed in deeply. "Wow, it smells great here."

"Well thank you," Sylvia replied with a short giggle. "Christmas is my absolute favorite time of the year, you know. What you're smelling are my very special rich roll cookies baking in the oven. And of course, there is the tree." Sylvia motioned to the other side of the room where a fat tree, its star touching the ceiling, stood in all its splendor. Tiny colored lights twinkled around the silver and gold balls that hung from its branches.

"It's real!" Grace exclaimed. She smelled the branches.

"Why of course it's real, pet. I wouldn't have it any other way," Sylvia laughed.

"I've never seen such a collection of ornaments," Helen remarked. "Each one must have a story."

"Oh yes," Sylvia chuckled. "And if I told you all about them, we'd be here until New Year's. But I'm talking too much. You must be tired from your journey. How about a cup of eggnog or some Chai tea? And some cookies?" The consensus was that eggnog, lightly spiked because it was the holidays, would be best, and they both joined her in front of the fire.

Sylvia, it turned out, was a retired high-school chemistry teacher who had taught in the local school system for thirty-five years. When her husband, Arthur, died several years earlier of a heart attack, she paid off the mortgage on their house. "It wasn't much," she told them, "but we had refinanced several times, so we could travel. Best thing we ever did. It's important to do the things in life you want to do, and do them sooner rather than later. If we hadn't done that, I would never have seen Arthur ride a camel in Egypt or get chased by a herd of sheep in England as we walked across the countryside. But I digress."

Sylvia continued with her story, telling them she had put in the pool that she had always dreamed of, but Arthur had said would be "a damned nuisance and a money pit." Then she installed solar panels on her roof, so she could heat the pool all year for pennies, and she opened an Airbnb.

"Most of my guests, and I have had many, have been delightful. Educated people like yourselves, with an appreciation for my home. Of course, there was this one man," she continued, her eyes twinkling. "I can't really call him a gentleman. He simply broke all the rules. He drank and cussed and put his feet on the furniture. He ordered me around and, finally, when he whumped me on my buttocks, I told him that he was no longer welcome here."

Helen and Grace looked at one another and both stifled a laugh. The idea of anyone whumping Sylvia on the butt seemed preposterous. Sylvia was sweet, but not granny sweet. She was the kind of sweet you earn when you've been in the trenches and fought your way upward past snitches and idiots and liars. She was sweet only if she felt you deserved sweet. Otherwise, she was tough as nails.

"Amazingly enough," she said and poured more eggnog, topping it off with golden whiskey. "Just swirl that around with your finger," she instructed. "Now, where was I?"

"Amazingly enough," Grace, entranced by the old woman, prompted her, swirling her cup.

"Oh yes," Sylvia picked up her thought. "He was gone without a fuss. I hope he found some program or other to help him get better. He was really quite nice until he started in on the booze. Mind you, I like a little whiskey in my eggnog during the holidays, but him—he drank like a whale. Oh, but I do go on, don't I? Perhaps you'd like to see your rooms?"

"Yes, please!" Grace replied enthusiastically.

"Rooms?" Helen queried. "But I only booked one room."

"I know, dear," Sylvia said, resting her hand on Helen's arm, "but I had a cancellation. Something about a blizzard in New York, so I took the liberty of preparing two rooms, at no extra cost to you. My Christmas gift to you."

"Aw. You're so nice," Grace gushed.

"But I can't possibly let you do that," Helen stammered.

Grace hushed her. "Mom, please stop. It's a gift. Just say thanks."

"I like this young woman," Sylvia said as she led them down the hallway to their rooms. They stopped midway, and Sylvia opened the door to the bathroom. It was all bright white and blues with mermaids everywhere.

"These are my girls. I'm afraid you'll have to share," Sylvia said with a wink.

"Not a problem," Helen said. "We've shared many a bathroom before."

Grace pushed her head farther into the space, mesmerized by the clear bowls of sea glass, the sun-bleached wedges of coral, and the shells. There were so many shells from the most delicate and minute angel's wings to the giant cups of abalone, shining iridescent in the light. And then there were the mermaids. Tiny green ceramic mermaids and glass mermaids, and beautiful porcelain mermaids sitting on a rock. There were pictures of mermaids, postcards of mermaids, and mermaids etched into the stained glass. There was even a mermaid soap dish and a mermaid toothbrush holder set.

"This is amazing! Where did you find all this stuff?" she asked.

"Oh, here and there. You know. When you live as long as I have, you collect a lot of treasures. If you focus on one thing you love and stick with it all your life, before you know it, you're a connoisseur," Sylvia told her new young friend.

"I had a friend in high school who collected pigs," Grace offered.

"Olivia. I remember her," Helen said wistfully. "You gave her that book, *Olivia*, about the little pig."

"That's kind of how it all started," Grace tried to explain. "She had wax pigs and pig mobiles and T-shirts and games and stuffed animals. But it got to be too much, and when she went away to college, she gave it all away."

"Was she a *Charlotte's Web* fan?" Sylvia asked.

"Not so much. She didn't really like to read. But I love *Charlotte's Web*. All the underappreciated creatures and critters who come together to create something magical. A piglet. A spider. A rat." Grace left these words hanging in the air.

"Well, it could have been worse," Sylvia chimed in. "She could have collected spiders."

"EEEWWW!" Helen and Gracie both exclaimed in one breath.

"Do you collect anything, Helen?" Sylvia asked.

"Just memories. I collect memories. And not all of them good ones."

"Well, that's a downer, Mom," Grace declared.

Helen just raised her shoulders, pressed her palms upwards into the air, and followed Sylvia as she took the two them to their room.

Chapter 14

*L*ater that same evening, Helen was nestled deep in an exceptionally fluffy white eiderdown that had turned the handsome king-sized mahogany bed into a soft cloud. Even with the huge bed, the room was spacious and secure. Sage green walls were decorated with various prints: photos of big black-and-white photographs of ponderous trees bending over an empty road like children playing "London Bridge" and of paths through woods with shafts of sunlight piercing the shadows like shining swords. One photograph, however, caught her attention. There was a wall in the foreground and its stones and lichen were visible in detail. Behind it was a field filled with fog that billowed up to the tops of the trees that rested on white-looking ragged crowns.

"That's my life," Helen thought to herself, and she gazed at the painting and sipped on the eggnog Sylvia had brought her. "That is either me moving forward or me moving back," Helen slipped off the bed to take a closer look. But one can look too closely sometimes, Helen discovered as she came face to face with the print. The detail became blurry and lost its shape. She could barely discern a signature inscribed very lightly at the bottom of the print. She couldn't read it, scribbled as it was. So, she'd never know. She'd never know who. She'd never know why. But that didn't make it any the less beautiful.

In the living room, Grace and Sylvia sat in the front of the fire, and it crackled and hissed happily, occasionally spitting out sparks. The Christmas lights on the tree twinkled, and the room shone gold against the blackness that had now made a sharp descent. It was cold outside, not cold enough for snow but cold enough to leave spidery snowflakes on the windows. Grace smiled.

"I didn't think I was going to have Christmas this year," she said, sipping her hot chocolate. The whipped cream formed a fluffy white moustache above her lip.

"Why ever not?" Sylvia asked.

"My mom and dad got separated not too long ago. They are going to be divorced. Mom didn't want to relive the memories at home. This is their first Christmas apart."

"That's got to be very hard on you. And them too. Although I think they have it easier. They were separate when they came together. You, on the other hand, have only known them together. They can recreate the old, but you must create something entirely new."

Grace thought about those words for a while, sipping on her cocoa. "You are very wise," she said at last.

Sylvia laughed. "Well thank you, pet. But I think the truth is I am just very old. I've seen a lot. Maybe too much."

"If it's not too rude, can I ask if you ever had children?" Grace looked over at the old woman whose skin she thought was the color of a fawn and still as soft as a baby's.

Sylvia rose and poked at the fire. She stood there for a moment with her back turned to Grace and took a deep breath, shaking her head gently.

"You loved Arthur, didn't you?" Grace asked, breaking the silence.

Sylvia turned around. "Oh yes, I loved him very much. But we both saw so much wickedness in the schools and out. We didn't want to become those parents, so we chose to give our love to our students and help them bloom and prosper in their own way." Sylvia sat down in the wooden rocker by the hearth. "I suppose we missed a lot. You know, like having a daughter as lovely as you, but we received a lot too. Many of the students who took courage from our support went on to live healthy, happy lives. I am a 'fairy godmother' to a dozen little ones, now of course not so little!" She laughed. "My life is full and rich. I wouldn't change a thing."

Grace stayed silent, lay down on the sofa, and pulled a Christmas throw, green with red cardinals in the snow, over herself.

"I suppose that's what Christmas is really all about, isn't it?"

"What?" Sylvia asked quietly.

"Giving. Really giving. Not things, but yourself. Loving people enough to forget yourself."

Sylvia smiled and rocked gently back and forth. "Now who's being wise?" she asked.

"You know, I came home because I wanted Mom to make everything all right for me again," Grace said, sitting up on the sofa cross-legged and clutching the throw close around herself. "I wanted to repeat the Christmases past, only without Dad. But now I think I see. I need to let her move forward. See the men she thinks she needs to see," Gracie said.

Sylvia stopped rocking.

"Men? What men?"

Grace put her feet on the floor. "Sorry," she said sheepishly.

"Don't be silly," Sylvia reassured her. "I've had men on that couch with big, calloused, smelly feet and dirty socks with holes in them. Sit on the couch cross-legged and tell me about these men."

Chapter 15

Back in her room, Helen turned out her bedside lamp and cuddled down into the soft pillows that cradled her head. She pulled the eiderdown up to her chin and shivered with delight. "Heavenly," she whispered and closed her eyes to sleep. But sleep did not come. What she felt instead was a surge in her brain, like an oncoming subway car spewing sparks from its sides. Thoughts poured into her consciousness. *What am I doing anyway? I made such a mess in Chicago, why am I here to see Micah again? Would this be another debacle? What about Grace? Shouldn't we both be home stringing popcorn and cranberries and watching* It's a Wonderful Life? *No, not that movie*—Love, Actually. *No, God no, not that one either. What about* Eloise at Christmastime *with the wonderful Julie Andrews and a man you could hate and another you could love? That's what I need. But here we are staying at an Airbnb on December 23. Who knows what Sylvia is putting in Grace's head, or if Sylvia is even her name! What if Micah wants to sleep with me?* she suddenly thought. *With Grace it would be more than complicated.* But then she thought, *what if he doesn't want to sleep with me? That would be even worse.*

Round and round and round the thoughts went until Helen was physically tossing and turning, so much so that she toppled out of the bed. It was quite a drop to the floor below. Helen sensed herself moving in slow motion, imagined her arms and legs all swimming and flailing, and then she hit the cold wood floor. Landing, as luck would have it, on her right elbow.

"Shit!" Helen cried out in pain.

Footsteps. Fast footsteps. The door to her bedroom flung open, and the light snapped on.

"Are you okay, Mom?" Grace asked, rushing to her side.

"I'll get peas," Sylvia called out and turned to go down the hall.

"Please, no peas! Just eggnog and double the whiskey," Helen cried out from the now tangled web of pillows and blankets. "Actually, just whiskey, neat. Two fingers. No ice." Helen placed her hand on Grace's smooth cheek. "Can you ever forgive me?"

"Forgive you? For what?"

"For all this. We should be at home."

Grace laughed. "Are you kidding? This is the best Christmas ever," she gently lifted her mom to her feet and led her into the living room.

Chapter 16

elen was invited to Micah's for Christmas Eve dinner. He wanted her to come early, so he could show her his antique shop. The plan was to attend Christmas Eve services at his church and then eat. That was all before Grace, thought Helen. So now what should she do? It was too late to call Micah and tell him she was bringing her daughter. But it was too late not to. Sylvia had already made her own plans with friends, and Helen was not going to leave Grace alone. Not on Christmas Eve. The truth was, Helen had a vision of it all: how Micah would look, how educated he had become, how connected they would feel sitting side by side on a wooden pew, and how their inhibitions would leave as soon as they got home. They would peel off their clothes like banana skins and leave them in a heap on the floor, and they would make wild and passionate love like they had done in college. Then they would smoke some weed. Then scarf down the meal he had prepared and go to bed.

Helen, she heard a voice say in her head. *That's projection. Stay in the moment.*

"Screw the moment," she said right back. "I got into trouble by staying in the moment during my marriage. If I had visualized a happy future instead of living a day at a time, I would have left him years ago.

You don't get it, the voice said and went silent.

In that moment, all Helen knew was that she was driving a little red Ford Focus with her daughter to see an old boyfriend in a small town in North Carolina. The sun was still shining and the massive magnolia trees that lined the streets reflected its glow in their shiny green leaves. The temperature was mild, by New England standards, and many of the folks were out in sweaters and vests, walking dogs of all sizes. On the high school tennis courts at the end of the street, two couples were playing doubles, albeit with hats and gloves on because it was Christmas Eve Day. "I could live here," Helen thought as she passed a small ranch similar to Sylvia's with a For Sale sign on the front lawn.

"Don't even think it," Grace warned, reading her mother's thoughts.

"What?" Helen asked, innocently.

"You know what," Gracie replied. "Whenever we go somewhere, you want to live there. Whenever you meet a man, you put your first name with his last name."

Helen chuckled. "You know me so well."

"Seriously, Mom, you've got to stop doing that stuff. What is it you say? Bloom where you're planted?" Helen instinctively knew her daughter was right.

Suddenly, the GPS navigator interrupted her reverie. "Turn left onto Center Street," the navigator's nasal voice barked. "In 400 feet turn left on Main Street," it barked again.

"Turn that damned thing off," Helen commanded.

"But we're not there yet," Grace insisted.

"It's Main Street. Does it look main enough for you?"

"You don't have to be so mean, Mom."

"Sorry, sugar plum. I'm just a little anxious," Helen confessed.

"Destination on the right," the navigator chimed in.

"It lives!" Grace laughed.

"It's not Christmas, it's Easter," Helen added sarcastically.

They found a parking space easily, and Helen swooped in with the car. She sat there, gripping the steering wheel with both hands. "This isn't exactly the quaint location I imagined," she said sourly. She looked out the window at train tracks on her left and old brick buildings that looked more like stage flats than anything else. If a strong wind came, who knew? Down the street was a ramshackle auto and tire store, neighbored by a urine-yellow insurance company and a desolate concrete Mexican restaurant that was also for sale. The cockles of her heart were not warmed.

"Look over here, Mom," Grace cried out excitedly. "Isn't that where they filmed that movie? I can't remember the name of it, but it was about that teacher who got stalked. Off Track or something. Anyway, aren't these cute antique stores? Look at that old hardware store with the red sled! And they turned the old train station into an arts center! How great!"

Perspective, Helen reminded herself. *It's all about perspective. Shakespeare was either a genius or a bore. Life is either a daring adventure or nothing at all.* Someone tapped on the passenger's side window. It was an old man, thin, balding, leathery skin from too much sun, but still handsome. Maybe five feet eleven inches. He was motioning for her to roll the window down. Helen rolled it down.

"Helen?" the man asked excitedly.

"Micah?" Helen asked.

"Helen! Welcome! And who is this charming young lady?" Micah opened the door for Grace and offered her his hand. Grace started giggling. Then he went around to Helen's door and offered her his other hand, kissing her cheeks—first one, then the other. Grace giggled again.

"It's been too long. I'm so glad you could come."

"Me too," Helen replied, now curious.

"You look as beautiful as ever."

"You too."

Micah laughed. "Don't be a liar. Time has not treated me well." He took both their arms and led them toward the store.

"You're still fit though," Helen commented.

"Don't be so sure. I have chronic back problems from all those years playing ball. But I guess I still have what it takes." He smiled.

"I beg your pardon?" The two walked into the store with Grace following close behind. The door bells chimed, and a youngish man came out from the back. Helen gasped.

"My sentiments exactly," Micah said. "I believe you've met my partner, Nicholas Kingsford."

In the soft light here, far away from the fluorescents of the airport, Nicholas was even more handsome.

"A pleasure to see you again." Helen extended her hand.

"The pleasure is all mine," Nicholas said, taking Helen's hand.

Micah walked over and put his hand on Nicholas's back. "Nick told me that he met you at the airport. I introduced him to your books, and he is now a dedicated fan."

"So he said," Helen added dully. "So, you two are…?"

"Together five years come May," they replied in one voice and laughed.

"How nice!" Helen secretly was mourning that she had lost two birds with one stone. She had invested more than $1,000 to an obviously lost cause. *MOST EXPENSIVE CHRISTMAS EVER,* she thought. Still, knowing how her face had a way of revealing her emotions, she pulled up the corners of her mouth into a smile, glazed her eyes with delight. She pulled Grace close, wrapping her arms around her daughter.

"And this is the love of my life!" she exclaimed. "Came all the way home from Jakarta to give me a Christmas surprise!"

"Just one of many, Mom," Grace whispered softly.

"And here's another!" Helen cried. She pulled a bottle of cold champagne from her oversized bag. "Let's all drink to the holiday!"

Micah looked for the vintage champagne flutes he kept in the back while Helen and Grace browsed the antiques that neither of them really cared about. Both had come looking for something, and neither of them had found it.

After the champagne and small talk, Micah led them on a guided tour through town, which took only fifteen minutes. To Helen, the lavish Christmas decorations on the 'olde' street lamps and in the windows seemed incongruous with the mild temperatures and snowless streets.

"No polar bear would be caught dead in a red wagon full of artificial snow," she muttered as they passed the hardware store window. The jewelry store glittered like ice with silver and diamonds scattered on a snowy background. Pandora! All Helen could think of was her lost hope. *Will I ever know love, buttercup love?* She was fully aware that the champagne was speaking. It had gone to her head and was creating the maudlin thoughts.

"Look at this, Mom! A beading store!" Grace's happy voice broke her reveries. "I love this stuff! Look at that necklace!"

Helen looked into the store window and saw a most beautiful thing. A small Christmas tree covered in tiny, circular peace sign brooches that were crafted out of delicate, multicolored crystals. "I like this tree," she said pointing at it.

"I thought you would," Micah smiled and put his arm around Helen's shoulders. "My little peacenik."

"I'm not a peacenik," Helen replied petulantly. "And what if I am? Isn't it the season to be one?"

"Every season is the right season for peace, Mom," Grace jumped in.

"My point exactly," Micah squeezed Helen's shoulder gently.

Helen shrugged him off. "Truth is, I don't want to be a peacenik anymore. I want to be a rabble rouser. I want to make waves."

She looked over at Nicholas. He was deep into his phone, texting. His dark hair fell over his right eye, and his lips were parted slightly. She had the urge to swoop over and kiss him smack right on the lips. To cup his privates in her hands and lead him off to bed. But these thoughts were stupid. He's gay, for God's sake, she reminded herself and brushed imaginary flakes off the bottom of her coat. When she stood up, she had her acceptable face on, and Nicholas was gone.

"You okay, Mom?" Grace asked gently. "You look like you're going to puke."

"I'm perfect. Just perfect. Just a little warm. That's all. Perhaps we could head back?"

"Absolutely!" Micah replied. "Not much more to see here anyway. Let's see how Nick's making out with the ham."

Grace clutched her mother's arm. She hated ham. Wasn't Christmas Eve supposed to be oyster stew with trifle? Helen squeezed her back, now feeling guilty that she had insisted that they do North Carolina for Christmas.

"It's okay, Mom," Grace whispered in her mother's ear. "My friend in Indonesia always tells me, 'no expectation; no disappoint.'" Helen smiled. The words were more something you'd hear in a Chinese Laundromat than a sage piece of needed advice.

Chapter 17

After drinks and appetizers to hold them over until dinner, they set out for church. The evening was endless. The Christmas service was a pageant and took ten times longer than usual what with all the readings and hymns. There was a live crèche as well, which was in and of itself a challenge. At first, it was charming. A young girl dressed as Mary in Carolina blue was escorted by a young boy sporting what appeared to be a fake salt-and-pepper beard. They stood with their backs to the congregation and then they turned around. Pop! There was Jesus. A real live child, probably about two months old was wrapped in swaddling clothes and sleeping soundly. Perhaps he had just been fed a bottle laced with Trazodone.

One by one, the animals arrived. A little boy and his father shepherded up a few sheep, who then wandered around the manger, eating the straw and bleating. Then came a donkey all alone who lay right down at Jesus' feet. The trick was when the cow and her calf were herded up the aisle to the makeshift stable. The cow pushed her way in behind the manger and lost herself in the straw in the stall. The calf had a harder time, doing splits on its spindly legs all the way up the aisle. The children in the congregation found this to be uproariously funny. The adults did, too, when they allowed themselves. The laughter got the sheep to baaing and wandering, though not too far because the sting of the switch held them at bay. The young man who was leading the calf up the aisle was dressed in long robes and had a fake beard, too. When the calf split a third time, the young man, who couldn't have been more than thirteen, pulled his beard down under his chin, raised his staff, and called out, "That's it, Lucy! Get your shit together!"

The congregation hushed. Very few sniggles were heard. The calf, taking that wise advice, did get her shit together. As soon as she arrived at the manger, she pooped right there at Jesus' feet. The donkey didn't budge. The crowd went wild. Even Helen found it hard to stifle a laugh.

"Mom," Grace whispered, jabbing her mother in the side with her elbow.

"Ow," Helen hissed back. "That hurt!"

"Behave," Grace cautioned.

"Why? Isn't that just what we all do? Shit on Jesus and expect things to go our way? I know I do." She laughed loudly.

The organist, his pipes set to play the quietest, sweetest tone, began to play "Silent Night." Little by little, the laughter died, and voices picked up the words of that familiar hymn. The music reverberated into the air and throughout the whole church. Magically, the poop was gone; the animals were still; and the baby slept soundly in Mary's arms. Helen felt a tear flow down her cheek. Grace looked and smiled.

"There, there, Mommy," Grace said. "It's all right. You always get this way on Christmas Eve."

Chapter 18

Dinner was Southern. Ham and grits with cheese, collard greens, sweet potato casserole, and biscuits. For dessert there was key lime pie.

"So, what did you think?" Micah asked the women as he laid his napkin on his empty dessert plate. "Is Nicholas a great chef or not?"

"An excellent chef," Helen agreed. "Apparently excellent at many things." She then raised her glass. "To Nicholas."

"To Nicholas," they all said, joining her.

"Hush," Nicholas commanded. "You make me blush! What about you, Gracie? Did you like it? I know you had your reservations…"

"I did," Grace confessed. "I am a traditionalist. Christmas Eve means oyster stew and Waldorf salad and trifle and snow…"

"It's always hard to be open to something new, isn't it?" Nicholas said quietly.

"It is. This is my first Christmas without my dad, and I'm spending it with two gay guys in a tropical climate!"

"Gracie!" Helen hissed, shooting her daughter a look that was more obligatory than heartfelt. She was feeling exactly the same way inside.

"Let her talk," Micah encouraged. "Go on, Gracie."

"Well, and then this food was so different. Ham? I never eat ham! And marshmallows in the sweet potatoes? Key lime pie!"

"I'm sorry," Micah started... "We just thought..."

"No, wait! It was all delicious! Better than delicious! It was superb! And you know what else? Christmas, I believe, is what happened at the church tonight. It's all about leaving our shit about traditions and expectations and how things are supposed to be at Jesus' feet and being open to new ideas, new perspectives. You opened your home to my mom and me and you've been super kind. Thank you. Thank you, thank you, thank you. It's been a wonderful Christmas Eve."

Silence. A clock chimed 11:30 p.m. Dust motes sifted through the air, tiny golden flakes. Micah clapped, then clapped again, and Nicholas joined him. Grace hid behind her napkin, but Helen joined in, clapping, beaming. Then the clapping stopped. The table was cleared. The dishes were rinsed and stacked. Before they left, Micah, who had been "taking care of something in the back" produced two red gift bags, a small one with green tissue for Helen and a medium-size one with white sparkling tissue for Grace.

"You shouldn't have!" Helen cried, angry at herself for not having thought to bring anything but booze. "We don't have anything for you!"

"Well then you can give them back," Nicholas kidded and laughed.

"You can take hers. I'm keeping mine." Grace clutched the gift to her chest. "Can I open it?"

"Don't see why not," Micah winked at her. "It's almost Christmas."

"No, I'd better wait," Grace said earnestly. "It's bad luck to open presents before Christmas."

"Another tradition?" asked Nicholas.

"Not really. I just made it up. I'm waiting to see if Mom comes around," Grace laughed. They all looked at Helen. She was sitting at the kitchen table, staring at the little bag. "I'm pretty sure it's not an engagement ring, Mom, if that's what you're worried about." And they all started laughing so hard that they almost didn't hear the clock chiming out midnight.

"Hush!" Micah said, holding his hand up in the air. "It's time. Time to forget outdated rules and traditions. Time to accept small gifts in return for the ones you've given. Time to say Merry Christmas and mean it!"

"Merry Christmas!" they all cried and hugged and kissed. At 12:05 a.m., Helen was wearing a small beaded peace sign pin that sparkled, just as her eyes were sparkling. Grace was in the bathroom fixing an antique silver and rhinestone tiara on her head. *How did he know?* Grace wondered. *How did he know this was just what I wanted? Even I didn't know.* She walked back into the room to more clapping, curtsies, and bows. More laughter. More hugs and kisses all around. It was truly Christmas!

❀

By 12:15 a.m. Grace and Helen were driving back to the Airbnb. The small streets of White Oaks were lined with houses etched in icicle lights and tall trees decorated with colored balloons, big as the moon that looked as though it had just washed its pale face and put on a smile. It was a quirky smile, a Peppermint Patty smile on a big old wafer moon, thought Grace, as she drove dressed in her twinkling tiara, feeling very silly and just a little important. Helen glanced at her beautiful daughter sitting behind the wheel.

"Quite a day, princess." Inside she still felt a delicious weightlessness. It had been a day of transformations, of letting go of expectations, finally opening up to God's love.

"I'm so happy, I could explode!" Grace exclaimed.

"Please don't. I had enough of that at church."

They both laughed, quietly at first and then in raucous laughter, punctuated by snorts and gasps (which only made it worse), and bouncing tears and runny noses. When they were quiet again, Grace pulled into the driveway and turned off the lights. They sat there for a long moment, holding hands.

"Just look at that moon, Mom. It has a face." And surely, the bright full moon, like the biggest Christmas ball, seemed to be wearing a smile.

"It does."

"I remember when I was little, you used to tell me if I looked really hard, I would see it wink."

"Only on special days."

"This is one of those days, Mom."

Chapter 19

Grace had been dreaming of snow, billowing snow, curtains of snow, veils of snow, all showering over her. In her dream, the snow, sparkling like diamonds, painted the Carolina blue sky!

She sat up in bed, swiping the white lace curtains away. The room was blue. The ceiling fan above sent waves of cool air down on her. Outside the sun poured down onto grass that was still green and onto shining, glowing gardenia bushes.

"This is not Connecticut," she told herself. "But it's Christmas! Yes, it is!" She walked across the carpeted floor, stopping to pick up the tiara she had laid gently on the white bureau with its huge attached mirror. She brushed her hair, placed the tiara firmly on her head. "I am in an Airbnb with my mom. No expectations, no disappointments," she told herself, and she waltzed out the door, wearing the only present she would get that year and trying to make the best of it.

She passed her mother's bedroom and peeked in the door. Her mother was hibernating under a huge, igloo-like comforter, snoring slightly like a little breeze passing in the air. *Best not to wake her,* she thought. Grace made her way down the hall to the bathroom and smelled something. Something good. Yeasty and warm. It was cinnamon. Cinnamon rolls on Christmas morning! *Perfect,* she thought, and she washed her face and brushed her teeth. Her image in the mirror told her she was happy. So far. No expectations, no disappointments. Sylvia had the fire blazing, even though it would probably be in the sixties and sunny. The Christmas tree sparkled, and the presents added a fine touch.

Presents, Grace thought. Had there been presents there yesterday when she put her mother's gift, a red Balinese scarf dotted with yellow flowers and bordered in apricot and gold, under that same tree? *Who were these presents for?* Certainly not for her unless her mother had brought some. She was tempted to look, but no. No expectations, no disappointment.

"There you are!" Sylvia appeared, carrying a mug of hot chocolate topped with whipped cream. She curtsied as she approached and said, "Your Highness." Grace giggled and took the cup from Sylvia, who was struggling to keep her balance and needed both hands to launch herself off her bent knee. "It's always the knees," Sylvia said, rising carefully from the floor. "I should be grateful they've held out this long. Let's get started, shall we?"

Grace looked at the elderly woman in her old lavender chenille robe and faded grey slippers pressed down at the backs. Grace glimpsed, from the little that showed beneath Sylvia's robe, white cotton pajamas with tiny Christmas trees all over them. A long silver braid fell over the old woman's shoulder. Grace half expected a bell to be tied at the end.

"This is what happens when you don't have a man around to dress for," Sylvia winked.

"I don't believe that for a minute, Sylvia, I bet that's the same way you dressed for Arthur, and he loved it."

"It was something like that," Sylvia replied wistfully. "He gave me a new pair of pajamas every Christmas, whether I needed them or not, because I told him one year that I liked them. That did it. Every year afterwards, he gave me a pair, like clockwork. Christmas pajamas. It wasn't very original, but it was sweet. Would you like some breakfast? These buns are warm."

Grace thought for a minute, sipping on her cocoa. Should she go ahead and eat those nice hot cinnamon rolls or should she wait and celebrate Christmas morning with her mom, for support? It was Christmas morning! Grace ran over to Sylvia and gave her a big hug. "Christmas morning, Sylvia! Good Lord! Merry Christmas!"

"Merry Christmas to you, too," Sylvia laughed, hugging her back. "You're a fine young lady. A true princess. Shall we go wake your mom?"

"We'll give her until ten o'clock." Gracie laughed. "It's not like we have anywhere to go."

Sylvia smiled, walked into the other room, and came back holding two items. One was a DVD, and the other was a game. She held them out to Grace, who put her finger on the side of her face and tapped thoughtfully.

"This is a tough one. I love *White Christmas,* and I'm dying to see it. We watch it every year. But we only have an hour until it's 10:00 a.m., and Mom loves it too. I'd really rather watch that with her. But we both love Scattergories too, and she'll be really sad if I play without her."

"We can always play Scattergories again," Sylvia offered pragmatically.

"True. Scattergories it is then. But first, is there more hot chocolate?" Grace asked.

"In the pan on the stove," Sylvia instructed. She pulled out the cards and pens from the box. "Whipped cream's in the side door."

Grace walked toward the kitchen. She passed the red dining room and looked in. Places were set. At one was a stocking, an old stocking, lumpy and fat and filled with goodies. Grace's heart caught in her throat. Everything about her shivered and said YES! This day was getting better and better. Then her joy burst. She hadn't done the same for her mother and her mother was the one who needed propping up. As she took her cocoa back into the living room, she asked, "Who is that stocking for?"

"Why you, of course, my dear," Sylvia replied.

"Did you do it?" Grace asked.

"Well, I'd like to tell you it was all Santa's work, but you wouldn't believe me, would you?"

"Probably not." Grace sipped her cocoa, slowly. "Thank you."

"Don't thank me. Thank your mom. It was her idea. I just provided the back-up," Sylvia chuckled. "All right. Here are our categories. Are you ready to toss the dice?"

Grace shook the fat dice in her hands, more than pleased that her mother had made the effort to turn this particular Christmas into something special for her. So much of her mother's attention went toward Grace's dad or her students, or to the books she was writing and the publicity she kept doing. Not that her mother didn't loved her, for what mother doesn't love her child, but this current gesture touched Grace in a powerful way. It was the "she loves me" that Grace had been waiting for.

"Grace?" Sylvia interrupted her reverie. "I think it's scrambled," Sylvia smiled. Grace threw the dice on the table. It was an R. The first category was Wild Animal. What else? Reindeer. The game took Grace's mind off her mother for a bit, but when there was a lapse in the game action, when Power Tools turned out to be too difficult a category for her or when she wrote down "umbrella" for something black when the letter was S, she thought about Helen. How would her mom survive? She was drinking more, crying more, sleeping more. This event in her life had not caused her to rise up and roar, but rather to lie down and weep. She was frantically searching for another man to fill the space where her husband had been. She played like it was only a "zipless fuck" she was after, but it was all too obvious that what she wanted was love—true love that would last forever. That's what Grace wanted too, after all. A mother who would love her and be there for her forever. Her mom was so preoccupied with work and finding a suitable replacement for her dad, that she wasn't truly there anymore. But then, there was the stocking, wasn't there? For that special moment at least, Grace didn't feel alone and unloved.

"Penny?" Sylvia's voice came out of nowhere. Grace looked up, a bit bewildered. "You are not wearing your Christmas face, dear," Sylvia told her gently.

"No," Grace agreed and breathed a heavy sigh.

"Do you know who Cardinal Newman was?" Sylvia asked. Grace shook her head. "He was a head honcho in the Catholic Church hierarchy. Whatever he was, he was very wise." Sylvia retrieved a small notebook from a side table drawer. "This is his philosophy, abridged." She read from the small book, "Dear God, you have not created me for nothing. Therefore, I will trust you, whatever, wherever I am. Though friends be taken away, though my spirits sink, though my future is hidden from me, yet will I trust you."

Sylvia took her glasses off and put them back in her pocket. She closed the book and put it back in the drawer. Then she came and sat by Grace and took both her hands in hers.

"I don't know what you believe in, Gracie. Maybe it's just love, which is really everything, of course. Trust love to see your mom through what it is she is going through. It is not for nothing. You too."

"Sure," Grace replied. But she had her doubts. The door to Helen's bedroom opened. Helen appeared, all ruffled and sleepy in white silk pajamas, a brightly decorated kimono, and red silk slippers.

"Wow, Mom, you look…" Grace stopped mid-sentence.

"Colorful," Sylvia laughed.

"Coffee," Helen croaked and gave her daughter a hug, kissing her head, being careful to avoid the tiara. "Merry Christmas, Grace."

"Merry Christmas to you too, Mom," Grace whispered, hugging her back.

As they all sat at the breakfast table, Grace felt slightly self-conscious about opening her stocking while Helen and Sylvia watched. At first, she tried to be nonchalant, taking a bite of egg here and opening a present there. She encouraged them to eat and talk too, but she was mesmerized by what she could, and could not, see, so finally she just dug into the stocking, forgetting them, so entranced was she by the contents of the red sock. Inside, there were old necklaces made of translucent gold and amber beads, a mood ring, a pair of red stone clip-on earrings, and an unusual pin with Russian spires and the Olympic insignia from 1968. There was a paperweight with delicate flowers floating inside the glass and a snow globe from Chicago that rained blue beads on the skyline when she moved it. A postcard from Prague with a troll was sending out a message. The translation on the back simply read, "I love you."

There was a miniature plastic whistle that barely made a sound and a tiny kaleidoscope whose innards displayed what looked like amoeba swimming. There was a small book titled *Pierre* with a definite moral: CARE. And then there was her favorite, the Santa tin her mom always put in her stocking. When she opened it up, inside there was always $5, $20, when she was older even $100 dollars for a pair of special shoes she wanted or concert tickets. Grace put the Santa aside. She would save the best for last. She pulled out a large chocolate Cadbury fruit and nut bar. Her favorite! And a handful of red and white peppermints wrapped in cellophane. Of course, there was also an orange. And a lottery ticket for $2 that had been scratched off and showed a prize of $10. Each discovery brought her a new wave of delight. By the time Grace got to the bottom, she was breathless with joy.

"Oh, Sylvia!" Grace gushed, throwing her arms around the old woman's shoulders. "This is so perfect! Thank you!"

"It was a joint effort," Sylvia reminded Grace. "Your mother did more than half."

"Of course, you did," Grace said as she went over to her mother to give her a kiss.

"You didn't open Santa," Helen prodded. "Open him." Grace went back to her seat and took the tin Santa in her hands. No expectations, no disappointment, she thought, and she popped open the tin. Out spilled bills, three bills, all curled one inside the other.

"Thanks Mom," Grace said, happy for the newfound $60. But Helen pressed her harder.

"Look again," she said. Grace took the bills out and pressed them flat on the white tablecloth. These were not $20 bills. They were $1,000 bills! Grace had never seen such a thing. In fact, she didn't even think bills like these existed.

"Is this real?" Grace asked her mother, who simply nodded her head and beamed.

"Yes, and extremely difficult to come by," Helen replied. "I didn't want you spending all your money on your trip home."

Grace burst into tears, and Helen knew she had scored big. Tears always meant either gratitude or desperation. Helen waited for Grace to wipe away the tears to hear what she would say.

"You never let me down," Grace exclaimed happily.

"Not if I can help it," Helen declared.

Still something hung between them that was not Christmas joy, and Sylvia noticed it.

"Let's leave these here and go open our presents in front of the fire," Sylvia rose from the table. "Anyone need a refill?" she asked before disappearing into the bowels of the kitchen.

"No thanks," Helen and Grace called out in unison. They went into the living room. Helen and Sylvia sat on the sofa, while Grace settled onto the loveseat, in front of the fire.

"Sylvia, where did you get all this stuff?" Grace asked.

"Like they always say in the ads. Recycle/reuse."

Sylvia was good to her word. The presents she had (re) gifted were throwbacks from an earlier time. Books for both of them. First edition mysteries by Lawrence Block for Helen. "Because you need a good page turner to take your mind off the stuff." *The Book of Clouds* for Grace. "I gave this to Arthur just before he died. I know, that's morbid. Right? But he loved to lay outside on the chaise and look up at the sky. 'That's where I'm headed, Syl', he'd say. 'Smack into that cirrus. Don't forget to look up for me.' That's what I'm saying now, Gracie, don't forget to look up." There was also an ice cream maker still in the box for Grace and a pretty Fossil watch that some guest had left, though Sylvia didn't know who. For Helen, there was a beautiful pashmina shawl and a silver rope bracelet that fit just right on her wrist.

"We can't possibly take all this from you," Helen declared.

"Hush!" said Sylvia. "This was all headed for the rummage sale at the church anyway. What am I going to do with all this stuff here? It just collects dust."

Back to the big presents they then went! For Helen, a vintage Coco Chanel suit, all confetti corals and orange and gold with solid burnt-orange velvet collars and cuffs and bars that bordered the pockets.

"Really, Sylvia, this suit is too much!" gasped Helen. "It must be worth several thousand dollars. I can't possibly take it from you."

"Is it worth that now? I didn't really know. Well, who cares!" Sylvia shrugged off Helen's concerns. "I think it will look lovely on you. Anyway, I've had my wear of it."

"Well, thank you then. It's a very generous gift."

"I was wearing that suit when I met Arthur. Maybe it will bring you luck now."

Helen hugged the suit close to her chest. "I certainly hope so."

For Gracie, Sylvia had dug up a pair of tall black riding boots topped in brown and a tight black crop. Gracie looked at her mother, now confused, when she saw them.

"Thank you, Sylvia. But I haven't ridden horses since I was a little girl."

"Well, there's no time like the present to take riding up again," Sylvia replied. "And if you don't want them, you can always sell them. Though I hope not. Arthur gave me these boots for my sixtieth birthday. He told me to be adventurous, have fun. I never used them. I wish I had. Still I found adventure in other ways. Here, open this…"

Sylvia handed Grace a smallish box. Inside was a moss green felt cloche. When Grace put it on, she looked like a woodland elf. All she needed was wings.

"Adorable," commented Helen.

"Is this from Arthur too?" asked Grace.

"No, that one I stole from my sister. I was mad at her, so I never gave it back," Sylvia laughed softly. Grace looked concerned. "Oh, don't worry, pet. She won't come and get you. She passed long ago."

Two boxes remained, and both were for Sylvia.

"This is the real reason I wanted company for Christmas, so I could give these gifts to myself without any guilt." With that, she opened a shoe box from LL Bean and pulled out a pair of shearling slippers. In no time, she shook off her ragged mules and sunk her feet into the plush shearling, closed her eyes and smiled in luxury. "Heaven," she sighed. One box was now left.

"Aren't you going to open it?" Grace asked a bit anxiously.

"I don't need it," Sylvia replied. "This is enough for me. You open it, Helen."

Helen took the large box and placed it in front of her. She took off the bow and delicately loosened the wrapping paper. Then she gently pried open the box and started pulling out sheets of tissue paper, one after the other, all the colors of the rainbow until the floor around her looked like a box of Crayola crayons had just had a meltdown.

"There's nothing in here!" Helen exclaimed, digging ever deeper into the pile of tissue, even putting her head in the box, and flinging the sheets of colored tissue paper in all directions behind her.

"Keep going," Sylvia said, calmly sipping her coffee.

Finally, Helen came to the bottom of the box. Lying there was a small white card with HOPE written on it in bold letters. Helen pulled her head up, blew the hair off her face and asked, "Is this some kind of a joke?"

"Your guess is as good as mine," Sylvia winked at Grace. "This came from my other sister. She has a real flair for the dramatic."

Helen picked up the card and saw it was not a card but an envelope with something inside.

"Open it, Mom," Grace said eagerly. Helen did. Inside there was a ticket. She gasped.

"I can't possibly take this," Helen sputtered, holding the ticket out to Sylvia, who put her hands up in silent refusal.

"It's for you," Sylvia said quietly.

"But it's a round-trip ticket to Paris!"

"Seriously?" Grace couldn't help but squeal.

"It's the very place for you to wear your Chanel suit," Sylvia remarked.

"But this is ridiculous!" Helen cried. "Your sister sent this ticket for you to use." Grace and Sylvia exchanged shocked glances.

"There never was another sister," Grace suddenly realized. "Was there, Sylvia?" Sylvia just smiled.

"Why? You don't even know me, know us. Why are you being so kind?" Helen was perplexed.

"Why?" Sylvia began. "Someday you'll know, if you're blessed. I'm an old woman. I have a good life. Now all I require is a pair of warm slippers, a good book, and a little fine Scotch. I know that it is more blessed to give than to receive. And a darned sight easier I might add. For twenty years, I have adopted families at Christmas because I know that if I make someone else happy, I am happy too. When you called me, you were frantic, even desperate. I knew you needed comfort, and I knew I could comfort you. I hope I have."

Grace went over to Sylvia and put her arms around the old woman. She kissed her on the cheek and sat down and held her hand. "Thank you, Sylvia, for everything. This has been an amazing Christmas because of you."

❄

From there forward, the day pieced together in happiness like a paper chain. A walk in the park, and for Grace, a jog. She did it once alone, twice with an old yellow dog, thrice with that dog and its owner, and a fourth time alone again. Helen and Sylvia meandered along behind her, stopping to admire the fragile skeletons of flowers and the bright and shiny holly bushes now dappled with clusters of red berries. The wind picked up and blew the last brown leaves across the pavement, letting them scratch the ground as if they were nails. Gradually, clouds covered the blue sky. Helen pulled her collar up around her ears and shoved her hands deep into her pockets.

"Let's head back," Sylvia declared. "We have a meal to prepare."

This time, Grace did get her Christmas meal of roast beef and mashed potatoes and roasted Brussels sprouts. A Christmas salad with bright red cherry tomatoes and slices of green avocado. And a trifle with its bright layers of raspberries, kiwi, custard, and lady fingers all topped with homemade whipped cream. Sylvia had dug up three mismatched Christmas crackers, and they all sat around in their colored crowns (Grace sporting both her tiara and the paper one) drinking wine, eating the wonderful feast, and thanking God, each in her own way, for this very special moment, indeed for all the moments of this day that they had shared together.

As Grace lay down in her bed that night and snuggled in for a long Christmas nap, she listened to the whistling wind and watched the mottled clouds race across the face of the moon. *No expectations, no disappointments. It had been a perfect day.*

Chapter 20

Leaving Sylvia behind the next day was hard. They had only known each other for a little while, and yet it felt like they had been friends for a lifetime. For Grace, Sylvia was the grandmother she had never had, but always wished for—that kind of *bippity boppity boo* Grandmother who knew your every wish and fulfilled it, turning rags into rich blue ball gowns and trimming Christmas in handfuls of wonderful golden stars.

"I'll miss you," she sniffled and gave Sylvia a huge hug.

"Well then, you'll just have to come back, won't you?" Sylvia patted the young girl on her back. "I'll miss you too," she whispered.

Then it was Helen's turn. She looked the old woman squarely in the eye, took both of Sylvia's soft hands into her own. "I can't thank you enough for all you've done."

"My pleasure, dearie. I'm just thrilled to see you're leaving a little more relaxed than when you arrived," Sylvia gave Helen's hands a squeeze. Helen sighed, reached down and gave Sylvia a hug, then she walked to the car.

As they backed out of the driveway, they rolled their windows down and waved at the old woman who had given them so much joy. Sylvia just stood there in her lavender robe and new shearling slippers, waving back and smiling.

"Don't be strangers!" she called out, as they drove off down the road.

Helen chuckled. "That's ironic."

"What?" Grace asked.

"We are strangers," Helen explained.

"Not anymore," Grace corrected her. "We've gone from strangers to friends."

"I guess so," Helen concurred and she slowed down to take a right onto Faith Road.

"It doesn't take much, does it, Mom, to move from strangers to friends? Just being open to it. Letting go of expectations. No expectations, so no disappointment."

"What has Indonesia done to you?" Helen asked rather incredulously. "Have you been ingesting massive amounts of fortune cookies?"

Grace was very quiet, so quiet that Helen could feel the air in their car thicken palpably, as if someone was building a wall. She swallowed, hoping the sensation would go away. Outside the tall trees swayed in the wind, and the black cows stood against the yellow fields like targets. Helen felt alone, wrong, and yes, mean. She wanted Christmas again and that feeling when the fire crackled and the lights on the tree twinkled and everyone laughed, the feeling that she was part of a whole pulsing happiness that made her feel complete. Now she just ached and wondered. "What am I going to do?"

Say you're sorry, the voice came to her.

Sorry for what? she asked the voice in her head.

For whatever it is that's making Grace cry. Helen looked over and saw Grace was indeed crying, wiping away big tears from her eyes and sucking the snot back into her nose as delicately as she could.

"I'm sorry," Helen said and slowed down to take a serious turn in the road. Grace just stared out the window and wiped her nose on her sleeve.

"Do you need a Kleenex?" Helen asked sweetly, wanting to help. Grace grabbed the Kleenex from her mother's hand, blew her nose, and then dropped the tissue on the floor.

"You don't have to be rude, Grace," Helen could not help saying.

"Rude? Look who's rude! You!!" Grace shouted.

"Gracie, what's gotten into you. What have I done?"

"Nothing. You've done nothing," Grace replied. "That's just it. I tell you how I feel about things, and you put me down. Make me feel like an idiot. You put yourself first above everybody and everything else. You think you can just waltz into people's lives, and they'll fall down and love you, but you don't give love in return. You take endlessly, think of yourself endlessly. All that while you are a victim of Dad's infidelity, Micah's homosexuality, and God knows what else. Just once, just once, I wish you'd put your work and yourself and your life truly aside and be kind."

Helen felt as if Grace had just run toward her as fast as she could, in full football gear, and slammed her head-on in the gut. She was having trouble breathing. Her thoughts spun in her head, zigzagging this way and that and crashing into each other. She looked desperately for the right thing to say.

I'm sorry you feel that way, she wanted to say, but such words sounded positively morbid.

Do you really feel that way? she realized would sound like a whiny response.

Tell me how you really feel would come across as sarcastic and psychiatric.

You don't get me at all would make herself sound like a victim.

I don't get you at all? Defensive.

You're entitled to how you feel? Offensive.

If she told Grace that she loved her, that she was the most important thing in Helen's life, would Grace believe her or just snort her disbelief, turn away, and look out the window at the horses galloping across the field, their wild manes waving like flags, their thunderous haunches flexing with a strength that she didn't feel?

Helen was lost and confused. But then another thought came to her. *What would Sylvia do?* She felt her heart open and her fear diminish, and she asked Grace very simply, "What is it really, pet?" She took her right hand off the wheel, laid it on Grace's slender thigh, and gave it a squeeze.

The flood gates opened. Grace didn't just cry. She wailed, rocking so violently that Helen feared she would either slice herself in half on her seat belt or roll their car into a ditch. A fire engine passed them, lights flashing, sirens blaring, going in the opposite direction. For a moment Helen couldn't tell who was louder, Grace or the emergency vehicle.

Helen pulled the car into a driveway by the side of the road and looked at her watch. They still had plenty of time to make their flight. Even if they missed it, so what? They could always get another. Then, she thought, what about

Grace's connecting flight to Indonesia? Helen sighed. She couldn't go back to Indonesia like this.

Helen looked over at her daughter. Grace's hair was tousled, her eyes red, and her nose swollen from blowing so hard. *Here is my baby girl,* Helen thought, *carrying a burden that is turning her from a dandelion tuft into a catastrophe. What if it's me? What if I did this? What did I do?* Helen was dismayed.

"It's not you," Grace said through a stuffy nose, as if she was reading her mother's mind. "I was wrong to say all those things to you. I'm sorry."

Be quiet, Helen's inner voice advised her. *Be quiet and listen.*

"The truth is, I met this guy in Indonesia…"

Helen felt her heart drop. She knew what was coming next. *Quiet,* she told her head. *No expectations, no disappointments. Please.*

"…but he's not Indonesian," Grace continued.

Thank God, Helen thought. *She's not relocating.*

"In fact, his name is Jake, Jacob Tanner actually, and he's from New York. City. The Village. His mother is a poet. You'd like her." Grace was cheering up a bit.

"You've met her?"

"Yes. A few months ago, his parents came to Jakarta to see Jake. He's a bee researcher, and he was there working with the honeybees."

"Jake doesn't teach like you do?"

"Oh, no. He travels all over the world researching propolis and honeybees and all. It's very important work. Propolis could be the cure for some cancers," Grace said brightly.

"What exactly is propolis?" Helen asked earnestly, although that was not the question she really wanted to ask.

"Propolis is the stuff on the inside of wood that honeybees suck out. I think. Not sure. I just know that Jake works with the Bee Lab at the University of Minnesota, and he's doing important research, and he's a really nice guy."

Helen could not stand the suspense. She felt like she was sitting in a dark theatre waiting for the cymbals to crash. Or better yet, waiting at the start of a race for the starting shot. "Well, this is all good news! Why all the tears, Lamb?" Helen asked again and stroked Grace's hair. Again. Her daughter was wailing, this time with her face buried in Helen's lap. Helen patted her daughter's head, took her daughter's swollen face in her hands, and asked her the big question.

"Grace, tell me. Are you pregnant?"

The very thought brought Grace sitting upright in her seat. "Pregnant? Hell no! But I'm married!"

Chapter 21

arried? Married! The word pealed in her mind like the ringtones on her phone. Not pregnant, but married! "That's wonderful, Sweetie!" Helen gushed, but then wondered if it really was. She had always dreamed of Grace's wedding. She imagined it being held outside in some bucolic venue with fields of wildflowers and blue skies. Grace would wear a simple, but beautiful, dress, maybe an Empire dotted Swiss with a crown of flowers accentuating her long blonde hair. Frank would give her away, and there the fantasy stopped suddenly, awfully. Frank had given her away long ago. In fact, he'd given them both away, and in her own anxiousness and despair, Helen had let go of Grace too, sending her off to boarding school and leaving her adrift in her adolescence while Helen struggled to put meaning back in her life. No wonder Grace had gotten hitched to someone she had known probably twenty minutes. "Were they at the wedding?" Helen asked her daughter. "Jake's parents, I mean?"

Grace nodded. "It was all just so spur of the moment. I didn't think you'd be able to come, what with school and all."

And the divorce. Helen felt herself sliding back into victim status. She was reacting to circumstances rather than responding to them. She silently reached for Grace's hand and asked what she should do. "I have to admit, I'm sorry I missed it, but I'm happy for you, if this is what you want," Helen spoke straight from her heart for once.

"Oh, it is, Mom!" Grace replied excitedly. "Do you want to see a picture?"

"Of course. Then we must really get to the airport," Helen replied. "You don't want to miss your connection to Indonesia."

Grace handed Helen a picture from her wallet. Grace was wearing a short white sundress. She had a wreath of bright flowers on top of her head. Standing beside her was a frankly gorgeous man, probably in his thirties, who looked like he had just stepped out of a Calvin Klein commercial. His white T-shirt hugged his chest, and she saw that his jeans fit like a glove.

"Wow!" Helen exclaimed. "He's really amazing."

"Isn't he?" Grace gushed. "He used to model, but he gave it up because he wanted to do something more purposeful with his life."

"Noble, too. And by the way, you look lovely. Not quite what I had in mind, but lovely. Will you two get a place in Minnesota?"

"Well, that's the thing, Mom." Grace started twirling the strands of her honey colored hair in her fingers. "He travels a whole lot, all over the world. I'd be alone a lot. And Minnesota? You know what they say about Minnesota. In summer, it's Minneskeeta; in winter, it's Minnesnowta.

That's all you get. We thought if maybe we could live closer to home, I would have family around whenever he was gone."

Helen had put the car back on the road and was heading down I-77 in what she saw was amazingly light traffic. "That sounds sensible. Will you be coming back in June, then, when your semester ends?" Helen asked, trying to sound respectful.

"Well, actually not. I'm not going back to Indonesia. I quit," Grace said quietly.

"What about your ticket?" Helen asked without thinking further.

"There never was a ticket, Mom. I'll give you your $3,000 back," Grace whispered.

"No, no," Helen replied quickly. "Consider that a wedding gift." In her mind, Helen called on Sylvia. *Sylvia. Sylvia.* She whispered the old woman's name under her breath. *It's all a daring adventure or nothing at all.* "So where, what will you be doing?" Helen asked politely.

"Oh, I'll still be working for the same company, teaching English, only it will be here in the U.S.," Grace said, quite pleased.

"Exactly where in the U.S. will you be working?" Helen queried cautiously.

"In New Haven. I'll be working part-time and going to Yale part-time to get my Masters in Teaching English as a Second Language."

Helen sucked in the air. "And you will be living, you and Jake will be living…?"

"See that's the thing, Mom. With Dad gone, there's lots more room because he doesn't have his stuff spread all around the house…" Grace paused.

"I think I know where this is going." Helen asked her daughter, "Tell me…"

"Well, we were hoping maybe we could live with you. Just until we can afford our own place, of course," Grace sounded hopeful.

And when will that be? A part-time ESL teacher and a bee researcher. Between the two of them they probably don't make enough a month to keep them in bathroom cleaner.

"The thing is, I was thinking about selling the house," Helen said. They had come to a standstill in the growing heavy traffic.

"Oh, well. That's okay," Grace replied, almost too quickly. "We'll find someplace else."

"Now wait," Helen jumped in quickly. "I said I was thinking. Only thinking. There are no for sale signs up yet. No one's made a bid. It actually might be nice to have some company. And you two could help with the food and utilities. It might be very nice. Of course, you can stay!"

Helen smiled, clearly startled by her own generosity and the ability to be flexible in her plans. This whole no expectations, no disappointment thing was starting to show some real results. The traffic started moving again, and Helen found herself in the flow in a way she didn't remember ever feeling before. She was at ease, not jumpy, relaxed and not rigid. She had the feeling that everything was going to be fine. Of course, that moment was fleeting because just then some aggressive asshole in a white truck darted across two lanes and slowed down dramatically in front of her. At the same time, Grace asked the question she'd been asking since she was four years old.

"Can we get a dog?"

Chapter 22

By the time Helen and Grace arrived home, it was almost five o'clock, and the winter sun had set. Only a residue of color remained in the sky like the colored lines on a scratch-off picture. Take away the black, and bright colors are revealed, only in this case, the black covered the light. It's all in one's perspective, Helen thought as she drove the Volvo onto the driveway, toward the darkened house, tires crunching on the snow.

"Home sweet home," she said and gently nudged Grace, who had fallen asleep the minute they had left the airport.

Grace rubbed her eyes and stepped down onto the driveway.

"Be careful," Helen advised. "It could be slippery." She pulled their bags out of the rear and released the handles. She gave the larger one to Grace, who stood waiting and shivering in the cold.

"It's warmer in Jakarta," she chattered. "Even in North Carolina."

Helen laughed. "You've gone soft, Sweetie. Don't worry. I'll make you some tea. Then we'll light a fire and wrap ourselves in big blankets."

"Sounds good," mumbled Grace, shivering harder.

"You can't beat this sky though," Helen observed as they climbed the stairs to the front door. Looking up, she saw a handful of stars, flung out into the deep and distant night, catching diamonds in its weave.

Helen reached out and put the key in the lock. Before she pushed it, the door just opened. "Shhhh!" Helen cautioned Grace. "I think there's someone inside."

"Mom, you're freaking me out," Grace hissed back.

"Go back to the car. Take your phone. If I don't come to get you in ten minutes, call 911," Helen instructed.

"Mom. Seriously. I'm scared," Grace whispered. "Can't we just call 911 right now?"

"It'll be all right, Gracie. Just get in the car," Helen tried to reassure her.

Grace hugged her mother close. "I don't want to lose you."

"I don't want to lose me either. It's probably just a fluke. Gloria must have come over half in her cups and forgotten to close the door." Helen placed her hand on her daughter's cheek. "I'll be all right. Promise."

Helen watched Grace get in the car and lock it. She pointed to her watch, and Grace gave her a thumbs up. Then Helen went inside. The house was black, pitch black, and Helen was at last grateful for the small penlight that Frank had advised her to carry in case of emergencies just like this one. She had kept the light not out of sentiment as much as forgetfulness. She simply had forgotten it was there. Until tonight when she really needed it. Sort of like faith. That thought made her think of Sylvia and what Sylvia would do in this situation.

Arm herself, Helen thought and ducked into the kitchen, which was just past the sitting room by the front door. She reached up to take down a heavy copper skillet from the carousel over the counter, but when she did, the pots and pans all started clanging. The more she tried to settle them, the worse it got. Now her heart was pounding frantically. She knew she had attracted the attention of whoever was in her house. All she wanted to do was run. Which she did, leaving her penlight behind and running straight into something wider than a coat rack but not quite as inflexible as the wall. Helen screamed a piercing scream and the thing put a hand over her mouth. "Please don't let me die. Please don't let me die," Helen prayed with eyes shut tight. Then it was light, and the hand went down, and Helen looked up and saw Frank. He was standing there with a fireplace iron in his hand.

"You!" Helen hissed. "What the hell are you doing in my house?"

"I'm here for Grace," Frank said quietly.

"What do you mean you're here for Grace," Helen spat the words like an angry cat.

"To give her my Christmas present. It's the least I could do," Frank said sheepishly. "I thought you were coming back tomorrow, not today."

Just then Grace came flying through the door. "Mom? Mom? Where are you? Dad! Dad, what are you doing here anyway? And why are you in your underwear?"

Helen looked at Frank more closely. How had she overlooked the fact that he was bare chested, wearing only his white boxers that seemed to glow in the dark? The answer came immediately as a woman's shrill voice shattered the still night air.

"Franky boy! Where are you? Bring that big dick back up here. I'm not done with you yet!"

Even in the darkness, Helen could feel her face, and Frank's, and Gracie's turning a deep shade of red. *What would compel a man like Frank to go for a girl like Stephanie? She was crass and wild, not like me,* Helen thought. *Was that the appeal?* Helen felt sorry for Frank that his mid-life crisis had taken this turn. She would rather have seen him sail off solo in a small boat to see the world, returning like Odysseus, penitent and grateful. Frank seemed to be stuck in Calypso's den.

Suddenly, there were blue lights flashing outside.

"I called the police," Grace whispered, barely able to speak. "I thought you were in danger."

"You did the right thing, Grace. You couldn't have known who was inside," Frank offered.

Truer words were never spoken, thought Helen as she opened the door for a dewy-eyed policeman who was traveling solo that night. When Helen returned with the officer in tow, Frank, now fully clad in jeans and a cashmere sweater walked down the back stairs to the kitchen. Stephanie followed behind him in a red minidress that stuck on her like a bandage, accentuating her enormous breasts and voluminous rear end. Neither of which went unnoticed by the cop. Stephanie pointed a frightening long red talon at Helen.

"She broke into our house!"

"I beg your pardon! This is MY home, thank you very much."

"Well, he paid for it," Stephanie pouted, clutching Frank's arm tightly.

"Is that the bullshit he has been feeding you?"

"Hush, Mom," Grace chimed in. "Don't engage. She is just baiting you."

"Are you baiting me, you whoring…"

"Mom! Let's take a walk!" Grace said, pulling her mother's arm.

"Wait! I'd like to ask you a few questions before you leave!" cried the young officer, who frankly couldn't wait to get back to the precinct to tell this story to his colleagues.

"Fire away!" Helen yelled.

"Who owns this house?" the officer asked, his pencil poised to jot notes in a small pad.

"We do," Helen and Frank answered simultaneously.

"Are you married?"

"Separated" was their joint reply.

"So, you both own the house?"

"In theory," Helen responded. "I live here. He is with her."

"So really, nobody broke in."

Frank looked relieved. "That's right, officer. It was all just a misunderstanding."

"Then my work here is done." The officer flipped his notebook shut and placed both it and his pen back in his pocket. Helen was fuming.

"You can't be serious! You can't just let him break into my home, fuck his girlfriend on my bed, and…"

"Legally, ma'am, there is nothing I can do. I'm sorry."

"YOU'RE sorry? You're SORRY?"

The officer made his way to the front door as fast as he could. When he opened it, he almost knocked over two handsome men standing on the front porch. One was carrying a platter heaped with ham, cheese, grapes, and rolls and the other held a plate of Christmas cookies, macaroons dipped in chocolate. The men were dressed in matching red sweaters and designer jeans.

"Care for a bite?" the shorter one holding the cold-cuts asked the officer, who took one look at the clearly gay men and made a bee-line for his cruiser. Helen took one look at the couple and shook her head.

"Don't get me started."

"Drama!" the men chirped together, following Helen back into the fray.

"You disgust me," Helen hissed at Frank. "And she disgusts me more."

"I'm sorry you feel this way, Helen," Frank replied, sheepishly.

"How am I supposed to feel, Frank? Tell me. For thirty years you have lived off the money I have brought into the house; you chose to have an affair at year twenty-two, an affair that you have perpetuated; you chose to leave your wife and child only to return at Christmas to give us the present we have always wanted—the indelible memory of you in your underwear as she yelled to you to, and I quote, 'get that big dick back up here. I'm not done with you yet.' Straight into the ears of our daughter."

"She's old enough to take it," Stephanie called out.

"YOU have nothing to add to this conversation!"

"Don't let her talk to me like that, Frank!" Frank just shrugged his shoulders. "FRAAAANK," Stephanie whined.

The two gay men, Lou and Ron, stood wide-eyed in the corner, barely breathing as they watched the drama unfold.

Meanwhile, Grace had disappeared into another room. This was all too much for her to bear.

"I didn't mean for it to be like this," Frank apologized. "I only came over to give Grace a surprise."

"Some surprise," Ron mumbled under his breath.

"Some surprise," Helen spat out the words.

Suddenly, Grace was back in the room. She went over and stood by her father, looking up at him with tear-stained eyes. Then she put her arms around him and gave him a loving hug. "Thank you, Daddy."

"For what?" Helen asked.

"For my surprise."

Chapter 23

When Helen walked into the living room, she saw Frank's handiwork. He had taken the tree down from the attic and put it up. For an artificial tree, she thought, it did look stunning. Nine feet tall, covered with hundreds of tiny white lights and gold and red balls, fully draped in icicles and dotted with tiny red bows. It looked like something from Macy's. Perfect every year. Such beauty, and all Helen could do was cry. If Frank was such a nice man, why did he have to go and cheat on her with a bimbo? He'd made a fool of her. Worse yet, she had lost hope that she would ever really know love in her lifetime. Frank was probably the closest she had ever gotten, and he had chosen someone else instead. Helen sobbed miserably, her shoulders shaking up and down. Then she felt two strong hands calm her shaking, and a deep voice whispered in her ear, "You are more beautiful than this tree, by far. You deserve better."

Lou. She could count on Lou to understand just how she was feeling, to say all the right things. If only Lou weren't gay.

"Are you sure you aren't just a little bit attracted to me?" Helen sobbed, as she stared at the magnificent tree.

"You know I am attracted to you, Helen. But not to your body, not sexually. I am attracted to your soul."

"I have no soul."

"Now you're just pissed off that I don't want to jump your bones to make Frank jealous."

"No! Well, yes. A little. But can't you be a little bit bi-?"

"Helen, Helen, Helen. When are you going to get that all this love stuff is an inside job?"

Helen thought for a moment, then turned around to face Lou. "You are the third person who has told me this. Or something like it."

"And?"

"I guess it is time to listen."

Lou leaned over and kissed Helen on the top of her head. "Just remember, you are the star on the top of that tree."

Chapter 24

"Mom? Mom?" Gracie's voice echoed down the hall. "Where are you?"

"Living room. Let's see what Daddy got you." Helen picked up a box from under the tree. She shook it, and whatever was inside moved, hitting the sides of the box like a pinball.

"Too light for a ring," Helen concluded. "What do you think? I think it's a padlock to a hidden treasure. Only you'll never know the combination," Helen quipped, thinking maybe the wicked Stephanie had had a hand in the purchase.

"That explanation doesn't even make sense, Mom," Grace laughed.

"You know what doesn't make sense is how your father knew that you were going to be coming back with me."

"Maybe it is gold nuggets."

"Maybe you should tell me the truth."

Grace was scrutinizing the box in her hands, clearly considering her response. "Yes, I told him. And yes, I wanted him here when we came back. I thought maybe if you saw each other and it was Christmas…"

"Oh, Gracie. I'm so sorry," Helen said as she took her daughter in her arms and stroked her silky hair.

"I didn't think he'd bring her. I'm sorry, Mom."

"Regrets all around. But let's not ruin the holidays! What do you think your bastard father put in that box?"

"Let's find out." Grace ripped the wrapping off the small silver box. Inside, there was a car key. Grace pressed the horn button and heard nothing. "I guess it's not inside," she laughed and walked to the front door. Lou and Ron were out on the porch smoking cigars. Gracie held her nose with one hand and swiped at the air with the other.

"Did anybody hear anything out here? Like a bleep?"

"Oh yes," Ron said, turning toward Grace. "Someone's car chirped in the garage."

Gracie skipped down the steps clutching the key in her hand. At the garage door, she punched in the combination, her birthday, 0715. The door lifted slowly, creaking and loud in the cold night, and a vehicle appeared. It was jet black, sleek, and wearing a large red bow. It didn't look like any Honda she had ever seen. And it wasn't. It was a BMW, the latest, fanciest, most well equipped and outrageously expensive model on the market. At least, that's what she thought. She unlocked the car and opened the driver's door. She sat down on the butter-soft leather and ran her hands over the smooth steering wheel. She put the key in the ignition and turned on the radio. Sound boomed out from every corner. The GPS lit up. Her seat grew warm. Fully equipped would be an understatement.

"You like it?" her father asked, leaning into the front seat, his arm resting on top of the door.

Grace turned the car off. She looked up at her father with fire in her eyes. "Is this what you think it takes, Dad, to make it all better? To make up for all those years you were cheating on Mom and left me to fend for myself? You think you can just buy me off with a fancy car and everything will all be all right? How insulting. How disgusting! If it had been a little used Honda, like I asked you for, I might have been okay with that. But this is just gross. Keep it. I don't want it." She started crying, got out of the car, and tossed the keys at him.

"You know, Dad," she continued, "you need to learn something about presents. The best present you could ever give me would be being present in my life," Grace said over her shoulder as she headed out of the garage. Then she turned to face him. "Normally, I'd say no expectations, no disappoint, Dad. But I fell for it again. I guess for the expectation that maybe you could do something different for once. Less selfish. Really heartfelt. And yet again, you just disappoint me. Bah Humbug and Scrooge you." Grace stormed off into the dark. Frank stood there with a plumber's helper in one hand and a set of keys in the other, looking as blank as bathroom tissue.

"Frank," Stephanie called out into the night, "Are you ready to go? I'm kind of over being around your ex and these two queers."

"Coming. You'll have to drive the van."

"The funeral van?" Stephanie whined. "But, Frank…"

"I'm taking the BMW," Frank told her.

"She didn't want it?" Stephanie cried out incredulously. "Of all the ungrateful little brats. You know what it is, don't

you? They just can't get over the fact that we're together."
Frank rolled his eyes. "I mean, Jesus, it's been over eight
years! Don't you think it's about time?"

Just then, Helen came to the door. "Where's Gracie?"

"She went for a walk," Frank responded dryly. "We're
heading home."

"Did you really think she'd like it, Frank?" Helen asked
quietly. "Really? You can't buy her off, unlike some people…"

"What's that supposed to mean?" Stephanie asked shrilly.

"Never mind," Frank replied, "Why don't you just go get
in the van."

"What if I crash?" Stephanie whined.

"Use your AAA card. You know, the one for Asshole
Adulterers…" Helen suggested dryly.

"Frank, don't you let her talk to me like that," Stephanie
ordered. "She has no respect for me whatsoever."

"You're so right. None," Helen whispered under her breath.

"You're not going to crash, darling," Frank said and gave
her a kiss. "Anyway, I'll be right behind you."

Frank walked Stephanie out to the road where they had
parked the van earlier. He stayed with her while she pulled
slowly out onto the road and waved, as she headed off down
the street.

Helen watched, her stomach tightening at seeing every
gentle gesture Frank made toward the other woman. She
didn't remember him ever being so kind to her. Maybe he
was at the very beginning, but for the last decade of their
marriage, he had simply been uninterested. The chivalry, if
there had ever been any, had disappeared. He didn't hold
doors, or give gentle kisses, or brush strands of hair out of

her eyes, or remember their anniversaries or birthdays. He was all work, no play, no sex. No love.

She'd taken it all to mean that she was the one who was unlovely, unlovable, unloving. She just worked harder to build the academic armor around her, constructing conferences and publications behind which she could hide. If she could be the foremost authority on Shakespeare in the country, she would be able to withstand rejection, infidelity and loss. Or so she thought. But watching the tenderness with which Frank treated Stephanie tonight made her ache. Not so much for Frank, but for love in general. Specifically, she ached for a love that could touch her gently and erase the lonely pain she felt so deeply in her heart. Helen sat on the front steps staring at the enormous red bow that Frank had left behind. Grace appeared out of nowhere, scooped it up like a used condom, and stuffed it into the trash. "He's an ass," she declared and sat down on the steps by her mother. "I can't even call him Dad."

"He'll always be your dad," Helen said quietly. Soft snow had started to fall. She could see it shining in the streetlights and on her sweater, where it flecked and stayed briefly, then melted away.

"Well, he's still an ass. An unfeeling ass. It must be because he's been around dead people for so long. It's killed all his emotions."

"He is who he is," Helen whispered.

"Oh, please, Mom! Aren't you mad? Don't you ever get mad?" Helen sighed. "Well, I think she's a cow. Nothing at all like you. She's just short and fat."

"She's voluptuous. Sexy," Helen sighed. "I think they're a better couple than we were. I need someone who is more intellectually spirited and engaging than your father." At just that moment, Lou appeared at the door.

"Ladies! It's freezing out here! Come on in front of the fire!"

Helen and Grace looked at each other and laughed.

Chapter 25

Three glasses of wine and as many logs later, Grace said she was going to bed.

"It's been a long day," she yawned, "but I'm glad I met you both. Finally."

Lou rose and helped Grace to her feet. "Likewise," he said winking at her.

Grace went over to her mother, who sat with her feet tucked under her, a fuzzy blue shawl wrapped tightly around her. She was drinking Scotch and had a woozy look in her eyes.

"See you in the morning, Mom." Grace leaned over and kissed her mother's cheek and whispered in her ear. "You'll never get laid if you keep friends like these." Helen smiled, raised her glass, drank a bit more Scotch, and watched as her daughter disappeared up the stairs.

"Those are clean sheets on your bed!" Helen yelled louder than she intended.

"Got it, Mom! Thanks!" Grace's voice drifted back.

Helen belched deeply. "Oh God, I'm drunk, aren't I?"

"A little." Ron giggled. "But not overly so."

"I'd better go to bed," Helen said and rose more than wobbly from the sofa.

"Only if you want to," Lou said agreeably.

Helen sat back down. More than sat, plopped, really. "Not yet," she slurred the words a little, reached for her glass, and then pushed it away. "So, what do you think of Grace?" she knew it was intended as only a rhetorical question.

"She's lovely!" Ron chimed in. "Beautiful. Intelligent. Devoted."

"The question I have is what is she doing here, Helen?" Lou asked pragmatically.

"She's moving back," Helen said, smiling briefly, then reached for the Scotch.

"When?" Lou and Ron asked in unison. They sounded like a couple of warbling birds.

"Tonight! Right now! She's back!" Helen forced a smile, knowing that she should be glad for her daughter's return, but believing more deeply that Grace's return meant her own loss of freedom. It was a devastating blow to her self-discovery. With Grace here, she would be forced to be a mother again. She would be catapulted into more tough confrontations with Frank. She felt her old co-dependency cloaking her again, and it made her feel stifled and sad. And yet, she loved Grace with all her heart, and that realization made her feel guilty and ashamed just because she did want to love herself more.

"Exactly," Ron agreed, nodding his head.

"Did I just say all that out loud?" Helen was now embarrassed.

"You did," Lou affirmed.

"Then it really is time for me to go to bed." Helen stood with as much authority as she could muster.

"Just one thing before you go, Helen," Lou said, taking her arm and walking her toward the stairs. Helen looked at him inquisitively. "What about Boston?"

"Boston?" Helen repeated, drawing a blank as to its significance. "Boston?" she asked again. Then she made the connection. "Oh my God, Boston!" She was supposed to go to Boston for New Year's Eve and spend time with her long-lost love, Webb. Of course, Webb didn't know that yet. She had planned to surprise him just as she had surprised Alan. *Look at how all that turned out, Helen. Who got that surprise?* Helen decided she would call Webb, give him a heads up, let him know she was coming to town. But what if he told her, "Don't come?" She didn't think she could bear rejection from her greatest and only hope. Maybe her last hope.

Turning to Lou, she said with a completely straight face, "I called him. He's expecting me."

"Good," Lou replied, paternally. "But what about the weather?"

"What weather?" Helen asked innocently.

"The blizzard. They're calling for a blizzard," Lou stated patiently.

"They're always calling for blizzards. Besides, I have snow tires," Helen brushed the warning off nonchalantly. "I need to do this, Lou. I need to do this for me. For Grace, to show her my life's not just going to come to a screeching halt just because she's coming home. I need to act decisively, to change my meticulously ordered and solitary life. I'll be free! No, I mean, fine. I'll be fine. If there's a blizzard, I'll just stay at Webb's or maybe a hotel. I'll be fine," Helen tried to reassure both herself and her friends.

"Well, I, for one, am proud of you!" Ron gushed. "Going after what you want! Pushing your limits! Living the dream! I say Brava! And Happy NEW Year!" Helen beamed and held onto the banister, as Ron crushed her in an awkward hug.

"Thank you, Ron. And as they say down South, I appreciate that!"

"Just remember," Lou warned, "This guy is two bulbs short of a pack. This adventure you're planning could be more than you bargained for."

"I take umbrage with that," Ron protested.

"Not you, him," Lou clarified his comments. "This guy Webb, by all accounts, is … What would you say, Helen?"

"Unpredictable. He's unpredictable is all, so I won't bet on anything. As Grace always says, "No expectations, no disappoints.""

"When are you going?" he asked as Helen began a slow, careful ascent up the stairs.

Helen stopped. "What's today? The twenty-seventh?"

"No, it's still the twenty-sixth," Lou and Ron twittered musically.

"And New Year's Eve is the thirtieth."

"The thirty-first," they crooned again, correcting her.

"Then I'll just go on the thirtieth. That will give me more time to spend with Grace before I go," Helen was thinking aloud.

"How about I take the Volvo and get it checked before the trip?" Lou offered.

"Would you? I hadn't even thought of that," Helen confessed.

Lou and Ron looked at each other knowingly. "Why don't you and Grace come to our place for dinner tomorrow night. I know she'll love my boeuf stroganoff. That will save you the bother of cooking," Ron suggested.

"Really? You guys! You are both so good to me. I couldn't ask for better friends. Now I must say good night, good night. Parting is such sweet sorrow," Helen disappeared with a final wave. "And do check the fire before you leave, would you? And hit the lights on your way out too?" Helen's voice drifted down the stairs.

Lou and Ron looked at each other and sighed, then smiled. "That's Helen," they declared in tandem.

Chapter 26

Helen arrived in Boston ahead of the storm. As she parked outside the tall brick apartment building on Chauncy Street where Webb Richards lived, her stomach began to turn and her heart began to pound a little harder. *Maybe this was a bad idea,* she thought, *putting all my eggs in one basket.* This basket, this Webb basket woven long ago. She had been the lover and he the beloved in their relationship. She had fallen in love with him with her whole heart, but he had not returned the favor. In so many ways she knew now he was just like Frank. Unemotional. Unsentimental. Uninterested. So then why did she love him so much? Was it those memories of teenage kisses in the hayloft where she lost her virginity with him? Or was it the fact that he was so inaccessible to her, but not to the other girls he married and divorced and divorced and divorced again?

She stared out the car window and watched the snow sift from one branch of the pine tree in the courtyard down to the next. A squirrel ran down the trunk, headfirst, then froze, and stood tall, then scampered on to where it had to go. That, and the fact she had found a parking space right in front of Webb's apartment, gave her courage, led her to believe that her visit was blessed, looked on with favor by the gods. She shouldn't freeze; she should scamper. So, scamper she did, grabbing her oversized bag. It held what she recalled was Webb's favorite drink, ouzo, though frankly it tasted like paint thinner to her, and she could never understand its appeal.

Helen walked to the front door and pulled the knob, but it was locked. She peered in through the glass door to see if anyone was there, but not a soul was in sight. She might have to call him after all, but that was not the way she had imagined their meeting again. She had imagined herself knocking gently on his apartment door and his opening it, standing there in a worn Irish wool cardigan, pipe in one hand and an Irish wolfhound at his side. Then Helen corrected her vision. As an Emeritus Professor he would be wearing a smoking jacket and carrying a French bulldog.

"Why Helen!" he would exclaim. "What a lovely surprise!" Helen's reveries were suddenly interrupted by a voice behind her.

"Did you forget your key?" asked a pretty young woman in jogging clothes. She was carrying a canvas bag brimming with vegetables and bottles of water. Her cheeks were as rosy as polished apples and her eyes a piercing Madonna blue. She was all youth and promise and good health. She waited for Helen's reply.

"Why yes, yes I did," Helen stammered.

"I do it all the time," the young woman smiled. "Here, let me get it."

"Thank you so much," Helen gushed. They entered, then parted ways inside. Helen was relieved the girl had taken steps to a higher floor. Webb lived in 10C, Helen reminded herself, and she set out down the red tiled corridor. Finally, she found his green door with the gold numbers. Taking a breath, a very deep breath, Helen knocked lightly on the door, and then curiously enough, it opened, ever so slowly, ever so slightly.

"That's odd," Helen thought. "Maybe he's out walking the dog and forgot to close it." She walked into the apartment. It had the potential to be quite nice with its high ceilings, wooden floors, large windows that looked out onto the courtyard, but the place was littered with newspapers, and clothes, and dishes crusted over with old food. It was then Helen noticed the smell, a piercing, noxious smell of urine and filth and God knew what else. Helen found a Kleenex in her purse, held it over her nose, and called out, "Webb? Webb? Are you there?"

The apartment wasn't big, just a foyer, a bedroom, a bathroom, and a kitchen. Dark walls made it almost impossible to see, but then she found him, bare chested at the kitchen table with a belt cinched around his bicep and a needle hanging from his arm. His head was back, and there was a permanent grimace on his face. Helen walked over to him very softly and whispered, "Webb?" She poked him through the Kleenex, but she already knew. She had seen enough death with Frank to last a lifetime.

Chapter 27

Helen felt the bile rise in her throat. She was paralyzed by what she saw. She knew that she had to move but she could not. "Shock," Helen said to herself. "You are in shock." She pulled out her cell phone and dialed the only number she could remember.

"911. State your emergency please," said a purposeful voice on the end of the line.

"My friend. He's dead," Helen said dully. "I came to visit him, and I found him dead."

"What is your location?" the voice asked, now concerned.

"10 Chauncy Street, Cambridge, Massachusetts. Apartment 10C."

"Stay on the line with me, miss. We'll have people over there to help you as soon as we can. Miss? Miss, are you there?"

"I'm here. I'm not going anywhere," Helen replied dully.

Indeed, Helen did not go anywhere at all for hours. She was questioned and interrogated by a plethora of cops and detectives. All seemed to want to connect her to the heroin they found on the table beside Webb's ruined body. Still blurry with shock, Helen answered their questions as best as she could.

"How long have you known the victim?" barked a policeman who smelled of too much cologne and stale cigarettes.

"Forever," she said sadly.

"Can you be more specific, ma'am," he asked tersely.

"We met in high school. 1969."

"Were you and the victim in a relationship?" the cop continued.

"Not really. Sort of. It was rather one sided," she confessed.

"Meaning?" a tall lanky cop with beady eyes probed her answer.

"Meaning nothing!" she cried, feeling suddenly paranoid. She knew where they were going with this interrogation. They were going to pin Webb's death on her, on the slighted woman who had had a hard on for this man all these years. It was all Helen could do not to vomit on their shiny shoes.

"Ma'am," an attractive woman wearing a grey pantsuit and a badge leaned over Helen and took her hands in hers. "You're freezing! Can we have a blanket over here?" she cried over her shoulder. Then she looked back at Helen. "No one is accusing you of anything. Personally, I think the only crime you committed was entering an unlocked apartment."

"Is that really a crime?" Helen asked, now shivering harder. "Who would have ever found him if I hadn't come in? Oh, I should have called him days ago. Maybe I could have stopped him," Helen leaned over onto her elbows and started crying.

The detective smiled. Helen looked at her badge. It said Delia. Delia Morse. "How did you know the victim?" Delia asked.

"Please, just call him Webb. His name was Dr. Webb Richards, and he was my friend."

"…did you know Dr. Richards was an addict?" Delia asked, this time more gently.

"Never," Helen stated emphatically. "I mean, he used drugs and alcohol in high school. We all did. But I thought he'd outgrown it."

"So, help me out, Helen. May I call you Helen?" Delia asked sweetly. "Why exactly were you visiting Dr. Richards?" Helen was pleased that this detective, at least, had credited Webb with his proper title.

"If I tell you, will you promise to keep it to yourself?" Helen asked.

"You know I can't do that, Helen," the detective replied.

"I know." Helen pulled the blanket more closely around her body. "Well, my husband of thirty years and I are going through a divorce. I found out he had been having an affair with his assistant for eight years." The detective shook her head as she scribbled some notes in a small wire bound book.

"Go on," she prompted Helen.

"So, after I sank into a depression, I decided to look up the three men I had been closest to in high school to see if any of them were still interested in me. Webb was one of those men."

The detective scribbled more notes, then looked up. "I assume you checked in with these fellows before you appeared on their doorsteps?"

"No. Yes, and no again," Helen admitted looking down at her hands. "The first surprise visit with Alan was such a debacle that I did contact Micah, the second, before I actually showed up. In fact, we had a very nice Christmas Eve together, he, me, my daughter, and his partner. But I'm deviating…"

"His partner?" the detective said, smiling. "I guess the surprise was on you, then?"

"Which is precisely why I didn't make a greater effort to contact Webb! I really didn't want to know the truth. And the facts you can get on Facebook. I just wanted him because he was my last, best hope at a relationship. I called him once and left a message…"

"When was that?" the detective interrupted.

"I don't know. Sometime yesterday. No, today actually. This morning. I was sitting outside the building…" Helen recalled dreamily. It seemed like years now since she had watched that damn squirrel.

"What building?" the detective asked.

"This building. I was watching the snow sift down from the pine trees and hoping he wouldn't turn me away." Helen stifled a sob with her Kleenex.

"Did anyone see you?" Delia asked a bit more gently.

"I'd like to say a handsome red-haired man with a Great Dane sporting a red sweater coat walked by and waved. But that didn't happen. My only witness was that rather clueless squirrel," Helen giggled. All this interrogation was getting to her. "Am I really a suspect here?" she asked bluntly.

"No. You never were. This is a clear case of an overdose," the detective explained.

"Then why all the questions?" Helen asked. She was now frustrated.

"You were pretty shaken up. Once we ruled out that you had anything to do with this incident, we needed to calm you down. Did it work?" Helen nodded. "Can I take you somewhere?" the detective asked. "Some friends, maybe? A hotel? There's a Sheraton at the end of the street."

Helen smiled. "Thanks, but no. I think I'll walk. Get some fresh air. Take all this in." She held out her hand to the detective. "Thanks for everything, Detective."

The detective's clasp was tight and firm. "Delia. It's Delia. And Helen, I hope you don't mind a little unsolicited advice. Maybe you don't need to go chasing after men. Maybe if you just stand still, one will find you. If that's what you want."

"You're probably right," Helen smiled, and they parted ways.

Helen left her car where it was and walked down the sidewalk to the hotel, which was only a few blocks away. A light snow was falling, speckling her black cashmere coat and quickly melting, leaving no trace. Helen felt tears sliding from the corners of her eyes and over her cold cheeks. She hadn't loved Webb for who he truly was. She had loved her image of Webb, the Golden Boy, head of the Student Council, perpetual altar boy, wrestling champ, and much more. But now she realized the signs that had led to his demise, the booze that he slipped in during orchestra rehearsals, the hash brownies that he snuck into study halls, the grass he always smoked, every day it seemed. She thought he had outgrown it all, but evidently that was not what happened. She knew enough about him to know that he had been in and out of three marriages and that he had

had a terrible accident while driving drunk. Why Harvard had kept him on, she couldn't fathom. He had never seemed all that bright to her, just handsome and irresistible, and now he was gone. She cried because she could have been a better friend, loved him for who he truly was, not who she wished him to be. But he was gone. That dull bell kept clanging in her head. *He was gone.*

Next to the hotel was a small white church with a sharp steeple piercing the now dark sky above. Strangers bundled in heavy coats and bright scarves trickled in through red doors. The church bells pealed out Christmas songs, the music streaming out into the dark night. Helen intended to check into the hotel and go to bed, but she found herself on the path leading into the church. She had no idea what she was doing. She hadn't been to church for years, not since Grace was little. Then they had all stopped going. For the life of her, she couldn't remember why. She didn't know what denomination this church was, but something pulled her in. It was as though she had an invisible cord attached to her waist, and someone inside was tugging on it.

Immediately as she walked inside, Helen felt calmer. The church, small, simple, and white, without all the curlicues and gaudiness like some she'd seen, was punctuated with white candles at the end of every pew. An arc of white candles behind the plain wooden altar flickered. Set against the creamy background were lush crimson poinsettias forming a chorus of red spilling down into the congregation. The coves of simple, dimpled windows each held a plant. Everything was bright red and white like the Danish flag.

Helen was reminded of her youth, when the Danish Gymnastics Team visited her school. Try as she did to conceal her admiration for the beautiful, healthy athletes—it was so uncool to be healthy in those days—still, she was mesmerized. To this day, she could hear the music that played as they performed on the balance beams and tumbling mats; she could smell the shiny rubber of their red balls and feel the sleek finish of their white hoops. Something about the way they moved and simply were, so polished and beautiful, stuck with her all these years. She remembered their names. Preuben Brandt. Annie Jensen. She remembered falling in love with their golden hair. Looking around the church, it struck her that what she loved the most about the gymnasts was the simple perfection of their lives. Something she felt was sorely lacking in her own, then and now.

Helen took a spot in a pew toward the rear. She had hoped to sit on the aisle for an easy escape, but a young couple arrived at the last minute carrying a very young child, all puffy with bright blonde hair like a dandelion and dressed in red velvet, her chubby legs covered in white cotton tights and black satin shoes. She stood on her father's legs just like Kate Winslet when she was leaning out over the Titanic and yelled "Hallelujah! Hallelujah!" until her mother whispered to her, "Quiet, Hopie!" putting her finger to her lips firmly.

The organ prelude transitioned into a Christmas hymn. Everyone stood and start singing. Helen rose with them, not having a clue which book to use or page to find. The mother took Helen's program, a thick book, almost as thick as a journal, and pointed to where they were. "It's all right here," she whispered.

"Thanks," Helen whispered back and began to sing. "In the bleak midwinter…" Then a man from the congregation made his way to the pulpit and read from the Gospel of John: "In the beginning was the word..." His deep voice boomed out over the masses. "And the Word was with God and the Word was God…"

Helen smiled. She could relate. It was all about words. Words could bring into being things that were real and not real. Words could destroy. An absence of words could destroy absolutely. If only she had said something to Webb when she had first had this brilliant idea, he might not be dead this night. All the things she had told herself about Alan and Micah, lies really, were trying to convince herself of lives that were unsubstantiated and untrue just to manufacture a feeling that she'd lost a long time ago. The feeling of being loved. Of being cherished. These men were never the men to give that to her, the people to give that to her. The feeling should have come from Frank. But he robbed her of that years ago. In her heart, Helen felt a very muscular pain, a deep ache that came not from a heart attack but a heart retreating into a small, dark space comprised of loneliness.

She looked over at the family next to her. The mother was buried in her pocketbook, feverishly seeking something. The little girl standing on her father's thighs, holding onto his pinky fingers, was bouncing up and down like an automated doll. The father grinned at his little girl's antics. That was us, she remembered. That was me, never present, always feverishly seeking something I never could find.

Just then a small angel from the choir, tiny in her massive robe, stepped onto a footstool, adjusted her tinsel halo, and began to sing.

"Sissy," the little blonde girl next to Helen cried, clapping her hands together and nearly knocking her head on the pew in front of her. But her father's great hands caught her just in time. The mother pulled out a video camera, handed it to the father, who began to tape the little angel. He handed over the baby to the mother, who had now found the pacifier to quiet the screaming child. She popped the lint-coated pacifier in her own mouth, sucked it clean, and gave it to the baby Hope. Some of the congregation laughed, and many smiled, but everyone also listened to the sweet high voice penetrating the cold air. "Lo, how a rose e'er blooming," the girl sang. She sang so purely it made Helen's heart ache. It was all so graceful, the baby clapping and falling, the catching, the swapping and singing like some beautiful dance that only God could create.

Grace, Helen thought, and then *Grace!* again. *I've left her alone all so I could chase an illusion that turned out to be dead.*

After the service there were refreshments to be served in the parish hall, so said the man with the booming voice who encouraged everyone to come. Helen decided not to join them, but just slip back to the hotel. She wanted to get some sleep and make an early start back home. But instead she found herself talking to the woman, Sharon, who was a Realtor. Sharon asked her to hold Hope while she checked her phone calls and text messages all while trying to coax the child back into her crimson coat. Her husband, Jeff, retrieved their other daughter, Julia, who had sung so sweetly. For some reason she didn't understand, Helen obliged and then was invited to their home on Linnean Street, just a few blocks north, to eat homemade Christmas cookies and have a drink. Jeff, who taught in the English Department at

Wellesley, knew Helen's work, and he wouldn't take her "no" for a final answer.

"Just a drink. And maybe spend the night?" he pleaded as they stood outside the church in the snow.

"Oh, I really couldn't," Helen explained. "I need to make an early morning of it. I've got my own Grace to get back to."

"Grace?" Sharon asked.

"My daughter," Helen smiled.

"That's a great name. We almost named Hope, Grace. How did you choose it?" Sharon asked, now curious.

"Oh, we didn't choose Grace," she said, feeling a sudden ache well up in her heart. "Grace chose us."

"Nice," Jeff nodded and winked at her. "Doesn't Grace choose us all?"

Chapter 28

The newly fallen snow was crisp and crunchy as Helen walked to her car, dragging her paisley bag behind her. It was dawn now, and the sun was just rising, covering the sky like a robust blush. Helen took in a deep breath. The frigid air tightened in her chest, and her nostrils stuck together for a moment, and then popped. She laughed. How could she feel so good this early in the morning with Webb dead, her hopes gone, and her vacation nearly over?

"Don't ever question your good luck," she told herself as she sat in the warming car and prepared to travel home.

The journey was uneventful, of course, until it wasn't. Helen was driving, noticing how the snow sparkled in the trees and thinking about the semester to come. Something in her was saying: *don't go back. Take a leave. Go to France. Meet a man.* But that's not really what she wanted to hear right then, so she turned on the radio and searched for something, anything—NPR, Rock, Classical—to occupy the space in her mind that was filled with nonsense. Outside the sky was opening into blue, and the roads were clear, but inside she was swirling. Bach didn't help. His frantic concerto only made her feel worse, claustrophobic, so she snapped the radio off with a sharp twist. The voices came back.

What should I do with Grace? Should I really let the two of them live in the house? What about selling it? But why leave? The house was paid for, so maybe I could turn it into an Airbnb. Not with all those people there. Has Frank ever really loved me? Did my parents ever really love me? My mom died at only thirty-four of cancer, and I was just an eight-year-old kid. And my dad, so broken, was never able to heal. "Oh, this is shit," Helen said aloud. "Why am I going over this again and again?" She grabbed the first CD she could find and pushed it into the disc player. Out wailed Eric Clapton's voice. Perfect, Helen thought. Ahead the road was shiny, and she was the only car in sight. *Smooth sailing ahead,* she thought, and she accelerated slightly.

Suddenly, the car began to spin. Immediately, her mind cleared of all the debris it had collected and focused on the problem at hand. *Black ice.* Helen's heart pounded. She gripped the steering wheel and forced herself to keep her foot off the brake. Her father hadn't taught her many things, but he had taught her how to turn in to a spin, keep her foot off the brake, and stay calm. Trust that everything would be okay. "I hope everything will be okay," Helen whispered as the car spun once, twice, three times across the highway. "Please God, if you're there, help me," Helen begged. Then with a hard bump that made her teeth vibrate, the car came to a rest in a house-high pile of snow. Helen sat in her seat, clutching the steering wheel, her head resting on both her hands. "Thank you," she whispered to anyone who might have had a hand in her salvation. "Thank you."

Someone tapped on her window. She looked out and saw a police officer, his features hidden by his dark glasses, his fur-lined hat pulled close to his cheeks, and his jacket zipped up over his Adam's apple. His car, blue lights flashing, was parked by the side of the road.

"You all right, ma'am?" he asked as she rolled down the window.

"Oh yes. I am now. Thank you, officer. You are so kind to stop."

"Step out of the car, would you please, ma'am." When Helen tried to move, she felt a dull pain in her neck and realized her whole body ached from stress. "You okay?" he asked again.

"Just a little sore," Helen said, rubbing her neck and breathing in the biting cold air.

"You're lucky it wasn't worse," the officer told her. "Truth is, ma'am, you hit that black ice going seventy-five. The speed limit here is only forty."

Helen looked at the officer plaintively. She was about to try to bargain with him and charm her way out of what she could only assume would be a hefty ticket and a day in court, when she heard herself say, "You're right. I was speeding. How much am I in for?"

"Have you been drinking?" the man asked earnestly.

"Not a drop," Helen replied honestly.

"Walk over there to my car, in a straight line, with your finger on the tip of your nose," he commanded. Helen did as she was told, although she didn't believe they still made such requests. Couldn't she just breathe into something?

The officer smiled. "Well, seeing as how it's New Year's Day and all, I'll let you off with a warning. But if I catch you again, you're toast. Is that clear?" the officer instructed Helen. She nodded her understanding. "Watch out for this black ice, ma'am. It's deadly."

"Thank you! Thank you so much! Happy New Year to you!"

The officer touched the side of his hat with two fingers, got in his car, and watched Helen slowly pull away.

All the way home, Helen reflected on how lucky she had been. Lucky not to have spun out and killed herself. Lucky there were no other cars on the road. Lucky the cop had been there to help her and even luckier that he hadn't given her a ticket. Whatever little demons had been floating around in her head, they were now gone. She laughed as she told herself, "Too much thinking can kill you."

She took out the Eric Clapton CD again—it always reminded her of the moments of passion she and Frank had actually shared. She inserted Andre Boccelli's Christmas album instead. It held nothing but happy memories since Lou and Ron had only given it to her this year. There was no history, no misery attached to this music.

When Helen pulled into the driveway several hours later, she was surprised to see a little grey Honda in the garage. For a split second, she wondered whose it was, but then she realized that Frank had taken Grace at her word and bought her a car she might actually use. "Good for you, Frank," she said. "And good for you, too, Gracie."

She went up the stairs and into the house. Grace was up, still in her Superman fleece pants and white tee, headphones in her ears, making a terrible racket in the kitchen, spatulas flying, whisks stirring, pans clanging. It sounded like a one-woman band.

"Mom!" Grace yelled, jumping two feet into the air when Helen kissed the nape of her neck. "You scared me to death!" Then she turned around and hugged her mother. "You're back early. Everything okay?"

"Yes and no." Helen laid her cashmere coat on the back of a kitchen chair. "When I got there, my friend was gone."

"Oh, that's too bad," Grace said flipping a pancake in the air. "Did you have to wait long for him?"

"I mean gone as in dead," Helen explained a bit too nonchalantly. "Did you make any coffee?"

"What?" Grace shrieked.

"Coffee," Helen said again.

"Dead?" Grace poured her mother a cup of Santa's White Christmas.

"Dead as in really dead. The police interrogated me for hours. For a minute or two, I was even a suspect." As Helen took the cup, a tremor coursed through her hands.

"Oh my God, Mom! That's awful. How did he die?" Grace now asked delicately.

"Suicide. Overdose. Something like that."

"You didn't see him, did you, Mom?"

"Oh yes," Helen stated matter-of-factly. "I saw him."

"You sure are handling it well."

"I'm still in shock," Helen said quietly, trying to calm the shaking in her hands. But the trembling would not cease and she spilled coffee on her lap.

"The truth is, he was my first, my only love."

Tears began to slip down Helen's cheeks. She wasn't sure who she meant—Webb or Frank. One was dead. The other might as well be. She fought her emotions, gulping hard.

She did not want to meltdown. Grace slipped away from the stove and put her arms around her mother's shoulders.

"Poor, Mommy," she crooned. "You sure do know how to pick 'em."

"Don't I!" Helen said and burst into laughter. "I hope you make better choices."

"Oh, I think she has," said a deep male voice coming down the back stairs. Helen turned and saw Jake. He was as attractive as his photograph, a knockout. He walked over to Helen and held out his hand. He was wearing a pair of jeans and a white V-neck tee.

"Jake Tanner," he said, grasping her cold hand in his warm one.

"Helen Ferry," she replied.

"Nice to meet you, Helen," Jake then grinned. "I've heard a lot about you."

"And I've heard practically nothing about you. Let's sit and chat." Helen sat down at the kitchen table and patted the chair next to hers.

"Hold on!" Grace cried. "He gets to call you Helen?"

"You can call me Helen, darling. If that's what you want." She sipped her coffee.

"No, I can't. You're my mom. You'll always be my mom." Grace emphasized her point by flipping a pancake. "You've just gone soft because of your friend."

"That's right. I'll always be your mom, no matter what you call me, just like you'll always be my Grace," Helen stated solemnly.

"Grace enough for two?" Jake said, putting his arms around his wife and kissing her golden hair.

"Grace enough for us all," Helen said, smiling. "Poor kid," she continued, apologetically. "I should have named you Cordelia or Portia. Something good and Shakespearean. Anyway, I've got to use the potty." Helen rose, her coffee mug in hand.

"You planning on spending a while there?" Grace teased.

"Only as long as it takes," Helen laughed and disappeared.

Chapter 29

When Helen came back, Grace and Jake were standing at the sink washing dishes and whispering secrets to one another, each giggle punctuated by a kiss.

"I actually did find something interesting," she said, interrupting their tryst. "Lao Tsu?" she waved a large black and white book in the air.

"Oh, that's Jake's," Grace explained. "He reads a page a day for his meditation and then starts over. Since today is New Year's, he'll go back to the beginning. Page one."

"I read that one. Made no sense to me," Helen confessed and laughed.

Jake and Grace laughed as well. "It's not meant to make sense, Helen. You read it with your heart. Stay open to its message. If you try to get it, you lose it," Jake then explained.

"That which was lost has been found," Helen murmured.

"What?" Jake and Grace said together.

"It's nothing. Just Perdita. *A Winter's Tale.* Another paradox. Speaking of that," Helen continued, "whose little Honda did I find in my garage?"

"Oh, that was Dad."

"I guess he heard you after all, Sweetie."

"Yeah. It's nice. I like it."

"He loves you. He's trying to do the right thing."

"Are you defending him?" Grace asked rather petulantly.

"I'm just saying that life's too short to hold a grudge."

"You have gone soft because of your friend."

"No," Helen disagreed. "I just think we need to love one another. Forgive, no matter what's been done by whom to whom."

"I'll never forgive Dad." Grace slammed some spoons into a drawer. "And I don't think you should either."

"The thing is, Gracie, if I don't forgive him, if I always keep focusing on how he hurt me, I'll be putting poison in my blood. I'll never be free to give or receive love the rest of my life. I don't want that. I want to be free." Helen sipped her coffee, blowing on it even though it was now cold.

"Wow! Are all your breakfast conversations like this one?" Jake asked. "At our house, the most profound thing anyone ever says is 'Pass the Fruit Loops!'"

The joke broke the tension, and everyone laughed. Grace scooped the remaining pancakes, an elephant and a heart, onto a plate and set them in front of her mother. "That's so you never forget how much I love you." Helen smiled, secretly wanting to decline the pancakes. She would rather have had a salad. It was, after all, past noon. But she saw the look on her child's face and weighed the cost of eating something she really didn't want against the price of disappointing Grace. Why did every little action in life have to be so damned complicated? She wrangled and wrangled over everything these days. Hadn't she told herself this morning that too much thinking would kill her?

She turned to Grace and said as gently as she could, "Sweetheart, I love that you made these pancakes for me, but I'd really rather have a salad for lunch. Can I save them for later?"

"Of course," Grace said and popped the pancakes into a Tupperware container. "They may not be here by then though. Jake loves my pancakes."

"I guess I'll have to take my chances," Helen replied and felt the dull ache of separation well up in her heart.

"Chill, Mom," Grace said putting her arms around her mother's waist. "They're only pancakes. Now, can I fix you a salad? Something with pistachios and pears and goat cheese?"

"That sounds delicious," Helen smiled. "Actually perfect."

Chapter 30

The weeks passed by quickly enough. Helen returned to school and settled into her routine but with a few alterations. With prompting from Sylvia, who had become Helen's confidante and guide, she balanced out her day with noontime walks and Vespers on Wednesday at 5:00 p.m. She was always home in time to make (or bring) dinner at seven, at which time she, Grace, and Jake (if he was in town) talked movies, music, the weather, and, only if they had to, the political events of the day. They would sit in the living room, sunk deeply into the plush sofa and chairs, and watch the landscape change outside the picture windows Helen so loved. The snowstorms and blizzards of January and February turned to flurries in March with a few golden days that teased her into thinking winter was done before BLAM more snow came. Still under the carpet of cold, brave little flowers unfurled until Helen's garden was dappled with snowdrops and crocuses and then a blanket of bright bonneted daffodils gently swaying in the warmer breeze.

Helen had wrestled all winter long with Paris. *To go or not to go?* That is the question she asked herself over and over until one night the decision became quite clear. She and Grace and Jake were playing Scattergories in front of the fire. It was March, and a late spring squall splattered the sky outside. The letter was H; the category was Dream. For Helen, it was easy. She said "happiness" without even thinking. Gracie and Jake both wrote "honeymoon."

"Where did you go on your honeymoon?" Helen asked, vaguely remembering her own with Frank as a Bermuda debacle when she contracted sun poisoning, and he fell off a motor scooter and sprained his ankle. Past history now.

"We didn't have a honeymoon," Grace replied.

"No money. No time," Jake chimed in.

"Oh," Helen said simply, but that night she went on her computer and booked a second ticket and hotels. She was so excited to be able to do this for them and frankly relieved she didn't have to go. She was off the hook now, not having to fantasize about sitting alone at a café in Paris and having some gorgeous Frenchman, a baron no doubt, ask if he could join her. Would she have said "yes"? Would she have said "no"? She was tired of her dream, that one day the right man would just come along. What was her dream? Happiness. And where did happiness really come from? Doing things like what she was doing right this minute, as Sylvia so often reminded her.

The kids were overjoyed. She drove them to the airport on a beautiful April day, April 4th, which turned out was their true anniversary. It couldn't have been better, Helen thought, as she drove home. The last thing Grace said to her as they passed through security was "No expectations, no disappointments, Helen!" Grace had actually called her Helen and then walked through the gate with her husband. Now, for a week, Helen would be alone. The house would be big and silent. She felt that empty feeling returning suddenly again.

No, Helen. Don't be ridiculous. You've been looking forward to this. A week alone. Sleep. Walks. Catching up with Lou and Ron. Then she remembered they had flown to Key West for Easter. Helen sunk deeper and deeper into a loneliness pit. *I thought you were over this! Snap out of it!* But all her self-scolding only reminded her of her ineffective, but cruel, father, who had a knack for making her feel bad about herself, like she was possibly just about the worst creation God had ever had the misfortune to create.

As she rounded the corner into her neighborhood, she was crying. Crying so much that her vision was blurred, and she almost ran over a bag in the road until, just in the nick of time, she realized it was a dog. A stupid dog, she thought, as she turned off the car. What creature in its right mind doesn't move when it sees 2,000 pounds of metal hurling its way?

"This dog," she said and walked up to the unfortunate creature. "Poor thing. You're a worse mess than I am." Then she stopped, unsure if the dog was friendly or fierce. She stood there and put her hand out calling, "Here doggie, doggie, doggie."

She didn't know who looked more foolish, her holding out peanut butter crackers that she kept in reserve in the glove compartment in case the car broke down somewhere and she needed something to eat, or this strange dog, all matted apricot curls and wiggles, shuffling over to her sideways-like, tongue extended and eyes too imploring.

"Silly dog," Helen felt for a collar and identification while the dog licked the salt off her hands. "Is this it? A dog?" she asked, turning her eyes to the heavens. "This is my significant relationship?" Then the dog jumped up onto the back seat of the Volvo, sitting there as if he had been doing it his whole life.

"She," the vet said when Helen brought the dog in to check for a microchip. "She's about two years old, a puppy really. No microchip. Bad fleas. Could use some shots. Unless of course you're just going to take her to the pound. Too bad. She's a pretty dog. I'd take her myself if I could."

Two hundred and fifty dollars later, the puppy had shots, a bath, a trim, and a new home. Unless someone claimed her, in which case "Perdita," as Helen named her, already had another home. From the moment Perdita was bathed and clean, Helen loved her. She was a cheerful little dog—well actually not so little, about the size of a footstool with a mop of curls and a buoyant personality. She followed Helen everywhere on her clickety clack toes, plopping down into a heap whenever Helen stopped, then looking up at her adoringly with round chocolate eyes. The feeling was mutual. Helen felt her heart swell whenever she saw the little dog and wondered how she had lived so long without one. Grace was, of course, overjoyed as well.

Chapter 31

So, spring passed for Helen. The deep ache that she had felt after Webb's death, the hurt and anger that she felt from Frank's betrayal, the loss of her dreams with Alan and Micah, all had become faint and hushed. She did not have a man, but she had her dog, her daughter and her son-in-law, her garden, and her job. It was enough to keep her distracted from the sadness that she felt inside. The lilacs in May were splendid, more robust and fragrant than any year she could recall. Harry Belafonte singing "Green Grow the Lilacs" simply made her laugh. "I've got everyone I need. No illusive 'you' is going to make this dream complete." She worked hard to convince herself that was true.

In June, the Shasta daisies formed a brilliant congregation, and in July the Stargazer lilies and purple coneflowers added color to the frame. All summer long she watered and weeded and hoed, tending her garden as Rabelais would instruct. Perdita sat in the shade and watched, licking imaginary things off her paws and snapping at bugs. *Il faut cultivar nos jardins* she thought as she dead-headed the golden coreopsis and the blue geraniums.

She also felt good about her own garden, the garden of her soul. Her relationship with Grace was solid and sweet. When Jake wasn't here, they spent good time together with Grace in the hammock and Helen stretched out on a chaise with Perdita beside her. They talked about nothing and were silent when they grew tired of that. Sometimes Helen ached for the years she had missed by being so preoccupied with her career, but the long lazy afternoons now were making up for that lost time. She was good with Lou and Ron, although they were always so busy with one thing or another that she rarely saw them anymore. She had lost touch with Gloria, but had kept up with Sylvia, who continued to be a source of inspiration and comfort. And, of course, clothes. More vintage suits had arrived and pillbox hats and gloves. "In the fall," Grace had said, "you should be Jackie Kennedy for Halloween."

She was even good with Frank, though that had taken a bit more doing. During a particularly rough spot when all she wanted to do was to blast a hole in him and Stephanie and to hell with the evening news, her priest at church just told her to pray for them. Pray that all good things would come to them too. She refused, of course, until she couldn't anymore. Then she started praying and gradually all the pain simply rolled off her. It didn't get to her anymore. Most of the time.

That their wedding anniversary was only a week away did trouble her. Would all this goodness melt away and drown her in self-pity again? *I won't let it,* she told herself resolutely. But could she stop it? *Can any of us know how we'll feel in a week, in a day, in an hour?* Life was a series of moments and that was all, just as Lao Tsu wrote. *What can we know anyway? Nothing.*

It all came back to nothing. Ingmar Bergman's *intighet.* The metaphoric crystal glass shattered by the silver spoon. Helen shook her head and sat up, dizzy from her dozing.

"You want some tea, love?" she asked Grace, who was rocking gently to and fro.

"I'm good."

Helen walked to the back door with Perdita following. "Who's my good dog?" Helen cooed. "You'll never leave me. Right, girl?"

Leave me. Where did that thought come from? Helen pulled the iced tea from the fridge and squeezed a lemon slice into it. Must be the twinge of autumn or that old worry that nothing this good can possibly last forever.

Sure enough, just like a magic trick, the flourish of the wrist that reveals that everything you believed was real is now gone, all the goodness transformed. Lou and Ron decided to relocate to Key West and open a Guest House. While it was sad and she would miss them dearly, it was not the end of the world. Then, her Realtor called her and asked, out of the blue, had she considered selling because if she had, he had a buyer ready to go. She wasn't considering selling, at least not until Grace spilled the beans she was three months pregnant. Wonderful news in and of itself, except they were going to move out and into a town home that Frank had given them the down payment to buy. In less than a week, Helen lost everything—her daughter, her home, her best friends. She kept waiting for the tears to flow, the ache to throb unrelentingly, but she felt nothing except joy for all involved. Herself included. No regrets.

Chapter 32

One month later, she was in her office at school. Perdita lay at her feet snoring as Helen graded the first batch of papers of her school year. She wondered how these kids had even managed to get into Yale, given how deplorable their prose was. She took off her reading glasses and rubbed her eyes. It had been a long day. She wasn't looking forward to going home to an empty house. It was just her and Perdita now, eating cottage cheese and fruit for dinner while she watched the news. Then, she heard a gentle knock on the door. She looked up.

"Enter," she trilled.

She did not know the man who nearly filled the door frame in front of her, he was so large. Not fat, just large. His hair was an over exuberant mop of jet-black curls. His wide hazel eyes sparkled, and his smile was broad and kind. His stature served him well in all his pastimes—club rugby, rowing (he had once been on an Olympic team), acting in Caerphilly's chapter of *Gilbert and Sullivan* (he was the Mikado in a recent production), singing in an *a cappella* group called Dod Gyda Mi, and dancing the Nantgarw, a type of Morris dancing, though he actually preferred ballroom and swing. He also mentored a waif from Cardiff whose family was desolate and had left him for lost. However, Helen would not know these things about Gerard until much later because he was a humble man, one of few words. He was a truly gentle man who, though of course experiencing the appetites of us all, leaned a little more toward sainthood than your average Joe did. What kept him grounded was his heart, his big heart, which told him that somewhere was a real woman, the woman of his dreams.

"Dr. Ferry?" he asked politely. He had an accent of some kind, but she couldn't detect it. Maybe Irish? Scot?

"Please, I'm Helen," she rose and held out her hand.

"Gerard. Gerard Ferguson," he said taking her hand in his own firm grasp. "Your jacket photos don't do you credit. Yours is, indeed, a face to launch a thousand ships."

"Surely you haven't come all the way from…"

"Wales."

"Wales, to tell me that."

"Oh. No, no, no. I'm on sabbatical here. From Cardiff."

"Well, welcome," Helen said, more graciously. "Welcome indeed."

"The Dean said you might be willing to show me about," he sounded a bit shy. "I'd be honored if you'd join me for dinner."

"I'd be delighted," Helen smiled. "Will your wife be joining us?"

"Oh, there is no wife. I'm solo," he blushed.

"Well, let me just straighten up my desk, and we can be on our way," Helen shuffled her papers together into a pile and put her pencils away, smiling the whole while.

"Are you certain? I can come back in an hour if that's better for you."

"Absolutely not. This is perfect. Just perfect." She came out from behind her desk, grabbed her coat and purse from the coat rack, and snapped the leash on Perdita. Then she swept her arm toward the door. "After you." Gerard walked through the door, and Helen hit the light switch and pulled the door shut. "Shall we?"

And they did.

The miracle of change is that it often begins without our being aware of it. The Universe simply graces us with moments that we later realize are the very core of a new and wonderful life. The moment Helen closed her office door, she accepted a gift that would alter her life forever. In blissful ignorance, she embraced love.

Chapter 33

"That went surprisingly well," Helen said to herself as she buckled up her seat belt and started home to Stony Creek. "Home," Helen then chuckled to herself. It was hardly home yet. Just an aging Cape filled with cardboard boxes in need of some TLC. The thought reminded her of the dinner she had just shared with Gerard Ferguson, the visiting scholar from Wales she had met only hours earlier, but who she hoped to count as a friend. A good friend.

What did her daughter, Grace, always say about strangers and friends? The difference was being open. Letting go of expectations. Since the divorce, Helen hadn't really felt ready or prepared to do that. Until now. She was suddenly ready to move into a new home, be a grandmother, and welcome a new man into her life. As a friend, for now. But then, who knew what might come later?

The sky was heavy and golden as she made her way from work to the little house that she had found by accident. She was scouting new neighborhoods for something with a different view from the one she had shared with Frank for thirty years. She wanted to be free of the massive gardens she had cultivated so lovingly over the years and of the work that had gone into each of the tiny plants she had nurtured and raised to maturity. Let someone else prick themselves while pruning their anniversary roses. She had spilled enough blood in her marriage, both figuratively and literally. The pruning, the weeding, the dividing. It all had produced a glorious effect of course, pungent and playful with butterflies and bees. But enough was enough. Now she wanted something less strenuous, more serene. She wanted water, and so she had set out to find the perfect little house with a gorgeous water view. Unfortunately, all the houses the Realtors showed her were massive structures with endless docks and factory-sized boat slips. They all came with a price tag that was longer than a list of Shakespeare's insults. So, she had given up. Almost. Until that day when she agreed to meet her Realtor one last time. She had gotten lost and found herself at the end of an old dirt road where smack in front of her was a small Cape, windows boarded, with yellow "No Trespassing" tape wrapped around the edge of the entire property.

Channeling the girl of her youth who had broken into chapels, cafeterias, and pools, Helen slipped under the tape and walked around the house, peeking in windows where she could and pricking herself as she moved branches of sweet pink roses out of the way so she could see the view. The view! What a view! It took her breath away. An overgrown lawn rolled down into a golden marsh that wound its way out to the Long Island Sound. The indigo Sound, smooth and flat, echoed the deepening colors of the sky. "This is Heaven," Helen said aloud, and she pulled out her phone and dialed her Realtor.

"Oliver," she said. "I found it!"

Now, several months and many hundreds of thousand dollars later, millions really, she owned it and was fixing it up to really make it her own. Her financial advisor had cautioned her against sinking her entire savings into the little Cape, but Lou, her old neighbor who dabbled in real estate and now lived in a multi-million-dollar home in Key West, encouraged her to pursue her dreams.

"It's a no-lose situation," he told her. "You fix it up and live in it for the next twenty years, and you'll have a sound investment. Hell! Five years and you'll double your money. You'll own the view and there is nothing that can ever take that away. It's priceless. Even if you just fix it and flip it, you'll end up better off than you were before."

Helen considered the renovations that would be necessary. The house needed a new roof and the kitchen definitely had to be updated. The bathrooms were in surprisingly good shape and not too dated, no avocado tubs or orange tiles. The downstairs bath did have brown wallpaper with orange and white flowers swirling around, but she kind of liked that and decided to keep it, no matter what. Of course, everything else needed to be cleaned thoroughly and painted and a pane or two replaced. But, she had friends who could help her. Even if she didn't, she could always do a lot of it herself.

Chapter 34

*H*elen had told Gerard all about her house at their first dinner, at the start of the semester in mid-August. The following week, when they met again, she shared her plans with him for Labor Day weekend. With the kitchen finished and the new roof on, she had arranged for the Habitat for Humanity crew to come over for the day and paint the interior rooms in what she was calling "a painting party." She asked if Gerard might want to join in the fun.

"I'd love to help," Gerard had offered when she told him about the event. "I'm a good painter, and I'm excellent with wood if you need bookcases built or cupboards and doors aligned."

Helen immediately felt uncomfortable with the offer. After all, she had only just met this man. Might he misconstrue her message and assume that she owed him favors in return?

"Not to be rude," she ventured, "but are you assuming that your generosity is owed favors, if you will, in return?"

Gerard threw back his head and laughed. "They warned me about you American women, how if I offered to take you to dinner, you'd assume I was asking for sex."

"Well, are you?" Helen asked.

"Good God! No! I just wanted to ask you for the whereabouts of a good cinema and if there's somewhere I might be able to stick my toes in the sand."

"Sorry," Helen blushed. "It's just some past experience..."

"I know, I know," Gerard replied, kindly. "Most men are louts."

The waitress arrived with a steaming plate of fried calamari. "Can I get you anything else?" she asked.

"I think we're good for now," Helen answered, then quickly adding, "I'm good. Do you need anything else, Gerard?"

"Another one of these," he said, chugging down his bottle of IBC root beer and putting the empty bottle on the waitress's tray. "Bloody good!" And he smiled broadly at Helen.

Helen looked at Gerard for a long time, then they simultaneously reached in and pulled out the baby octopi and dipped them in marinara sauce. Their hands touched, and a moment passed between them. Finally, she broke the silence.

"So, what's your story?" she asked. "Are you married? Divorced? Widowed? Gay?"

"None of the above," Gerard smiled, "I'm a confirmed bachelor."

"All these years?" Helen asked a bit too gently.

"Forever. Until I meet the woman of my dreams, that is."

"Surely you must be a little Irish," Helen laughed and Gerard's face broke into a wide smile, punctuated by two deep dimples in his cheeks.

"Welsh," he replied, "through and through."

"Ah Wales," Helen nodded. "The land of Dylan Thomas."

Gerard smiled again. "I'm hoping to find my Caitlin someday. I'll settle for nothing less."

"Well, in the meantime, come help me paint this weekend. You can stick your toes in the water at my beach, although it's starting to get cold here."

Gerard smiled again. "I'd love to. But how shall I get there?"

"I'll come get you. I have some stuff to pick up from my office in the morning anyway."

"Perfect," Gerard replied. The waitress cleared away the calamari and set down two enormous hamburgers smothered in mushrooms and onions and surrounded by sweet potato fries.

"God Bless America!" Gerard laughed, raising his root beer bottle to Helen. She laughed and raised her lemon water in return. They clinked their glasses, and she felt something. *Hope*, she thought. Hope that this easy-going Welshman might just be the friendship that she had been looking for.

Chapter 35

_T_he next morning at home, Grace was practicing her Tai Chi in front of the large sliding doors that looked out over their small brownish yard and the brick building next door. Not exactly the view Grace had hoped for, but it was what she and Jake could afford. They had enough room, two bedrooms and a bath, a manageable kitchen, and a living room/dining room that blended one into the other. The Home Owners Association had allowed her to plant a garden, so they had fresh tomatoes, peppers, basil, and squash all summer long. There were trails all around the complex where she would be able to wheel the baby when she was born. "She," Grace giggled, "hard to believe there's a little girl inside me."

Grace glided through her movements like a heron slowly winging its way across a cerulean sky. As she held the vessel gently and then turned to grasp the swallow's tail, she felt something in her belly. She stopped and lay down on the sofa, closed her eyes, and inhaled a few deep breaths. That's when she felt it, a burst, the first burst ever, in her belly. It was unlike anything she had ever felt before. No burps, no gas, no heartburn ever felt this way. It was a knock, a tiny kick from inside. Then it came again! Grace placed her hands on the spot where the kick had come from. She closed her eyes and breathed very slowly and quietly, waiting. Tears ran down her cheeks and under her chin, and she licked them away, laughing. "My baby likes Tai Chi!" she said aloud. Then she reached for the phone to call Helen because Helen needed to know. She'd track Jake down later; he was en route to Dubai. But Helen needed to know and know now.

"Mom," Grace said breathlessly when Helen picked up the phone.

"What is it, Gracie? Is everything okay?" Helen asked, immediately concerned.

"Fine. I'm fine. We're fine. It's just that I felt her kick!" Grace squeaked.

"Oh, Sweetheart, that's wonderful!" Helen replied. "Isn't that just the best?"

"Actually, it's kind of weird. But cool. I'm lying here hoping she does it again and soon." Grace was, in fact, lying on the sofa with their fat grey cat, Hero, stretched out beside her, purring heavily.

"Well don't hold your breath," Helen cautioned. "If she's anything like you were, she'll choose her own time and place to make herself known. What does Jake think of all this?"

"He doesn't know. He's on his way to Dubai."

Helen hated that Grace was alone when such a momentous occasion occurred. "What are your plans for this afternoon? Evening? Would you like some company?" Helen asked.

"Thanks, Mom, but I have a big test online tonight. I need to study."

"What about tomorrow, then?" Helen persisted. "I'm having the whole Habitat crew come out to the new house and paint. All day. Free lunch. Swimming. Are you in? I could pick you up early, and you could either help or spend the day sitting on the one piece of furniture I have in the place," Helen cajoled her daughter with promises of a grand day.

Grace thought for a moment, then agreed. "Sure. Sounds like fun."

"Great! I'll see you around seven. Good luck on your test!" Helen hung up, fully aware that she had not mentioned Gerard. Indeed, Grace had made it clear that she was not particularly interested in who her mother might be dating now that the divorce was finally over. Helen had struck out twice with online arrangements. The first was a charismatic Irish lawyer with a beautiful tenor voice. His sparkling blue eyes and wild white curls could not make up for the fact that he was a raging alcoholic. Helen had narrowly escaped with her sanity intact. The second "date" was a very fit, athletic fellow who spent his life at the gym. A retiree from the water business, he was charismatic until you got to know him. Then he was arrogant, opinionated, and sexist. That was what pushed Helen over the edge; that, and the fact that he was small, very short. At five feet eleven inches, she towered over him. His mouth came just to her breasts, exactly where she did not want his mouth to be. At first, she overlooked it, but after one peanut butter and kale smoothie with him, she folded and walked away, well actually limped away because by then she had developed *plantar fasciitis* and her gym days were done for a while. She left him lifting weights in front of the mirror, taking long pregnant pauses to gaze on his always glorious self. Grace was less than impressed with Helen's choices and made no bones about voicing her concern. "You are settling for less, Mom! You are better off by yourself than with one of those losers," she said.

Who knew what would happen with Gerard? So far, Grace had been quiet on the subject. Still, he might turn out to be the biggest lout in history. But really, she was just looking for a friend right now. Someone to go to dinner with, and the movies. So far, he seemed pleasant enough, but tomorrow would tell her more. Much more.

Chapter 36

*T*he next morning broke with perfect skies and air as clear as a choir boy's pitch. *I couldn't have asked for a better day for painting!* Helen thought as she walked to her car. The sun was shining, and the air had a touch of fall. She knew that by the water there would be a little breeze, and she would open all the windows to help the paint dry more quickly and air the place out. Tonight would be her first night at the new house. The movers were coming to the old house today. She had left Frank, who had decided to keep the house and had paid her handsomely, in charge of overseeing the operation. She wasn't a bit nervous. Frank, for all his lying and scheming, was still an honest man; he wouldn't cheat her out of anything she was owed. Stephanie's taste was not Helen's taste at all, so Helen was sure the bitch couldn't wait to be rid of any vestige of Frank's first wife. She had even heard from a secret source that his new wife intended to rip out the gardens and install a swimming pool set in a sea of concrete.

Helen felt the anger well up inside, so she turned her attention to the road and was amazed that she was already at Grace's. *How did that happen? I'm driving without knowing I'm driving. It's frightening, dangerous really, but I do it all the time.*

Grace climbed into the front seat and kissed her mother on the cheek.

"Back at you, sweetie," Helen said and took off down the road.

Grace turned to look in the back of the Volvo and saw all the paint cans and paraphernalia. "Looks like you robbed the store." Grace laughed.

"Just about. I am hoping to get it all done today, though."

"How'd you rope the Habitat kids into doing this on the holiday weekend?" Grace asked.

"One of my students is the President of Habitat at Yale. She's a sweetheart and a real go-getter. She persuaded the rest of the crew that earning hours this way would mean they could forgo a trip to Alabama in the spring."

"But don't they go to underserved communities? How do you qualify as underserved?"

Helen just feigned shock. "Are you kidding? A sixty-year-old woman, recently divorced, with medical issues and a limited income?"

"You have medical issues?"

"*Plantar fasciitis.* I can barely walk."

"I thought all that was cured."

"Well, all right. But I'm still too sore to paint a whole house on my own. And too poor to hire anyone," Helen's voice had taken on an edge. "Besides, I made a sizable donation."

"I'm not trying to be mean, Mom. I just wanted to get the whole picture. It sounds like you've got a great situation worked out for yourself."

They drove on in silence, Helen brooding and Grace calculating, but neither willing to speak any more about it. When they turned to go into New Haven, Grace offered, "This is the way to town."

"I have to pick up something from my office," Helen smiled.

"What something?" Grace asked a bit skeptically.

"Someone, actually," Helen replied, knowing where their conversation would lead, but not wanting to go there.

"Anyone I know?"

"Just a friend. Gerard," Helen stated as casually as possible.

"Gerard? Who is this Gerard? Not another online…" Grace looked annoyed.

"Of course not!" Helen interrupted. "He's a visiting professor. Just a friend," Helen continued, of course thinking to herself that she hoped he would be a friend. "Anyway, he knows how to paint, so I recruited him for the day."

Helen pulled in front of her building. Gerard was sitting on a bench reading a newspaper. His reading glasses sat on the end of his nose, and he was wearing old khakis, a T-shirt with a blue work shirt over it, and a pair of well-worn sneakers.

"There he is," Helen said to Grace. "You-hoo," she called out the window. "Gerard! We're here!"

"You-hoo?" Gracie said in disbelief. She unbuckled her seat belt which for some reason was malfunctioning. She could not escape into the backseat before Gerard arrived.

"Hello!" Gerard said cheerfully and climbed into the car.

"Sorry, but the seat belt is stuck," Grace took a closer look at the dashing Gerard. He was certainly large, but he was movie star handsome. He was younger than Helen by a good twenty years. Funny how Helen had failed to mention that small detail.

"Not to worry," Gerard said amiably. "I'm perfectly fine back here, unless you'd like me to try and free you from your imprisonment. Gracie, is it? Well, you're every bit as lovely as your mother."

"Careful, Mom," Grace whispered. "He's got an Irish tongue."

"Welsh," Helen corrected her, pleasantly. "Well, let's get going, shall we? We have a long day of painting ahead." They drove in silence until Grace could bear it no longer.

"What did you pick for colors?" Gracie asked, searching for an impersonal topic.

"Where shall I begin?" Helen giggled and pulled out into the steady stream of traffic toward her new home.

Chapter 37

Forty-five minutes later, they arrived at the "dream house," as Helen had taken to calling her aging Cape. The Habitat crew was already there on the lawn, munching on egg and bacon sandwiches and sipping hot coffee. As Helen pulled into the drive, a wholesome looking strawberry blonde in white painter pants and a tie-dyed T-shirt stood up and waved.

"That's Abigail." Helen waved back and parked the Volvo on the lawn by the back door.

"Morning, Professor Ferry," said Abigail as she arrived breathless at the car. Standing with her was a very tall, very thin young man wearing the same outfit, but not breathless at all. His name was Mike.

"Good morning, Professor Ferry." He grinned.

"Look you two, none of this Professor Ferry stuff," Helen commanded. "Helen will be fine."

"Well, Helen, it looks like you've stocked up well," said Mike, taking charge. "We'd better get the troops assembled." He put his fingers to his lips and let loose a shrill, piercing whistle. It chased the small birds from the wires overhead and sent the Habitat crew scampering like sheep.

When everyone had gathered around, Abigail called out, "Everyone, this is Helen. Helen, everyone."

Helen smiled. "I wish I could learn all your names, but suffice it to say I want to thank you for coming today. I can't tell you how much I appreciate it. This is my daughter, Grace." Grace stepped forward and gave a little wave. "She'll be in charge of lunch, so you'll want to keep an eye on her. She's also our water girl, so if you're thirsty, just shout out. It's important you stay hydrated. God knows we don't want anyone fainting while painting. Oh dear, that's an awful rhyme." Helen's comments were met with laughter, which she knew was not always the case with students this age. Still, she reminded herself, these were not ordinary students. These were students who have given up a part of their Labor Day weekend to help a stranger out. She loved them for that. Helen's happy reveries were interrupted when Gerard cleared his throat.

"Oh yes. This is Professor Ferguson. He will be helping us out today," Helen continued.

"It's just Gerard," he insisted as he stepped forward. "I may be a visiting professor with a charming accent, but today I am just another one of the lackeys. I expect you to treat me as such!"

"Oh, we will treat you 'as such!'" called a raspy voice from the back of the group. An old man, his skin tanned and leathery, made his way to the front of the crowd. "Hello, Helen."

"Jack," Helen cried and flung her arms around him in a hug. "Everyone, this is Jack O'Toole. My angel. He has almost singlehandedly brought this house back from the dead."

"Horse feathers," he replied, modestly though obviously pleased with the praise. "Heard there was a little painting party going on today. Thought I might join in. Well don't everybody just stand there! Get to work!" he exclaimed.

Abigail and Mike loaded Gerard up with drop cloths, brushes, and tape and instructed him to take it all inside. Once all the paint cans were inside, the elves began to tape. Helen, Abigail, and Mike walked around the house distributing the colors: silvery-brown in the dining room, creamy white in the kitchen, ivory in the living room, teal in the first bedroom, honey in the second, and mossy green in the den. Upstairs, the master bedroom, which took up almost all of the top floor, was a pale twilight blue, and the bathroom was a deep plum. The bathroom downstairs was already papered in a vintage orange flower design on brown, and Helen loved it. Grace was sure her mother would change her mind within a few weeks and suggested she purchase a gallon of deep orange paint, but Helen held fast. This was her dream.

"Wow," commented Abigail when they were through with the tour. "It's going to be quite a transformation here."

"That's what we're aiming for," Helen smiled. "I'm at a fairly transformative place in my life."

Mike started taping the plum bathroom-to-be, while Abigail stood with Helen at the top of the stairs. She took out her camera and snapped photos of each of the rooms in their current state of disrepair.

"What an excellent idea!" Helen exclaimed. "I should have thought of that!"

"I always like to photograph a site in its original state and then later," Abigail explained. "Before and after. It's satisfying to see the change."

Helen considered the profound significance of her words. She wished she had photos of her spirit before, when she was so frightened and hurt by Frank's betrayal, and then her frenzy period when she tried to fill the hole with a new man, to right now when she felt so excited about creating her own space, her own home, and living free of any desire to share it with anyone, except Grace and Jake and the baby. Yet even as she said that, she realized that it wasn't totally true. She wanted to share her life, but just on her terms, with someone who would be loving and loyal and passionate and sincere. A true companion. But given as she had yet to meet such a paragon, because most of the men she met were either drunks or dullards or self-absorbed asses, she had pretty much given up hope. She disguised her despair as a new spirituality, attending church again and reading books by New Age authors about self-actualization and self-love. She believed if she could convince herself she was living a more spiritual life without sex and conflict, she would be all right. The problem was that she couldn't, and she wasn't.

She just wasn't there yet. She wanted the warmth of a large hand wrapped around hers in the cold, or the playful teasing of shoving someone into a pile of leaves or the delicious taste of a deep kiss. The truth was, she wanted to be able to take a man out of her wardrobe and wear him like a friend that suited her mood and her desire at that particular moment. She wanted a man with a remote, be able to push one button for comforting attention and another one for raucous joy.

But people aren't dolls, Helen told herself, and I'm not a doll either. So that was that.

She looked out the window at the harbor and the big sailboats that were now rocking to and fro. Their lines and masts tapped each other and chinked, tinkled like a company of friends toasting in a new year. Her mind wandered back to the last New Year's, when she found Webb dead in his apartment. There had been no conviviality, no toasts, just the dull thud of the end of a significant quest. Her life seemed to be peeling away layer by layer.

"Are you okay, Helen?" Abigail's voice broke into her thoughts. "You look sad." Helen only smiled and laughed.

"Just thinking. Always a dangerous activity. I think I'll go check on things upstairs." She turned to mount the stairs, then turned again. "Abigail, I want to thank you for all you've done, are doing. There simply aren't enough words."

Abigail smiled her wide smile. "It's what we do. We help each other. It's what keeps us all spinning."

"Well, spin away then." Helen walked upstairs and into her bedroom. Gerard was there alone, painting. He seemed so focused on what he was doing, making sure of his long strokes and the even distribution of paint that he didn't realize she had come in until she cleared her throat.

"Hello! Have you been here long?" he asked, continuing to paint.

"Not really. It's looking good." She realized that he really was a good painter and that his offer to help had not been an idle one.

"Absolutely," he replied. "I love this color by the way. I was expecting more of a flat, pale blue, but this shade is more bluey-purply-pink. It shines!"

"It's called 'Luminescence.' It does glow actually, sort of like twilight does. That's why I bought it."

Gerard smiled, laughed a bit and put his brush down. "Funny. I would have thought you would have chosen green, sea foam green actually, to offset your eyes."

"And why would I do that?" Helen was now curious.

"Well, most beautiful women like to look their best in all circumstances," he said, winking at her.

"That's ridiculous! I'd have to walk around all the time with palm leaves behind my head. Besides, I'm over green. I'm looking for more color in my life."

"Be honest, Helen," Gerard continued. "Your last bedroom was green. Grey green. Am I right?"

"What if you are?" Helen returned his question with a question, refusing to give him the win.

"No matter. I didn't mean to offend you."

"No offense taken. Though I wonder, if you are such a confirmed bachelor, how is it you know so much about women?" Helen teased.

"I said I was a bachelor, not a monk," Gerard answered grinning again. "Now, about lunch…"

"Soon, I think. I hope you like turkey subs and potato chips."

"Delicious. I'm going to have to roll home to Wales at the end of the semester. My colleagues won't recognize me," he laughed.

Helen had nothing at all invested in Gerard, after all, they had barely just met, but still she felt a twinge at the thought of his leaving. He had just arrived and brought some new interest into her life, but already he was tossing about his departure like a Frisbee that lands in the Sound and is carried swiftly out to sea. It was hard to hold on to hope when people insisted on dragging you down all the time.

Gerard picked up his brush again and resumed his long, slow strokes. Helen watched him, sitting on the cot she had brought to sleep on until all the furniture arrived on Monday. She watched the way that he almost caressed the walls with the brush, and she imagined he was likely a very gentle lover, attentive to a woman's every need. Or maybe, she thought, checking her thoughts, he's just a good painter. He reached the last corner of the wall and finished the first coat. He wrapped the brush in plastic and wiped his brow with a paint-speckled arm. "This would be a good place to stop, I think," he said.

Grace's voice shattered the silence. "Mom! I'm going to pick up lunch!"

"Do you want me to come too?" Helen hollered back.

"No problem. Abi's going to ride with me. I'm taking your purse though."

Lunch arrived and was devoured by all. The second coats of color were applied, and Helen wandered through the house with Abi continually snapping shots of the now resplendent rooms. The color lifted the house which had before seemed to slouch and sink like an elderly man. Now it held itself upright, erect. Everything glistened, from the wide pine floors to the ceilings. Helen swore she would never wear beige again. It would all be magentas and plums and golds from now on. She would also stand straighter and declare her place in the world.

She had arranged for the neighborhood ice cream truck to stop at her house around 3:00 p.m. as a treat for the workers. Sure enough, at three o'clock on the dot, just as the brushes were being washed and the paint lids knocked back on tight, the tinny Butch Cassidy theme floated through the air. Eyes opened wide and then smiles abounded.

"Ice cream is on me!" Helen called out and the Habitat kids swarmed over to the truck.

"Thanks, Helen!" they chimed one after the other as they munched their strawberry shortcake bars and licked their chocolate popsicles.

"My pleasure! Thank *you*!" Helen grinned and slipped Jimmy the ice cream man a sizable tip. "And thank you, too." He just tipped his hat, smiled, and drove away.

The ice cream finished, the crew donned bathing suits and ran en masse down to the beach, where they dropped their towels, kicked off their sneakers, and plunged into the water. Helen was pleased by the laughter and youthful antics of the teens, because that's what they were, teens, or maybe just brushing twenty years old. What young people in this day and age actually took pleasure in helping an old woman out by waking at the crack of dawn, painting on a hot summer's day, and then engaging in water and chicken fights when they must have been bone tired?

Helen decided she would have to throw a Christmas party for this special group to show her gratitude. Then she remembered Grace was due on December 17, and the semester ended the week before. There were papers and exams, always a flood of them. Maybe she would have to forgo the party and send them gift cards to Starbucks instead. How impersonal. She would work it out though.

Meanwhile she sat on the beach with Perdita, Gerard, and Grace and watched the kids frolic.

Turning to Gerard, she asked, "Do you want to go get wet? After all, that's what you came for, isn't it?"

Gerard responded with a smile again. "Not entirely. You really are most lucky, you know," he told her. "This is an absolute slice of Heaven. It's different, but it totally reminds me of home."

"Come on, Gerard," Grace said, rising. "Let's go see if the water feels the same as it does in Wales."

Gerard hoisted himself off the sand and sauntered down to the beach; his iridescent white skin set off indigo blue swim trunks. He towered over Grace, who waddled a little, and Perdita, who bounced a lot. Helen watched them all— the teens, the man, the gulls, her daughter, and her dog, all the diamonds on the water.

"Lucky indeed," she told herself, thinking of how she had stumbled on this place. Yet she knew, too, that luck had nothing to do with it. The moment her marriage had started to go sour, nine years ago now, she had started to sock money away from her salary. She saved every penny from book sales and lecture tours; she never spent a cent of the gifts she received from fans for years. Then, there was Uncle Ted. Her only uncle, and she, his only niece. To support an Army buddy, he had invested in a hotel in the 1940s. It had gone on to become one of the biggest chains in the hotel business, with more than 1,400 locations. Over the years, he had amassed a sizeable fortune. When he died, he had left a small portion of it to her. The rest he had sprinkled over various charities in Vermont, the state he had loved and chosen for his retirement. Maybe luck did have something to do with it, she had to concede. Whatever it was, she had somehow known there would come a day when his gift would come in handy, and this was that day. She was glad she hadn't squandered it on expensive toys and trips for Frank, a feeble attempt at healing the wounds in their marriage. She might have lost him, but she had this. As she looked out over the golden beach and the blue water, she imagined her granddaughter spinning in the sand, arms outstretched, laughing, just as Grace was laughing now. Helen knew she had finally made the right choice.

Grace returned with a soaked and sandy but happy Perdita, and happiness did matter, after all.

"You'll have to bathe her," Grace instructed.

"Good thing there's an outside shower," Helen replied. "You can take her in it with you when you go in."

"Seriously, Mom? That water's freezing," Grace whined.

"I'll do it," Abi piped up. She and Mike had plopped down on a towel beside Helen several minutes earlier.

"You're a darling," Helen said, patting Abi's arm. Across the towel, Grace scowled and pouted. "But not as darling as my darling Grace is. She's my super-special girl."

Abi grinned. "Of course."

Seagulls wheeled overhead, bright white missiles streaking against the cloudless blue sky. It was late afternoon, and the sun was losing some of its power as it descended. Still, the Habitat crew played in the water. Helen and her entourage sat on the shore, licked by the breeze and calmed by the beauty around them. Up the beach a way, a well-proportioned woman in a black tank suit that looked as if it had been painted on her was walking an Irish wolfhound. Perdita, excited to find a new friend, leapt up, bounced away to go say hello. Abi caught her just in time, holding her while Helen attached the leash.

"Pity you can't just let her run," Gerard observed.

"I know. I hate keeping her tied up all the time."

"I couldn't help but notice you've started a new fence," Gerard stated.

"It was supposed to have been finished weeks ago, but the workers disappeared," Helen lamented.

"If you'd allow me," he said, "I could grab two of these strapping fellows, and we could have it finished by tomorrow's end."

"Mike and I will do it," Abi chimed in. "We're used to digging holes. Remember that site in Florida, Mike? That's all we did, dig holes there for an irrigation system."

Mike groaned and Gerard laughed. "This will be easier. We have augurs and the soil is loose. The job will fly by," he reassured them both.

"We're in then," the two agreed in unison.

"Perfect," Gerard grinned.

"Be my guests," Helen added, waving her hand in the direction of the posts.

"I'll go take a look," Gerard said, rising. Abi and Mike went with him, leaving Grace and Helen to stare out at the water.

"Well, you certainly let him direct the show," Grace noted. "He's like a bull."

"I know," Helen agreed, "and I kind of like it."

"Don't like it too much, Mom," Grace cautioned. "You know what happened with those other guys."

"I know, but somehow I think this guy will be different."

"Spoken like a true addict," Grace retorted.

"No, seriously, Grace. This time it feels different. I feel different too."

"How long did you say you've been seeing this guy?" Grace asked pointedly.

"I'm not seeing him," Helen clarified her situation. "We're colleagues."

Grace rolled her eyes. "Seriously, Mom? And you're trusting him with the key to your house?"

"Who said anything about a key?"

"The fence. They're going to need a place to pee," Grace stated what she felt should have been obvious to her mother. "What pregnant woman doesn't constantly think about where to pee?"

"So, I'll supervise."

Grace looked shocked and a bit hurt. "I thought you were going to go shopping with me for the nursery stuff. We were going to have a girls' day out together tomorrow…"

Helen stifled a serious sigh that would have given away her frustration at having to be a mother and a grandmother when all she really wanted to do was get her house in order.

"You still want to go, don't you?" Grace's voice was plaintive.

"Of course, I do, sweetheart. I guess I'm just going to have to trust Gerard, that's all. Maybe I'll ask him to turn over his passport or something."

Grace laughed. "There you go. Now you're thinking."

"I'm sure it will all be fine."

The sun dipped further below the horizon, and the tired workers trudged up from the water, bathed in its rosy light. There was talk of a bonfire, but there was no wood. No s'mores. No dinner. So as suddenly as the sun set, Helen found herself suddenly alone with Gerard and Grace. As she shut the lights off in the house and locked the door, she sighed. This day had been a very good day indeed.

Chapter 38

On Sunday, while Abigail, Mike, and Gerard toiled away building a new fence for the yard, Helen and Grace took a day trip to IKEA. They knew that every serious bargain hunter who had a modicum of taste shopped there. For Helen, every decorated showroom was like reading a page in a book. Complete and well organized, these designs helped you chart a course, consolidate your possibilities, partner items you'd never dream of putting together. Today Helen and Grace were looking especially for baby items, a crib, a changing table, a bureau. Those tasks proved too easy to accomplish, so after they chose a pretty white set with simple lines but sturdy construction, Grace decided to accessorize. They wound their way through the aisles looking for lamps and rugs and a rocking chair. Of course, they found plenty.

"Mom, wouldn't this be perfect in your new kitchen?" asked Grace and held up an eight-ounce glass speckled with red and gold.

Helen cinched her nose. "I think I'm all set on glassware. But wait, let me see that one. Do they come in a larger size?" Helen then rationalized her purchase by convincing herself that they were inexpensive, necessary, and part of the new person she was now choosing to be. The old glasses could go to Goodwill. They had been wedding presents, so they were lucky to have lasted this long, but, when she went to smash the thick, blue-ringed Mexican glass after Frank filed the papers for divorce, she just couldn't. Now, at least, they would find a new home.

"What about these?" Grace asked, holding up a couple of juice glasses with red roosters on their sides. "Aren't they precious?"

"Thanks, sweetie, but I'm good," Helen said and held up a dazzling blue teakettle. "But what about this?"

"Don't you already have a black one?" Grace asked as she placed the juice glasses carefully in their shopping basket.

But it's old and black, Helen thought. She kept the blue one. "I like this one better," she said.

By the time they loaded their goods into the car, they had the crib set, a ceiling lamp that looked like a dandelion puff, a white rocking chair with black and yellow striped pads, a wastebasket that reminded Helen of a bumblebee, a set of rooster glasses for Grace, sets of eight ounce and sixteen ounce speckled glasses for Helen, two violet pillows with Queen Anne's lace for Helen's bed, and a set of violet flannel sheets imprinted with stars. They had bought two area rugs for the downstairs bedrooms, the cobalt blue kettle, one stuffed elephant, and three pounds of Swedish meatballs for the workers back home. They were done.

"That was fun," Grace said as they drove home. "Thanks for all the great stuff."

"My pleasure," Helen smiled. She was happy that she could help, that Grace hadn't shut her out of her life long ago. She had been so absent then. But that was then, and this is now. People change. She had definitely changed since her divorce. It was almost two years now. Grace was pregnant. Frank and Stephanie were God knew where. She had bought a new house, found a new man. She paused then. Or had she? The jury was still out on Gerard; he still hadn't made any advances. Of course, she had only known him for less than a month. But she wondered what was up with the delay. She was a good-looking woman. At least a lot of people thought so. She was independent, but not militantly so. She still had a soft side that yearned for a man's touch. Maybe she just yearned too much. Maybe if she stopped yearning. Maybe…

"Look out, Mom!" Grace screamed, as Helen swerved into the next lane, almost hitting the car beside her. Helen quickly jerked back, averting disaster but not the ire of the other driver whose mouth blasted a thousand invectives while his middle finger stood strong like a monument on his right hand.

"Sorry, sweetie. It won't happen again," Helen reassured her daughter.

"What were you thinking?" Grace asked, still breathless.

"Nothing. I wasn't thinking anything. Well that's not true. I was thinking everything. A little about everything."

"Are you alright?" Grace asked, suddenly genuinely concerned.

"I'm fine," Helen replied. "Are you okay?"

Grace nodded. "But please, don't think anymore. Don't think. Just drive."

Helen stifled a snappy retort. She wanted to say, "You know I've done very well driving for a long time without your instructions." But she knew that wasn't true. She'd had many mishaps when she drove because she was always thinking about something in the past or something still to come. Grace talked about living in the moment. For Helen, that was almost impossible. In fact, it had been a problem her whole life. She thought too much, about what was or what would be. And here she was doing it again with her pregnant daughter in the car with her no less.

"Talk to me!" she cried to Grace a little louder than intended. "Let's play a game! Let's go through the alphabet and find names for the baby. You start."

"But we already have a name. Miranda."

"Humor me," Helen pleaded. Grace thought for a moment.

"This is hard. Nothing sounds good together."

"Just blurt out something," Helen prodded. "It's not like you're writing it in stone."

"Alright. How about Adele," Grace said, "because I like her music."

"Ariel," Helen countered, "because you loved the Little Mermaid."

"Bambi," Grace giggled, "because…"

"No more reasons. Just names." Helen thought for a moment and then said, "Beatrice. Bea."

Grace perked up. "Wait, I like that one—Bea Miranda. Miranda Bea. I bet Jake would love that. His little Bea."

"Hold that thought," Helen encouraged. "Now C."

"Cassidy."

"Catherine."

And so, the game went until they found themselves at the letter H.

"Hope!" Grace exclaimed. "She can be saddled with a ponderous name like I was."

"I never knew you didn't like your name, Sweetie," Helen said, now feeling sad that she had started their game if it was going to reveal those kinds of truths.

"Get over yourself, Mom. I love my name. It's just that it's more than a name. It's a way of life. Didn't you know that? Now you go. H. What have you got?"

Helen thought for a moment. Honesty. Honor. Hero. All those heavy names were stuck in her head. Try lighter, she told herself. Henriette. Hattie. Hallie. Helen. A bit sweeter. Maybe Honey.

"How about Honey?" Helen asked Grace. "Honey Miranda. Jake would love that name too."

"That's it!" Grace said bouncing in her seat. "That's perfect!" They talked about Honey all the way home and about how the room in Helen's house was perfect for her. By the time they reached Grace's house, she was tired and needed a nap, so Helen dropped her off with her rooster cups and her stuffed animal and a promise that she would come get her tomorrow morning once the furniture was all moved in.

Back at her house, the lights were off, the door was locked, and the fence complete. Helen let Perdita out in the backyard, where she roamed free, sniffing every blade and marking the new territory as her own. Helen picked up the little dog who was standing at her feet, wagging total approval.

"I feel you," Helen said, kissing Perdita's curly head and then setting her down to run again, probably chasing an imaginary squirrel.

Helen sat on the stone stoop, which felt cold against her thighs, and looked around. The house was painted. The kitchen was rehabbed. Tomorrow the movers would come. *Life is good,* she thought, and she sat there watching the sun go down and the moon rise. She fed Perdita a can of food while she ate a pear with blue cheese and went to bed. Well, actually a cot. Her bed would be here in the morning.

Helen woke to a knocking on the door, loud knocks that set Perdita yapping and bouncing up and down. "Coming," she called out as she pulled on her kimono robe. "Coming!" she cried again, thinking it was the movers. When she got to the door, she saw it was Abi, Mike, and Gerard, laden with coffee and scones.

"I couldn't bear the thought of you rearranging all that furniture on your own, and these two are relentless. Really relentless. They insisted on coming along. Something about finishing a fence," Gerard smiled broadly. Abi and Mike just giggled.

"Sorry, but I don't have much to offer you in the way of chairs," Helen reminded them. The young people just plopped down on the floor.

"We're good."

"Yes, you are," Helen agreed. "Now if you'll excuse me, I'm going to throw some clothes on," she said and she glided upstairs. When she returned, she saw Gerard holding Abi's hand. "Telling fortunes, are we?" she asked.

"A very good fortune, I surmise," Gerard replied. "Tell me, is that a bijou I see on your finger?" he asked the blushing

Abi, who nodded with a smile. "It wasn't there yesterday," he added.

"It was the full moon," Abi explained shyly. "So yes, we're engaged!"

"Engaged!" Helen cried, joining in on the conversation. "That's wonderful! Have you set a date?"

"Oh, it will probably be five years from now when we are both through school and settled in our careers," Mike said soberly. "But I didn't want to let her go," he said and looked adoringly at his fiancé.

"I know the feeling," said Gerard. Helen suddenly felt her stomach turn. *He couldn't possibly be talking about me, or could he? We barely know each other.*

"Helen, would you like a scone and some coffee?" Abi broke into her reverie.

"Yes, of course, dear. Thank you. Where will you be getting married? You're welcome to this venue, if you're thinking small." Mike squeezed Abi's hand happily.

"That's so nice of you," he said. "We'll certainly keep it in mind."

"I was hoping you'd say that," Abi said to Helen. "This place would be perfect!"

Helen smiled. *How funny it was that her little sanctuary was turning into a childcare center and a wedding venue.* All she wanted after the divorce was peace and quiet, but life kept rushing in, unstoppable. She was beginning to realize that it was not in books and words and internal dialogs that she was going to find peace, but rather in her interactions with others, lending them a hand.

As they sat drinking coffee and eating scones, Gerard regaled them all with stories of Wales, being chased by sheep, the truth about love spoons, and what most people really didn't know about *Noson Gyflaith (Taffy Evening)*. Which brought him to the story of his aunt who was sent to an English girls' boarding school. There she was tormented, called Taffy, and teased mercilessly. But she was a relentless gal. She ran away, determined that all she wanted was to go home and stop being a stranger in a strange land.

Suddenly, Helen asked Gerard, "Are you homesick?"

"Good heavens, no! I love America! There are enough freaks here already that I never stand out in a crowd!"

"But you've only been here, what? two weeks?"

"I know what I want when I see it," he said, and looked Helen earnestly in the eyes, so intently that she quickly looked away. His sincerity took her breath away. She finally exhaled when someone knocked at the door. The movers had arrived.

It was decided that Helen and Gerard would work with the movers while Abi and Mike finished the piece of fence that needed completion. Perdita was oblivious to the hole, which was a good thing, Helen thought. She contemplated what might have happened had her little dog escaped.

The day went slowly, deliberately, even though the movers were like little worker bees scurrying down the metal ramp carrying armchairs and bureaus that made their arms strain and the muscles on their calves as pronounced and defined as a fancy wood carving. Helen kept Perdita on a leash and stood at the front door directing traffic. Soon her empty cottage became smaller and cozier, as it filled with tables and chairs and plump sofas and beds. What had been merely a lovely painted building now became her home. She especially loved how her red Adirondack chairs sat on the patio facing west and how the tips of her four-poster bed almost reached the ceiling, but not quite.

Helen of course knew that "home" was more than nice furniture and a good view, but those two were a good place to start. Frank had often teased her about her need for beautiful things, mercury candle holders, velvet pillows, fabric shower curtains that reminded her of a song.

"There's no reason for it," he would say. She could hear King Lear's words rising in her mind. "Reason not the need!" However, Helen didn't put too much stock in reason anymore. What was it that the philosopher Blaise Pascal said? "The heart has its reasons which reason does not know." So here she was, in a serious standoff with reason. Reason told her it was too soon to get involved with Gerard Ferguson. Reason told her she had everything she needed for a peaceful life at last. Why complicate it? Reason told her that she wasn't ready to be in a relationship with anyone but herself. So, what did she do? She walked outside to where Abi and Mike were finishing up and gave them $100 to have a nice dinner on her, with her sincere thanks. Then she found Gerard in the nursery, where he was putting the crib together, and said, "Thank you so much for all you have done, are doing. I appreciate it more than you know."

"My pleasure," he said, looking up at her.

"I've sent Abi and Mike off to have dinner. I was hoping you'd stay here and eat with me…" Helen began, then stopped.

"I'd love to," he replied immediately.

Helen's heart was beating in her chest as she took the next move. She walked over to Gerard, leaned over, and took his face in her hands and kissed him. Still holding his face in both her hands, she whispered, "And then spend the night."

Gerard put his large hands over hers and whispered back, "On the couch or in your bed?"

"My bed," she said, and she blushed. "Why are we whispering?"

"Delighted!" Gerard cried in full voice, nearly knocking Helen down. He was grinning from ear to ear.

"Give me fifteen minutes," Helen said, and she disappeared up the stairs.

Chapter 39

*F*ifteen minutes later Gerard climbed the stairs too, this time expectantly. He knocked on her closed door gently, full of hope and desire. He didn't know what to think, nor did he care. He had no expectations, so when Helen quietly invited him in, he was neither disappointed nor surprised.

Helen sat on her bed, fully clothed, her knees tucked up under her chin, her arms wrapped around her knees. Her face was buried beneath her long copper colored hair that fell forward like a veil around her face. "I'm sorry," she mumbled, her words muffled by tears. "I can't do it."

Gerard was dumbfounded, hurt, and little pissed off, but not at all surprised. Helen looked up at him and wiped her nose with the sleeve of her shirt.

"It's not you. You're handsome and sexy, and I'm very attracted to you." Her words weren't making it any easier for Gerard. "I guess I'm just not ready." Though that alibi was, as she well knew, a bald-faced lie. Since divorcing Frank, she had had sex with several men. But that was sex. This was more complicated. "I like you very much," she began. Gerard held up his hand to stop her, but she persisted. "Maybe we could just get to know each other a little better and then see what happens. Just be friends first."

"I thought we were friends," Gerard replied.

"For what? About two minutes?" Helen laughed. "I'm sorry, Gerard. I just can't manufacture affection, and I don't want to settle for anything less."

"We obviously are coming at this situation from different perspectives," Gerard said simply. "I am attracted to you. I'd like to have sex with you. The friend element is a delightful addition, but not at all necessary in my book."

"Well that's disgusting," Helen declared. "You just want sex for sex. I could be a duck or a horse, and it wouldn't matter to you!" As soon as she said the words, Helen realized what a hypocrite she was. She may have always masked her strong desire for sex in romantic fantasies and fluffy love, but what she wanted deep down was a man inside her and an orgasm that sent execution style shock waves through her entire being. So why was she resisting having just pure sex with Gerard? Because it wasn't pure sex; it was sex with hope attached, hope that this kind, interesting, handsome man might become more in her life. She was afraid that that dream would never come true. Thus, it was best to shut it down before she went too far, to the point where she waited, expectantly, for the magic words every woman wants to hear.

"On the contrary, you fascinate me as no other woman ever has," Gerard said, as if he were reading her thoughts. "Your mind, your spirit, and yes, your body. I don't want any other woman on this planet, or any other creature for that matter. It's you I want. I want you."

Helen was floored by his confession. She looked at Gerard with his deep hazel eyes and his pouty, kissable lips, and she wished that she wasn't afraid, not so much about getting involved but of getting hurt again. His would not just be a zipless fuck. In the past, she might have slept with him out of a sense of obligation, because he had helped her, but not now. She heard a voice, felt an internal tug, that told her not to settle, not to sell herself short. It made her sad because she so wanted real intimacy and that feeling of connection, but she knew if she went through with this moment today, she'd feel lonelier than before. Still, she reasoned, he was a friend, and she didn't want to lose him. But she didn't want to lose herself more. She bit her lip and made clenched fists of her hands, let go, and exhaled a long, slow breath, and with that breath came the words, "I can't. I'm sorry."

Gerard put his fingers to her lips. "It's fine. I understand. I'll show myself out." He rose to his full height and stood proud, not at all a broken man. For a second, Helen wanted to throw herself at him and tell him she had made a terrible mistake.

"Does this mean…" Helen asked.

"It means that I'll hail an Uber now."

"Are you sure? I could drive you," Helen offered.

"I'd rather you didn't," Gerard replied.

"You're mad at me," she said now sounding childish.

"Look, if you want me to say I'm pleased with the way things turned out, I'm not. But does it mean I'll banish you from my life forever? Not a chance. You have too nice a place out here. Besides, you've already invited me for Thanksgiving."

Helen burst into laughter. "You're quite a man, Gerard Ferguson."

"And you are quite a woman, Helen Ferry," Gerard replied.

"Friends?" Helen asked. She rose to give him a hug.

"I'll call you," he said and held out his hand. Then he walked out the door and closed it behind himself leaving Helen tightly hugging a pillow and wondering what the hell she had just done.

Chapter 40

*A*s soon as Gerard left, her phone rang, the playful little bells that Alan, her wicked ex-boyfriend in Chicago, had hated so much. Helen agreed now. The celebratory chiming was incongruous with her mood. She snatched the phone up to turn the chimes off, but not before seeing that it was Micah, calling from North Carolina.

"Micah!" she exclaimed. "What a surprise!"

"Pleasant, I hope," he replied.

"Of course. Always. What's up?"

"In the South, we would have waited five beats before we asked that question. But since you asked, I'll tell you. We're moving."

"Really? Where? Why?" Helen rattled off the questions in a flurry.

"Nicholas wants to make a go of it in the entertainment industry."

"So, you're going to LA?"

"New York."

"Wonderful! You'll be closer to me!"

"Closer than you think, actually," Micah continued. "I'm looking to buy a friend's antique store in Madison."

"That's right next door!"

"Don't you live in Madison?" Micah asked, now confused.

"I actually moved to Stony Creek recently. But it's close."

"Does your offer still stand to visit for a few days while we get our affairs in order?" Micah asked. "We think we've found a place."

"Of course! I'd love to have you. When will you be coming?"

"We were thinking the thirteenth through the seventeenth if that works for you. We won't be any trouble. We'll have our own car. Just wanted to mix pleasure with business." All the while Micah was talking, Helen was thinking about beds, linens, dishes, towels. She had a lot of unpacking to do to get the place ready for company. Good that this was just the beginning of the semester and she wasn't too busy yet. Still, she would issue a warning.

"That's perfect, but you know, I've just moved in myself and things may be in a bit of a mess."

"If you'd rather we didn't stay…" Micah leapt in immediately.

"No, no, no!" Helen cried. "Of course you'll stay. Bring your bathing suits. I have a beach."

"A beach?" Micah sounded amazed.

"Yes, I have waterfront property. It's quite lovely," Helen said proudly.

"My heavens, you did settle well."

Helen felt herself bristle a little. The insinuation that she was where she was solely due to Frank's largess. "Actually, I managed to save quite a bit over the years. And we settled the house for an obscene amount, but largely I've done all this on my own."

Micah laughed. "Down girl! I wasn't suggesting you took your ex to the cleaners, though given what he did, you were certainly entitled. I'm thinking more selfishly about me and Nicholas."

"What about you and Nicholas?" she asked.

Suddenly Micah's voice grew soft and tender. "He's just come in. I can't talk now. We'll see you on the thirteenth!" he explained brightly.

"Looking forward to it," Helen replied and hung up.

She sat back down on her bed, thinking about the events of the day. In and out. In and out. The furniture came and made her place a real home, one that she could share. Out went Gerard because she had misinterpreted her own emotions, mistaking lust for intimacy, and wounding his ego in the process. Then right in stride, Micah and Nicholas soon filled the gap, although temporarily. Life was an accordion with its pleated ways. Helen was a little scared to move, however, lest something else fall away.

She quickly came back to the jobs at hand and began a search for Perdita, which took no time at all because the little creature was just where she should be at 9:00 p.m., curled up in her plush doggie bed at the foot of Helen's four-poster. That wouldn't last long. Helen smiled. Soon after Helen pulled the covers up to her chin, Perdita always climbed the little set of wooden stairs that Helen had hired Jack O'Toole to build especially for her dog. As stealthily as a chubby puppy with tinkling tags could move, Perdita would then climb up and curl herself into the small of Helen's back and sleep blissfully, snoring slightly, sometimes whimpering and shuddering until morning, when she would climb back down, look up adoringly at Helen, and bark once very clearly at her for the day's adventures to begin.

"Our revels now are ended," said Helen as she walked downstairs. She locked the doors, turned out the lights, and poured herself a glass of water. As she stood in her new kitchen, bright white-and-glass cabinets shone in the light that spilled from the small, paddle-shaped fixtures and bounced off the pale yellow counter tops and deep red appliances, she thought of the dress she had worn as a child when she was out with her mother, right before her mother died. The dress had had a white top and yellow skirt and a thick red belt embroidered with daisies. Helen wore shiny red Mary Janes and a beautiful ivory-colored coat with gold buttons and white gloves. Her mother had on gloves too and a beautiful blue straw hat decorated with silk flowers to cover her head, where her hair had once been. It was Easter, and her father refused to set foot in a church since the prognosis.

Helen sat beside her mother and cried and cried. She cried because she didn't understand how people could be so cruel, killing someone as nice as Jesus. She cried because she didn't understand how her mother could be so sick and dying. She cried because she didn't understand why God would do this to her, leave her alone with a man like her father, who was weak and helpless and full of fear, but who could turn his anger on her like a torch and hate like a whip. She hadn't gone to church again until Grace was small. But nothing changed. The story was still cruel. People were still angry and mean and full of hate, and she was alone. A tear ran down her cheek. She now had this beautiful house and a darling dog and an even more darling daughter with a granddaughter on the way. So why was she crying?

She picked up the phone to call the only person she knew who could answer that question. The phone rang and rang and rang, and just before she pressed the button to disconnect, a voice answered.

"Hello?" said a rather feeble voice on the other end of the line.

"Sylvia? It's Helen. Did I wake you?" Helen asked.

"Oh no, dear. I just haven't really talked to anyone all day. I'm so glad you called. Is everything alright?"

"Okay. Actually terrible. Oh, Sylvia," Helen said and broke into tears. "How do you do it?"

"Do what, dear?" Sylvia asked gently.

"Live without Arthur."

"You're not missing that scoundrel of an ex-husband, are you?" Sylvia asked a bit sternly.

"No, not him," Helen replied. "But someone else."

"Still spinning the same tale," Sylvia chuckled.

"I know!" Helen agreed. "I feel like I'm going crazy! I don't know how to escape this feeling that I must have a man in my life."

"Escape is the key word," Sylvia said. "Escape implies running away from something. Dark tunnels. Big trees. I prefer to visualize letting go, lifting my arms to the sun and letting whatever is holding me hostage trickle up through my body, out my fingers, and into the universe."

As soothing as Sylvia's words were, nothing could erase the hopelessness Helen felt. She was despondent. She tried so many things that Sylvia and Grace had suggested: Balloons. God boxes. Burying articles from the past or burning them. Meditation. Medication. Prayer. None of it had done any good. She still wanted a man in her life. She wanted love. Suddenly an idea burst forth.

"What if the man I am really missing is my dad?" Helen said aloud. "Of course! How could I not have seen this? I'm so stupid! I keep going to men who are inaccessible, just like my father. Then, when someone comes knocking, a wholesome man like Gerard, I shy away because I am secretly afraid that if I love him, he will hurt me. I'm really just afraid!" Helen now was shouting into the phone.

"Gerard?" Sylvia asked, her voice resonating with concern. "Is he your latest?"

"Don't put it like that. He is different. We are just friends."

"But I gather you'd like that to change."

"I don't know! I thought so, but then when the opportunity came…"

"You couldn't."

"Is it my conscience? Fear of being abandoned again? A real desire to live alone?"

"Sounds very possible," Sylvia said diplomatically.

"Not helpful."

"What if it is a bit of each?"

Helen's enthusiasm quickly deflated. "Well, that's all very well and good, but where does it leave me?" It didn't take long for Sylvia to understand and respond.

"Love," she said.

"Love? That's it?"

"Self-love. You have to love yourself, know that you are perfect the way you are, away from those punishing, critical voices of the past, before you will ever be able to participate in a harmonious relationship."

"So how do I do that? Go for weekly manicures? Take a month-long trip around Europe?"

"If you like," Sylvia responded and laughed. "Though I actually see it as more of an inside job. It starts with changing the tapes in your head. No more 'I'm stupid' or 'I can't.' If you fill your head with positive affirmations of yourself, it will go a long way. When Arthur died, I thought 'How will I do this? An old woman all alone?' Then I stopped and told myself, 'I am not alone. I am abundantly blessed with friends and good health.' I tell myself that every day, and do you know what? Wonderful people keep coming into my life like peach blossoms in May. I feel more alive and vibrant than I have any right to feel at my age."

"I just tell myself lies…" Helen stated cynically.

"These are not lies," Sylvia interrupted. "They are truths you have not yet accepted. But say them anyway. Act as if you believe them. You will see a change. I guarantee it."

"So that's it? This will solve my man problem?" Helen asked.

"No, but it's a beginning and a mighty good beginning at that," Sylvia replied. "Start with that. Then, do one nice thing for yourself every day. Lastly, help someone else. Smile. Hold a door. Call a friend. If you do these things, you will change. If you want to change, do these things."

"You have never steered me wrong. You and Gracie," Helen sighed. "Why has it taken me so long, Sylvia? Why didn't I get all this down pat when I was Gracie's age?"

Sylvia laughed. "Pet, you're getting it now, and now is all we ever have."

After Helen hung up, she filled one of her new red and gold speckled glasses with filtered water again and climbed the stairs back to her bedroom. Her head and her heart pumped rapidly with both hope and fear. She changed into her pajamas, washed her face and applied her anti-aging cream, brushed and flossed her teeth, and swallowed her medicine. She didn't always do all of these rituals, but tonight she felt righteous. She wanted to take care of herself as no one else could. She slid in under the cool sheets and pulled the covers up under her chin. Perdita climbed up and curled herself as always like a comma into Helen's back.

Telling herself that her life was abundant and was richly blessed was a bit too much of a mouthful for Helen to handle at ten o'clock at night. So, she closed her eyes and whispered to herself over and over, "There's no place like home. There's no place like home. There's no place like home." She hoped that when she woke, she would be surrounded by loving and trustworthy friends as Dorothy had in *The Wizard of Oz*. She closed her eyes, clicked her bare heels under the sheet, and prayed. In a blink, she was asleep.

Chapter 41

$\mathcal{T}$he next day, she met Grace for lunch.

"How'd you swing this?" Grace was devouring a hefty Chef salad, a napkin spread full out over her swollen belly. "Don't you have to work?"

"I have a lecture later this afternoon," Helen took a bite of her salad. "I wanted to see you."

Grace looked at her mother a bit skeptically. "So, what's up?"

"Nothing," Helen replied. "Can't I just have lunch with my girl?"

"C'mon, Mom. What is it? Is it Gerard?" Grace probed deeper.

Helen sighed and put down her fork, then took a long swallow of lemon water. Of course, it was Gerard. He had left and hadn't made contact today at all. But it was not even twenty-four hours, so to worry would be excessive, addictive even, she told herself. Besides, she wasn't really sure she wanted him to call. What was it that was bugging her? She wanted to start doing things for herself, things she would enjoy that would nurture her soul. She had thought having lunch with Grace would be one of them, but now she wasn't so sure.

She had a spoken to Grace about Jake on the phone that morning. He was flying in this evening from Georgia (the Russian one) and, God willing, would be staying home until the baby was born. Maybe longer. They would travel to his parents in New York for Thanksgiving, and then they would celebrate Christmas with her. Well, partially with her, then partially with Frank. Helen felt lonely and lonelier as she watched her only child slipping away into full adulthood and motherhood.

"I talked to Sylvia last night," Helen blurted out, changing the tapes in her head.

"Really! How is she?" Grace asked excitedly.

"She's good. You know Sylvia. Unstoppable."

The two women munched on their lunches for a few more moments until the silence was more than Helen could bear. "She says I should do three things—use affirmations, help others, and do one nice thing for myself every day."

"That sounds like good advice," Grace agreed. "Jake and I try to do that too. So what good thing are you doing for yourself today, Mom?"

"Having lunch with you," Helen replied quickly.

"That doesn't count. It needs to be for you, all for you. Like buying a magazine you usually pass over. Or going for a walk and finding the perfect stone. Or playing some music when you are alone and dancing to it. Stuff like that," Grace instructed.

Helen did not understand why having lunch with her child, whom she adored and missed and wished she saw more often, didn't count as a nice thing to do for herself. She figured she had a lot to learn about self-love.

"It's about being good to *yourself*," Grace said as she leaned into the car to kiss her mother goodbye. "Not doing it for anyone else. No one else at all."

Helen smiled. She felt that somewhere, sometime she had actually been good at this stuff. She bought designer outfits when she pleased. She traveled to foreign countries and stayed in fine hotels while Frank minded his business and Grace was off at school. She ate good food, healthy, organic, and drank the best wines. She had spent a fortune in planting perennials to build beautiful gardens. She knew that was not what Grace and Sylvia were talking about. They were challenging her to a simpler, more humble kind of love. The love a child propagates when she takes the apple seeds from lunch and plants them in a hole and waits and watches every day for them to sprout. Or when she sets a tea party on a fat leaf with mountain laurel blossoms filled with dew as their cups, and shares them with her imaginary friends. Or when she drifts away from home in her Sunday best, only to be found curled up next to a calf in a nearby barn, her black lashes long and curled, her copper hair in rings framing her beautiful, child-like face.

"Run outside and play!" her mother had often told her when she was young.

So here she was now, back at square one, being encouraged to be a child again, find delight in little things. And all this was supposed to help her? How? Up ahead, she saw a Dairy Queen. As if drawn by a magnet, yet all the while telling herself she shouldn't, she shouldn't, she pulled in and ordered a small vanilla dipped cone, something she hadn't had in years. She sat under the bright orange umbrella on the patio and nibbled and licked her way through the treat. As she did, something happened. She felt laughter bubbling up inside her like a rising effervescence, and she couldn't stop smiling.

This is fun, she thought. *I like this.*

As she finished her cone and threw the napkin away, aware that she might, in fact, be late for her class if she didn't hurry, Helen noticed a young woman who had just sat down with two toddlers and a baby who was wailing. The toddlers were tugging at their mom with ice cream dripping down their chins. "Just a minute," the frazzled mother snapped. Helen scooted into the store and came back out with a handful of napkins.

"Will this help?" she asked the mother.

"Yes. Thank you. You're an angel," she smiled.

"My pleasure," Helen replied and walked to her car. *Helping someone. Nice.* Helen ticked off her resolutions. As she backed out of the parking lot, she caught a glimpse of herself in the rearview mirror.

"I'm an angel," she whispered. An affirmation. She laughed, pleased that she had taken a first step, one further down the path that had already chosen her.

Chapter 42

"September, I remember," Helen sang the Simon and Garfunkel lyrics quietly to herself as she changed the calendar to a new month and reflected on what had transpired these last few weeks. Of course, there had been the visit from Micah and Nicholas. She had anticipated an edge based on Micah's cryptic comment about being taken to the cleaners and entitlement. Helen had assumed there had been some infidelity, that the gorgeous Nicholas had stepped out on his aging friend. Micah, old and showing it, couldn't let go of Nick. Like Hillary Clinton with Bill when the Monica fiasco erupted, Micah hung in there, unable to let go. For Hillary, Helen thought, it was all politics and self-aggrandizement; for Micah, it was love. At least that was what Helen thought until they arrived and announced that they were taking legal residence in Connecticut, in part, so they could get married. As soon as possible. They had waited long enough. Helen couldn't have been more surprised.

The rest of their visit was a celebration. Grace's baby. Helen's house. So much to be grateful for. They took long walks on the beach with Perdita tagging along and savored the rich, golden days of early fall that sank into the Sound silently every evening until the black night was fully speckled with stars.

"Pure magic," Micah said one night as they sat outside on the Adirondack chairs.

Helen couldn't have agreed more. Lately, she was seeing magic in everything. In Grace, who had swelled to the size of a pumpkin. In Abi and Mike, who ate dinner with her every Thursday night and filled her with hope for our world as they dedicated themselves to new causes that would make the planet a better place. In Jake, too, with his honeybees, working to keep the world alive. In princes who gave their fortunes to charity and children who sold lemonade to raise money for a friend who had cancer. In Jack O'Toole who kept her in firewood at little cost and fixed her plumbing for free. There was magic in the world, abundant magic, if she just stopped and looked for it.

The most magical of all was when she saw Gerard on campus. She didn't hide away behind a stack in the library or seek refuge behind a lamppost or a wall. She caught his gaze, nodded, even smiled warmly, and walked on. How hard it had been at first, but then gradually, the meetings became easier until by the middle of November, she actually looked forward to coming across his path. One day, after they had passed, he called out to her. She stopped and turned.

"Um, Helen," he said a bit shyly. "I was wondering, is that invitation for Thanksgiving still open?"

"Of course," said Helen smoothly, though inside her heart was beating turbulently. "Come over any time."

"Come over any time," Helen repeated quietly to herself as she walked on, totally delighted with how casual it all had been. She was certain that Sylvia's three suggestions had contributed to her ongoing transformation, and indeed to her response to Gerard just now.

On the weekend before Thanksgiving, Helen switched on the television, something she rarely did these days, although, as she often confessed, more now that she was doing something nice for herself every day. Not that the news was nice, hardly, but *Blue Bloods* with that handsome Commissioner Reagan was her idea of fun. And then there was *NCIS* with the enigmatic Agent Gibbs. She couldn't really decide which of the two types of men she preferred, so she allowed herself to indulge in both, like serving both mashed potatoes and rutabaga at Thanksgiving. It wasn't necessary, but it was delicious. Choose? I'll just choose both, and she smiled.

Speaking of which, she told herself, *I should get to the store.* The weather girl was predicting a massive storm for Wednesday. "I may have no one here for the holiday, or I may have a dozen," Helen said aloud. "Certainly, Micah and Nicholas and Gerard. Also, Jake O'Toole, who is a widower and all alone. And who knows, maybe Abi and Mike and even Grace and Jake." She wished it would be so.

So off she went to the store. She stocked up on the biggest turkey she could find, stuffing, celery, onions, green apples, potatoes, garlic, butter, rutabaga, and parsnips. Then chestnuts and mushrooms, Brussels sprouts and cranberry jelly. And, of course, biscuits, pumpkin pie makings, apple pie makings, cider, and wine.

She stood in the baking aisle, a chorus of spices at her back, and thought about what else she might need. The shoppers everywhere swirled around her grabbing the essentials off the shelves until the sugar and flour were decimated and all that was left were twenty-one varieties of brownie mix. This would be her first Thanksgiving in her new house, her new life. If everyone was going to have to stay over because of the storm, she thought, she'd best get eggs, bacon, coffee, cinnamon buns, and half and half. An avocado too, because Grace loved avocados, and some ruby-red grapefruit because that's what she liked to eat with honey and a cup of black coffee.

Helen suddenly realized she was blocking the aisle. She moved to the checkout, where $254.36 later, she gathered her goodies, placed them all gently in her car trunk, and drove home. "Damn," she said as she pulled in the driveway. "I should have bought a pecan pie for Micah. Oh well."

True to predictions, the blizzard came roaring through, sheets of snow flying sideways across an already white landscape, trees bending and waving their branches like hysterical women who have lost a child, the wind wailing and moaning in the background, as windows rattled and outbuildings shook and the snow accumulated inch upon inch to a foot and more. The water from the sound inched up too until it was dangerously close to the fenced-in backyard. Helen knew no chicken wire was going to keep that water out, and for a moment, she was afraid. But she lit a fire and held Perdita in her arms and spoke an affirmation to herself over and over again. "I am safe. I am loved. I am fine." She continued to speak it as the fire crackled and Perdita wriggled in her lap to try and find a comfortable spot. She said it until her eyes grew weary and her heart stilled. And when the wind lessened and the snow stopped, she called Grace.

"Sweetheart? How are you?"

"We're good. Are you okay?"

"Never better. Just sitting in front of the fire with Perdita on my lap." Helen smiled.

"You sound good, Mom."

"I am good, sweetie. Never better."

"That's the second time you've said that," Grace now probed a bit. "Is something going on that you're not telling me?"

"Nope. It's just me here with Perdita and a twenty-five pound turkey with all the trimmings."

"Are you expecting a crowd?"

"Not expecting, but I'm prepared." Then, because she couldn't help herself, Helen asked, "Will you be heading to New York?"

"Seriously, Mom? In this awful weather?"

"You're welcome here."

"I was hoping you'd offer."

"Why don't you come now, in case everything gets worse," Helen suggested. "Of course, if you feel more comfortable waiting…"

"I think Jake wants to wait until tomorrow. It's supposed to have blown by us by then."

Helen stayed silent, batting the unnecessary thoughts in her head. *Jake doesn't like me. He'd rather be with his parents. Don't be ridiculous; you two have always gotten along. It's not about you, Helen. Of course, it's about me! No, really, it's not.*

"You okay with that, Mom?" Grace asked.

"Of course. Whatever works for you. I'm just going to sit in front of the fire with my Perdita, eat a grapefruit and honey for supper, and go to bed. I'll be up bright and early to put old Tom in the oven!"

"Tom?"

"The turkey, silly!" Helen giggled.

"Mom, are you sure you are alright? Have you been drinking?"

"Nothing alcoholic, if that's what you're asking. Can't I just be in a good mood for once? There's a fresh blanket of snow, a refrigerator full of good food, enough to feed an African village, a blazing fire, and no school! A snow day! Actually, it's a holiday. But life is sweet. Great cause for being in a good mood!"

Grace laughed. "If you say so. Personally, I feel like I'm carrying a fifty pound watermelon in my belly. My back aches so much it stings, and my legs are about to snap. I can barely sit or walk."

"It won't be long now," Helen reassured her daughter. "Isn't it just three weeks?"

"Yeah. The seventeenth. But the midwife said the baby has dropped, so it could be any day now." Grace did not sound pleased. Helen stifled the urge to be a cheerleader and offer her happy thoughts. Instead she just offered up a prayer that Grace would have the strength and the courage she was going to need.

"Did you hear me, Mom?" Grace insisted. "I swear half the time you don't even listen to what I am saying."

"I heard you, and I was just thinking that no matter when this little girl comes, I know my own little girl will have the strength and courage to handle it. You're going to be a wonderful mother, Grace. You have all the love and wisdom and playfulness of a good mother."

It was Grace's turn now not to speak. After a few moments, Helen broke the silence.

"Are you there, sweetie?"

"I am," Grace replied, sniffling as she spoke. "Thank you for that, Mom. I have to admit, I am a little scared, but I know everything's going to be all right."

"Of course, it is, pet," Helen said, now channeling Sylvia. "We'll see you tomorrow?"

"Yeah. If I don't have this baby tonight, we'll be there in the morning."

"Great. My suggestion is do something relaxing. Take a warm bubbly bath. Get Jake to give you a massage. Drink raspberry tea. I'll see you in the morning."

There were air kisses into the phone, and then both hung up. At either end was nothing but love.

Chapter 43

By the next morning, the storm had passed, and the skies were bright blue. The sun danced merrily off the deep blanket of snow. Helen was up early, shoveling a little space for Perdita to do her business, stuffing the turkey and putting it in the oven, and stacking wet firewood in the mudroom to dry for later. She ate a little breakfast, this time a sticky cinnamon bun and two poached eggs. As she started peeling vegetables, Gracie and Jake arrived.

"Hello!" their voices chimed with the string of Indian prayer bells that Helen had hung on the back door, prayer bells which had actually come not from India, but from Disney World. It had been one of the few trips she, Frank, and Grace had taken as a family. They held sweet memories of an easier time when Frank laughed freely, and they still functioned as a family—two young parents and a child swirling in the Kali Rapids, squealing and laughing together when they got doused.

"Just leave your coats and boots in the mudroom," Helen instructed. "Did you have any trouble getting in?"

"Not at all," Jake said and kissed his mother-in-law on the cheek. "Who'd you get to plow your drive?"

"Jack O'Toole," Helen replied. "He's a sweetheart. He's done most of the renovation of this place, you know." Helen pulled hard on the waxy skin of the rutabaga.

"Here, let me help you with that," Jake offered. Helen obliged, washing her hands and then walking over to Grace, who was perched uncomfortably on the end of the sofa, her belly protruding onto the coffee table. Helen moved the table so Grace would have enough room to sit.

"How's it going, Love?" Helen asked, stroking Grace's hair.

"Fine. It's fine. Just uncomfortable, and she's stopped moving. Do you think she's okay?" Grace sounded concerned.

"I think she's getting ready to launch," Jake laughed from the kitchen.

"Stop it!" Grace yelled back. "You're just a boy. What do you know!"

"I think he may be right," Helen whispered to her daughter. "Let's go look at the nursery. Have you seen it since I put on the finishing touches?"

Helen helped Grace stand up, and they shuffled off to the nursery. When Helen flipped the light switch, Grace gasped. The honey-colored room was all decked out with a white crib, a changing table, and a rocking chair resting on a beautiful Pottery Barn rug. It was all pinks and whites and yellows that matched the walls. In the crib was a pastel-colored patchwork baby quilt and over it was a sturdy mobile with bees and a Winnie-the-Pooh standing at the center. Helen wound the key, and out came the Pooh song. On the walls were two framed posters, one with Piglet and Pooh and the famous quotation—"Promise me you'll always remember…"—and the other, Mackenzie Thorpe's humorous "Owen with a Bee on his Nose." The dots on Owen's body were picked up in the playful design on the white curtains, fat yellow dots with a black band and black antennas. It was the sort of thumbprint impression of a bee that a child might make.

Helen took Grace by her hand and led her into the room and over to the bureau in the corner. She opened the drawers and the cabinets. Grace gasped as she saw that, not only had Helen stocked up on diapers and burp cloths, but also onesies and footsie pajamas of all colors and patterns imaginable. Grace held up a light-blue suit with yellow ducks. She held it to her cheek and began to cry, a soft, sweet sob of appreciation.

"It's perfect, Mom. Thank you so so much."

"I just wanted to let you know that if she comes tonight, she'll have everything she needs."

"Grandma," Gracie gave her mother's hand a squeeze. Then yelled out loud like a bar maid, "Jake! You've got to see this!"

By noon, Micah, Nicholas, and Gerard had arrived. The Southern boys had brought a homemade pecan pie; the Welshman, some wine. Not too long after, Abi and Mike appeared on skis. By then, the house had filled with the rich smell of roasting turkey. The men were watching football, and Grace had decided to take a nap. Helen plopped down some chips and guacamole and a bowl full of pistachios for anyone who might be feeling a bit hungry.

"Thirsty? You're on your own," Helen had ordered. "There's beer in the fridge, wine on the counter, seltzer on the floor, and cider sitting in the snow at the back door. I'm going to go take a shower, and I'll return in about forty-five minutes." With a smile and a wave, she sashayed up the stairs.

Forty-five minutes later, Helen reappeared, dewy and refreshed, wearing a pair of magenta corduroy pants with a black cashmere turtleneck and black velvet slippers. Around her neck was the red Balinese scarf Grace had given her the Christmas before. Shot through with apricot and gold, it set off the copper hair that cascaded over her shoulders shimmering and her Irish green eyes sparkling in the light. For a moment, all eyes were on her, though no one dared speak. Then someone on the TV ran for a touchdown and fumbled, and the ball was intercepted and the spell was broken. Only Abi still gazed, admiring. When Helen looked her way, Abi gave her a two-thumbs up, which Helen returned with an air kiss as she made her way to the kitchen. Grace lumbered in from her nap, and Jake and Nicholas, disgusted by their losing team, took off on skis for one quick burst of activity before the eating began.

Before the final preparation lap took place, Helen sat in the living room, sipping a glass of wine and wondering, as she looked around the room at all the friendly faces, the fire, the walls, her walls, *how did I ever get so lucky? How did I get all of this?* Of course, she knew it wasn't luck, and it wasn't her hard work. It was, as Grace would say, the Unnameable. The Invisible. The Divine. Whatever it was and however it was working in her life, she didn't care. She was just appreciative, grateful, and glad to have it all.

Soon, Helen had Gerard mashing the garlic potatoes, while she simultaneously seasoned rutabaga, roasted parsnips and Brussels sprouts, kept an eye on the biscuits, and scooped the stuffing out of the bird. Helen waited for

Gerard to say something, anything, to break the awkward silence that hung between them. Finally, unable to contain herself any longer, she spoke.

"I am glad you were able to make it today."

"Wouldn't have missed it. Abi and Mike have been regaling me with tales of your Thursday dinners. You are quite the cook." Helen was taken aback. It hadn't occurred to her that Abi, Mike, and Gerard might actually be friends, sharing stories, talking about her. She wondered if Gerard was interested in her still? Distracted, she sliced her finger with a sharp paring knife.

"Shit," she said as she wrapped a paper towel around her bleeding digit.

"Let me help," Gerard offered, coming to her aid.

"No, I've got it. I just need a bandage. There's one in that second drawer." Gerard retrieved the bandage and applied it carefully to her finger.

"At least let me carve the turkey," he said, smiling. Helen told him she was leaving carving to Nicholas, the ex-chef who kept tasting things and adding a little of this, a little of that. His efforts once would have affronted her, but today she didn't mind. She actually welcomed the help and truthfully, she could have used more.

Once they were seated with steaming plates in front of them, Helen asked them all to hold hands.

"Here goes," Grace whispered to Gerard. "Some things never change."

"I heard that, Grace. So now you say the blessing," Helen laughed.

Grace bowed her head. "I am grateful today for friends present, friends past, and friends to come. May all of us, present or not, enjoy the gifts of this meal and the promise of love."

Everyone looked a little baffled at her words, but Micah, ever the diplomat, raised his glass.

"Hear! hear!"

"Hear! hear!" everyone chimed in, and then they all dove into what they immediately said was the best Thanksgiving meal ever.

Chapter 44

The next few weeks were a whirlwind for Helen. It was the end of the semester, and students stood in long lines outside her office waiting hopefully for their chance to convince her that she needed to grant them one last extension or review a grade from nine weeks ago that displeased them. The smart ones brought mugs from Starbucks steaming with latte or hefty slices of lemon cake. They appreciated how hard she worked, they always said, and now could she appreciate their situation as well? Have mercy? It was always the same, she would look over her confetti-colored reading glasses, glance at the paper or the situation, and she'd cave. Wasn't she young once too and up to her ears in deadlines like they were? She would not let them out of their obligations, but she did soften the process a little, and everyone went home a bit happier.

"Merry Christmas, Professor Ferry," pealed out like so many bells. And then, her phone rang. It was Jake. Grace, who had been miserably uncomfortable since Thanksgiving, had finally gone into labor. Helen quickly gathered her handbag, gloves, and scarf. As she struggled with the sleeves of her coat, she called Jack O'Toole and asked if he could watch Perdita for the night.

"Of course. Now go," he replied. "Best to our girl. And be careful out there. The roads are slick."

"Thanks, Jack." Helen left her office and walked out into the frigid air. The snow, which looked blue in the evening light, crackled under her feet. A big, full moon hung high. Helen inhaled a deep breath, and her nostrils pressed together slightly. The winter air gushed down her throat and into her heart. It seemed that they had all been waiting for this day forever, but now that it was here, it seemed to have happened so fast.

Helen took the drive carefully as the roads were slick, as Jack had said. The last thing she wanted was to end up in another snowdrift and to miss the birth altogether. How long ago that had been. A year to the day, almost, since she found Webb dead in his apartment. So much had happened in a year.

It was late, and Helen was one of the few travelers out that night. She was grateful for the quiet roads, the coming child, the moon. Life had given her so many blessings this past year. It hardly seemed fair that she should have so much.

As she passed by the hospital, with its screaming sirens and insistent lights, she was glad that Grace had chosen to have her baby in the birthing center. With its cozy rooms and comfortable décor, it seemed more like a home than a hospital. More natural than medical, though the midwives were certainly qualified practitioners. Helen wondered how Grace was doing. She was eager to be with her only child.

Helen reached the intersection just before the birthing center, in good time. It was then, stopped at the red light, that she noticed the car in front of her. A black BMW with the license plate #1LOVER. Stephanie's car. Suddenly, her mood deflated. Of course, Grace would want to have Frank there, but Helen hadn't banked on Stephanie coming too. She wasn't even a step-mother; she was just the live-in girlfriend who stole Grace's father away. Helen considered getting out of the car and instructing the bitch not to show her face, but she reconsidered. All she wanted for Grace right now was peace and loving support. Maybe this was the time to start seeing them all as a new family. Yet, she was still so angry with Frank, and disappointed. What an idiot he had turned out to be.

Just then, the light turned green and Frank pulled forward into the intersection. What happened next seemed to take place in slow motion. Helen saw it coming. Another car, dark and sleek, slid across the intersection from the side and slammed into the driver's side of Stephanie's car, as if they had never seen the light. Helen prayed that the "NO!" she felt inside would be enough to stop the collision. It did not. The sound of metal on metal was intensified by the cold, crystal air. Helen was sure she heard the *whomp* of the air bags inflating as she sat, paralyzed. She could not believe what she had just seen. With trembling hands, she reached for her phone and dialed 911.

"There's been an accident."

"Are you hurt? Is anyone hurt?"

"I am sure they are. I'm fine. Can you send someone right away?"

"What is your location, ma'am?"

"I am at the intersection right by the birthing center. In Madison."

"Someone is on the way. Stay where you are, please."

But my daughter is having a baby, Helen wanted to say. Instead, she hung up and walked over to the car, cautiously peering in the windows. What she wanted to see was Frank rubbing his head, looking dazed. What she saw was Frank slumped over the steering wheel, his face resting on the pillow air bag, unconscious. Stephanie was too. Helen told herself *They are going to be all right.* She was sure of it. They had to be all right. This had all just been an inconvenience, something to steal the thunder from Grace's big day. She took out her phone.

"Jake? There's been an accident."

"Are you all right?"

"I am fine. It's Frank. We are waiting for an ambulance. I am right outside the birthing center. I will be there as soon as I can."

"Do you want me to come out?"

"NO! You stay with Grace. We will all be fine."

The medics and the police arrived. While the police took Helen's statement, the medics extracted a very groggy and frightened Stephanie from her car. The other driver, too, was taken safely from his vehicle and placed in handcuffs as he, drunk and belligerent, blamed the accident on the ice.

The medics brought a gurney over to Frank's side of the car and removed him gently from the vehicle. They laid him down and then pulled the white sheet up over his face. Frank was gone.

Helen felt the bile rising in her throat. Her eyes filled with tears and her face was hot and prickly. Frank dead?

How could this be? This night was meant to be a magical night with the birth of their grandchild. The baby would bring their families all together. But now he was dead? Oh, the horrible things she had been thinking just before he was killed. Helen wished she could take those thoughts back and send him good ones. He hadn't been a bad husband and father. There had been many good times.

Helen's impulse was to go to Stephanie and give her hand a squeeze. She must be hurting now too. But that altruistic part of Helen was not yet fully operative, and instead she let the girl weep, alone.

"May I leave?" Helen asked an officer standing near her.

"We have your statement?"

"Yes."

"Then you are free to go."

Helen walked back toward her car.

"Oh, ma'am. One more thing. You are the ex-wife, right?"

"I am."

"Do you know where we should send the body? The girlfriend isn't all that helpful."

"She never was. Send it to the Court Funeral Home. They will know what to do with him. He is Frank Court."

Helen sat in her car clutching the steering wheel. The blue police lights still whirled round and the ambulances pulled away, sirens blaring. Her hands were trembling, her whole body was shaking, her teeth were chattering as she clutched the wheel and prepared herself to make the next move. *What is a person supposed to do with all these emotions,* she wondered. *Death. Birth. Love. Regret.* She wanted to call Gerard and have him make her feel better. She knew she should not. She would call Sylvia. Sylvia would help her through everything.

✳

By the time Helen arrived at the birthing center, Grace's water had broken and she was fully dilated. Helen washed her hands thoroughly and dried them, then one of the midwives said, "You'll need a gown and gloves." As Helen suited up, she took deep breaths, blowing them out loudly to keep herself calm. The midwife misunderstood her anxiety.

"Your daughter's going to be just fine, ma'am. Everything is looking good. You ready? You don't want to miss the birth."

Helen knew that this day would never be the same for Grace. It was the day her first child would be born. It was also the day that her father died. That awful reminder would be etched on little Honey's birthday for the rest of her life, a tragic legacy to hold.

But all her morbid thoughts disappeared as Helen entered Grace's room and found her tiny daughter pushing like a workhorse to try and deliver the precious creature inside her into the world. The contractions were fierce and frequent. Grace had tried to dismiss Jake, who would later say Grace had called him a bastard and was responsible for all this and he was not to touch her ever, ever again. Helen squeezed in beside the midwife whose hand Grace was locked on to. She leaned over her daughter, wiping her brow with a cold, moist cloth, and spoke to her in low, reassuring tones, as the midwife instructed with hands poised for Grace to push hard, push hard, push harder. Grace pushed with all the might she could muster, then let loose an earsplitting cry, and the baby popped out. The pressure was over. The midwife put a tiny baby girl, wrapped in a soft pink blanket, into Grace's arms. Grace looked at that little face with those big dark eyes and that mop of black hair and laughed. "Look,

Jake! Look at all this hair!" Gazing down on her child, Grace beamed and stroked the petal-soft face with a single finger. "You're not Honey. You're Bea. Beatrice Miranda Tanner. Our little Bea. Welcome to Earth."

Not a dry eye was to be found, not even Officer Ken, the policeman who had helped her get there in time. He had stood outside the door to the room anxiously eating donuts, waiting for the baby's first cry.

Jake was beside himself. Everything had seemed manageable, even as unmanageable as it was, until the midwife had asked him if he wanted to cut the cord. Which he did. Surreal. He couldn't take his eyes off his baby girl and the miracle she was. One minute she had been in Grace's belly, the next wrapped in a pink blanket and wearing a tiny pink hat and sucking on something that no one could see. As he held her, his whole world changed. Nothing would ever be the same. He knew there are no words. He leaned down to Grace and whispered softly, "I love you now more than ever. I couldn't have done what you just did."

"Damned straight," Grace replied with a big smile, and everyone laughed. "That's why God made girls. Where's Dad?"

Helen was quiet, standing in the corner of the room watching her own baby and her grandbaby. She looked over at Jake, whose gaze moved up from his new family to Helen. Helen just shook her head. Jake registered the loss and turned to Grace. Helen hoped with all her heart that he would not steal this moment from Grace, who lay in bed with her baby girl in her arms, smiling. In fact, Jake just kissed the top of her head and kissed the tiny fingers that were curled around her mother's.

"Let's give them a little bonding time, shall we?" the midwife said, putting her arm around Helen's shoulders and ushering her from the room. Once the door was closed, she turned to Helen.

"Officer Ken just told us what happened. We are so sorry for your loss."

"It's Grace I am worried about. She is going to take it hard."

"She will. But you can't keep it from her."

"I know."

"Now is a good time."

Helen knocked lightly on the bedroom door. "May I come in?" She pushed the door gently open. How should she do this? How do you tell a brand-new mother that her father is dead? Gracie had made some unkind comments about her father, but Helen knew that deep down she adored him. How was she to break the news?

"Grace? Why don't you let Jake take the baby for a minute? I have something I need to share with you," Helen said. Grace looked up at her with tear-stained eyes as she clung to her child.

"I know. Dad's dead. Jake told me." Helen was speechless. Her roles as wife and mother both seemed to have disappeared. She wasn't sure whether to feel resentful or relieved. She looked at the baby in Grace's arms and felt such pity for her, that she had elected to be born into a world that both favored you with blessings and forced despair at the same time.

"Beatrice Miranda Tanner," she said, "You have no idea what awaits you."

"She's not Beatrice Miranda anymore. I want to call her Frances Miranda. I want to call her Frankie."

"That's lovely," Helen smiled, wiping tears from her eyes.

"Mom, I know it's selfish, but I don't want to think about him right now. I'll do all that grieving later. Right now, I just want us to enjoy our little girl." Helen nodded her head agreement.

"Absolutely. Understood. You do that, Gracie. There will be plenty of time to mourn. I'm going to leave you three now," Helen said as she moved toward the door.

"Mom?" Grace called out. "Did she make it?"

"Yes, she did."

Chapter 45

Because of the holidays, the circumstances, and the weather, both Frank's memorial service and Frankie's christening were set for the same day. "Why not kill two birds with one stone?" Grace reasoned. "This way, people only have to make one trip." Helen concurred, the only position she was prepared to take at this time, riddled as she was with emotions.

As Helen stood in the receiving line, shaking hands with both friends and complete strangers, she marveled at the support Frank had amassed. To hear folks speak of him, he was charming, thoughtful, funny, and wise. *They can't all be bullshitting. It can't all be about trying to make his family feel better. Or could it?* Perhaps she had misjudged Frank. Perhaps she had not given him the opportunity to show his better side. She had always considered herself the better half of the marriage. What if she was wrong? The thought made her feel nauseous. She felt the heat rise in her face and that pre-vomit hollow fill her gut. The last thing anyone needed was for her to puke on the guests, so she quickly excused herself and made a dash for the ladies' room.

Helen stood in front of the large, gilt mirror dabbing cold compresses on her neck and chest. When Frank had been killed, she was shocked. Dismayed. But there was a part of her that felt that he deserved it for running off with Stephanie, for leaving her to fend on her own. She regretted that thought, as she had begun to regret many things about her marriage, most of which had to do with her behavior. But what was she to do about that now?

The door to the ladies' room opened and a woman about Helen's age walked in. She was tall, maybe six feet, and imposing in her red velvet bolero, white silk blouse, and black velvet pants. Helen did not know her, though she looked vaguely familiar.

"Helen?" the woman said. "Aren't you Helen Ferry?" Helen turned to face the stranger.

"I am. Do I know you?"

"Kerri. Kerri Tanner. I am Jake's mother," she said as she held out her hand. "I am so sorry for your loss."

Once again, Helen was assaulted with emotions. She was embarrassed, slightly, that she hadn't recognized this woman who was the spitting image of her son. Grace had shared pictures of Jake's family many times, but Helen did not connect. She had thought Kerri, a poet, would be wearing long robes and elephant pants, not a conservative outfit straight from J. Jill. Damn people for not sticking to their stereotypes! And her loss? Really, she had lost Frank so many years ago. Maybe it wasn't the loss of Frank but, rather, the loss of what she had hoped she could be with Frank.

"Helen? Is everything all right?"

"Yes. Yes. It's just all so much."

"I understand. If I can help…"

"Thank you. I'd better get back."

No sooner had Helen returned to the reception room than she saw another mourner whom she had hoped to avoid. Stephanie stood by Frank's casket, sobbing. Helen didn't know whether to be angry and instruct the staff to remove her from the room or to let the girl be. She did neither. Instead, she walked over to Stephanie and gently laid a hand on her shoulder. *This can't be me doing this. Surely, I am possessed.* Stephanie turned and faced Helen, grief on her face. It was then that Helen noticed that the girl was standing on crutches and that she wore a black cast with silver stars decorating it. Stephanie reached into her coat pocket. Helen wasn't sure what she was going to remove—a gun? a handkerchief? a pair of thongs? Stephanie placed the item on Frank's chest. It was a sand dollar, perfect and white, etched with the markings of a flower at its center. Helen was baffled.

"He loved these things. One day we found fifty on the beach. He said we would never be richer than that day. That's the day he told me he loved me."

The pain that Helen felt at that moment was unlike any she had ever known. Frank had never shared with her his love for the beach or for sand dollars. He had always cautioned her against sun poisoning with her fair skin. What else was there that she didn't know? Had she been married to a stranger for thirty years? Had she slaved away to give them a good life when all the while he had been out beachcombing with her?

"I know this is a difficult question," Stephanie continued, "but what are you going to do with the ashes? I'd like to take some, if I could, to spread at the beach and also to toss into the sky. Frank loved the stars. Even more than the beach. I'd like to send him home."

Helen had enough. She heard enough to know that she knew nothing. She didn't know Frank, not really. And she surely didn't know Stephanie except to say that the girl seemed genuinely to love Helen's ex-husband. It was all so confusing. She wanted to hate somebody, but she didn't know who to hate, and she surely didn't want to hate herself.

"Mom?" Grace's voice interrupted her thoughts. "Is everything okay? You really should be back in the line," Grace said as she gently guided her mother away.

"Do you think it was my fault?"

"What?"

"Everything."

"No, Mom, I don't think anything was your fault."

"Funny. It feels that way."

Chapter 46

hree days later, Helen sat on the sofa in front of the fire with Perdita snuggling up beside her and a glass of wine in her hand. It was the twenty-first of December. The kids had wrapped their three-day-old baby up and driven off to spend Christmas in Manhattan with Jake's parents. That was only fair since the kids had been with her on Thanksgiving. But that was before there were three, and before Frank had been killed, so now Helen pouted. She would be alone. Not that she would have spent time with Frank anyway. Nor Micah and Nicholas either, as they had flown off to St. Martin's. Abi and Mike had both gone back to their respective homes. Even Jack O'Toole had someone to be with for the holiday.

She looked over at the space she had made in the corner for a tree. No one would be there to enjoy it with her. She would let it stand bare this year, maybe just string a few lights and toss some pinecones at it. It wasn't the Christmas she had hoped for. She was better though, better than last year. Although she wasn't Sylvia yet, she was generally content with herself. Despite the conversation at the memorial service. She could hang garlands and drink spiced eggnog, all the while singing "falalalalas" as she slid through the holidays alone. If she chose to. Instead, Helen put on Joni Mitchell's Blue album. "I wish I had a river I could skate away on," she sang along, as she got up to get another glass of wine.

As she stood at the kitchen counter, the bottle poised to pour another drink, she thought, *Who am I kidding?* She poured the rest of the wine down the drain. Reaching for her phone to look up the number for the soup kitchen, she decided to volunteer on Christmas Day. She would find out when they needed her most and she would give back, just as she had been given to so often. Feeling much better, even slightly sanctimonious, she dubbed herself a saint for spending her holiday that way. She wouldn't tell anyone. This would be her secret, her way of thanking the universe for all she had been given this past year. Of course, no one answered the line, so she left a message, then put on a cheerier Christmas album of the Westminster Boys' Choir singing carols, laid a fresh log on the fire, and put Perdita on her lap, patting the little dog's curls. But then Perdita jumped down, barked at the door to go out, so Helen grabbed her coat, hat, gloves, and leash. Time for a walk in the snow.

Jack O'Toole had kindly cut a path down to the beach, so Helen didn't have to wade hip high in the white stuff, as he called it. The air was brisk, but not biting. Perdita bounced along, searching for new smells. When they arrived at the beach, the sand was wavy, a slight frosting of snow blowing across the gold. Helen walked down the beach as far as she could go until she touched the sound. Her cheeks were so cold they blazed, and the tips of her ears felt frozen. She wanted to feel this way, alive and cold and vibrant. It was something that would wipe away her earlier blues.

Still, she had to face it. She was alone, with her dog. Grace, Jake, and Frankie were a family now. Micah and Nicholas had each other. Abi and Mike were hitched. Sylvia was, well, Sylvia. That left Gerard, and who knew what he was up to. She hadn't seen him in days and assumed he was gone forever. Was it the cold wind blowing hard that made her tear up, or was it the recognition that even if she worked for the homeless from now until New Year's, she would still feel the same ache? *Live with it,* Helen told herself. *Do something nice for yourself, something no one else can do. You may be alone, but you're not a loser.* She threw a stick for Perdita to chase, wiped the tears from her eyes, and headed home.

As she walked through the door, already planning a dinner of artichokes with lemon-caper chicken, the phone rang. Assuming it was the homeless shelter, she pulled off her gloves and hat and picked up the cell. Much to her surprise, it was not the shelter. It was Gerard.

"Hello?" she said tentatively.

"Helen. Good. You're there. I was afraid I'd missed you." Gerard was breathless.

"Where are you?" Helen asked.

"In town. At your house. Your back door actually."

Helen looked over at the door. Sure enough, there was Gerard in his big coat, holding his phone to his ear. He gave a little wave. "May I come in?" he asked.

"Of course," Helen laughed and let him in the back door with its tinkling of bells. "So, what's going on? I thought you would have headed home by now."

"Yes. Well that's just it. I'm scheduled on a flight tomorrow evening…" Gerard began.

"It's sweet of you to come say good bye. I've really enjoyed meeting you. I'm just sorry…" Helen started.

"That's just it. It doesn't have to be over. You see, I bought you a Christmas present, a round trip ticket to Wales. To spend Christmas with me. You'd be back by the twenty-seventh. No strings attached. Please say yes. I'd love to share my home with you." Gerard stopped suddenly, totally spent.

Helen didn't know what to say. It seemed a little presumptuous and reckless to just go ahead and spend $1,000 dollars on a whim. But maybe it wasn't a whim. Maybe he had been thinking about it for a while. Maybe since Thanksgiving. He had seemed to have a good time. She certainly did. And face it, she had been thinking of him these past three weeks, looking for him in the hallways, waiting for a call. It's not like she had anything else to do this Christmas. There was Perdita, but she could call Jack. She'd never seen Wales, and Gerard was, after all, a friend. Right?

"Okay," Helen said simply.

"Okay, what?" Gerard said, still holding his breath.

"Okay, I'd love to go," Helen smiled. "Thank you. I think it will be lovely."

Chapter 47

*L*ovely was not the word for it. Magical, surprising, enlightening, exhausting. Fun. Those were the words that came to Helen's mind as she reflected on the eight days she had just spent with Gerard. First, there was the flight over. She generally traveled first class when she went overseas, but he had booked them both tickets in coach. Anticipating a tight and uncomfortable flight, she had expected the worst. But somehow Gerard had booked them on an almost empty flight, and with the pillows and blankets, she had stretched out three seats across and managed to get a good night's sleep. When she woke, Gerard was watching *The Holiday*, one of her favorite Christmas films. She imagined the little house he lived in was tight and cozy, just like Kate Winslet's cottage in the movie.

Nothing could be further from the truth. They arrived in Caerphilly (or "carefully" as she liked to think of this whole adventure) at mid-morning, just in time for elevenses. Caerphilly was not a small village. It was a bustling town with a plethora of shops and restaurants all decorated for

Christmas, and there was a giant castle. As for his house, Gerard took her to Court Street. The irony was not lost there. His was a surprisingly large stone home with a wrought-iron gate that kept unwanted company away. They paid the cabbie and hopped out onto a cobblestone drive bracketed by greenery that led to a majestic front door, not at all what Helen had anticipated. The interior was not what she expected either. She had labeled Gerard an antiques man with aging rugs on the floor and dust motes sailing through the air, the scent of pipe tobacco lingering everywhere. In reality, the place was ultra-modern, all white gleaming walls and shining oak floors. There were big leather sofas and chairs and a huge flat-screen TV in one of the two front rooms. The bookcases and side tables were all Danish and new. The other front room was a little cozier with softer fabric and gentler curves, but still, the house was all angles and light in the four bedrooms and the exceptionally modern bath. Helen was confused. When she stood in the huge kitchen, she wondered what Gerard did there. Did he even cook? Why have such a house if there was only one man living alone with no pets even?

"Come," he said. "I want to show you the best part." He took her hand and guided her out the back door of the kitchen onto a slate patio, then directed her gaze toward the backyard beyond. The lawn seemed to stretch forever to a wall at the rear that looked out over a spectacular view of the castle. On either side of the lawn, which would be perfect for Bocce or Croquet, Helen thought, were gardens. Dormant now, but in the spring and summer she could tell they would be glorious.

"I just couldn't let it go," he said quietly.

"If I were in your shoes, I wouldn't either," she agreed, but then realized she had in fact let go of the hundreds of hours she had put into making that little bit of Eden that her family had enjoyed in their own backyard. Now it was a pool. Stephanie had paved paradise and put up a parking lot.

"This used to be my parents' home," Gerard said. "But they died, as I think I've told you, in an automobile crash in 1994. I inherited the house and quite a bit of money, so I rehabbed it all with the intention of raising a family here. Of course, that never happened. I sometimes rent out rooms to students at the University. While I was gone, I just left it empty, which is what you see now. Not nearly as cozy as your little Cape, but it's all mine, and I live here free. And, as I said, I could never give up my gardens."

After a snack of tea and biscuits, they took a ride to Caerphilly Castle, a huge and impressive structure with thick, blackened walls and a section that leaned like the Tower of Pisa.

"Rumor has it, there's a female ghost somewhere here," Gerard teased her, as they walked through the cold and eerie halls.

"Good thing I don't believe in ghosts," Helen laughed, although secretly she felt a chill go down her spine. She was glad when they left.

The next day, they shopped for food and gifts, baked, took naps, and talked about going to church. Helen wanted to attend a Christmas Eve service so she could hear the music and smell the candles and surround herself with the beauty of the moment. Did that make her a hypocrite, attending church once a year? She thought not. Even if she didn't know how she felt about Jesus, she could thank God for putting Jesus on this Earth and providing that beacon of light to follow.

"We actually have an ancient custom here in Wales of attending church from 3 a.m. to 6 a.m. on Christmas Day. Would you like to give that a go?" Gerard smiled. Helen told him she would, knowing that she could sleep all day afterwards if she wished. But not so! On Christmas afternoon, while the turkey roasted in the oven and the sun shone, he took her to a forest, not too far from his home. They were going to take a nine-mile walk, but when Gerard checked, he saw the trail was closed. They settled instead for the three-mile Bluebell Path, which better suited Helen anyway since she still had vestiges of her old *plantar fasciitis.*

One mile in on the trail, they came upon a most beautiful structure, a free-standing arch with wings and filigree. It was a little piece of Heaven on Earth. The sign next to it said it was the Kissing Gate. Helen immediately suspected Gerard of foul play, as she supposed that he had known this gate would be there all along. Given the flutters in her stomach, she hoped that was so, because getting to know this man over the past few days, she had come to like him much more. She hoped that the feeling was mutual.

Helen stood frozen, waiting for something to happen, but nothing did. Gerard didn't turn her around and take her in his arms. He didn't plant a friendly kiss on her lips or even on her cheek. He just called out to her, "You ready?" Helen's heart sank and then rose again, as she told herself softly, "It's okay, Helen. You're okay."

Dinner that evening was delicious. Gerard was a good cook and a fine host, waiting on her and keeping her entertained with stories of his youth while she sipped wine and watched him prepare the mashed potatoes, gravy, stuffing, Brussels sprouts, and all. He had bought a plum pudding, which they doused with brandy, then lit, and ate in front of the fire along with some custard, and then he indulged in a Christmas tradition in his house. Just as his father had done year after year, he read Dylan Thomas's *A Child's Christmas in Wales*. Helen had heard it once, but never this way. In the half-light by the fire, with Christmas in her stomach and wine in her head, she heard Gerard's voice in a new way. Deep and sonorous, bringing each image to light and creating suspense when needed, Gerard made the world seem real. Helen laughed and dreamed and was caught up in every moment of the story, and she wished she was with Grace and Frankie. She wondered what tradition they might be starting without her.

"A penny for your thoughts?" Gerard asked, closing the book and laying it on the table next to him.

"Just thinking," Helen replied. "This has all been so nice. But I miss my granddaughter and my daughter," she confessed.

"I imagine you do," he said sweetly, coming over to her and laying his hands on her shoulders. "Is there anything I can do to help?" Helen placed her hands on his hands and looked him squarely in the eyes. They didn't say anything for a moment, and then Gerard leaned in and kissed her sweetly on the lips. It wasn't a passionate kiss that led to clothes being ripped off and naked bodies thrashing in bed. It wasn't a friendly kiss either that led nowhere. It was a kiss full of sweetness and sincerity, desire and respect. All Helen could think of was Chai tea and how much she loved it. Then Gerard pulled away.

"Oh, don't stop," Helen pleaded. Gerard took her into his arms and held her.

"I wanted to do that earlier," he confessed.

"Why didn't you?" she asked. "You could have."

Gerard was silent for a time, just holding her. "I'll take you someplace special tomorrow. We'll need to leave early, as it's quite a way from here."

"Where are we going?" Helen asked curiously. "Tintern Abbey?"

"You'll see," Gerard said, kissing the top of her head. "Good night."

The following day, they rose early and drove to Swansea to visit Dylan Thomas's house. The ride there, through the countryside and along the coast, would have been enough to satisfy Helen's appetite for sightseeing, but she was totally pleased when they arrived in Swansea and she could actually experience some of what Gerard had read to her the night before. Besides, she loved Dylan Thomas's poetry. "Do Not Go Gentle into that Good Night" was one of her absolute favorites, especially the "rage, rage against the dying of the light" line. She might not be on Death's door yet, but she wanted to live life to the fullest, while she had it, every, every minute. *So maybe*, Helen mused to herself, *I should move to Wales. I could get a job at the University. If not Cardiff, then London,. A man like Gerard only comes along once.* She then thought. *And I'm not getting any younger.*

They ordered fish and chips and wandered along the water, Gerard telling her that the next time she visited, they should ride horses on the beach. She smiled, sadly aware that she had a flight to catch the next day. What was the likelihood of her seeing Gerard again? A single tear fell onto her coat and then another and another.

"Did I say something wrong?" Gerard asked, clearly concerned.

"No, no," Helen brushed it off. "It's just me. I guess I'm overtired. We've had such a good time." Then she said quietly, "I really like you, Gerard."

"And I like you," he said, squeezing her hand.

Then it was over.

Chapter 48

*H*elen cried most of the way home on the plane as she tortured herself over lost opportunities and wasted time. *Is this what it feels like when someone dies,* she thought, and then she remembered that she had never grieved this way, not even when her mother died. She was too young then and didn't really grasp the enormity of that situation. And when her father died, at the time, she didn't care. Or so she told herself, totally denying that she had ever had any feelings for him and aching at his lack of feelings for her. And Frank, what about Frank? Lost to her the last eight years of their marriage and now, really lost. But she didn't care, she told herself again. She'd picked herself up, made a plan, and marched on, never really grieving the loss of a life she'd treasured even if it hadn't always been that good. She had told herself that she didn't care that these people had left her. Only she did care, and this realization made her howl with an anguish so loud the flight attendant came running and asked if there was something wrong.

"Wrong? What's wrong? I've spent my whole life building walls between me and the people I love. I know they'll just leave me, which they all have done, and I'll be alone. Which I am," she spluttered to the dazzled, but overly professional flight attendant, whose name was Cath and who spoke with a brogue. "Do you know what I mean?"

Cath nodded a little too violently and tucked a pillow behind Helen's head.

"I've kept myself so busy, I haven't had time to feel. Only now, I have time. And I have a man whom I love who makes me feel happy in a way I never have before," Helen cried.

"Well, that's really lovely," Cath remarked in her dulcet Irish voice. "So, everything's good then."

"Nooo," Helen wailed. "I pushed him away. I just left him, and I will probably never see him again. I should have slept with him when I had the chance."

"Let's lower our voices, shall we," Cath whispered, snuggling Helen's blanket around her.

"I'll never forgive myself. If only…"

"You know what they say," Cath smiled. "'If onlys are lonely.' And as for not forgiving yourself, I can tell you, if you don't forgive yourself, you'll never move on."

"But I don't want to move on. I love him," Helen cried.

"Move on, but not from him. From the thing that has been holding you back. From the thing that kept you from sleeping with him when you had the chance."

"How will that get him back?" asked Helen, taking the glass of wine that Cath now offered her.

"Maybe not him, but someone. Someone that you are willing to risk losing. You know, life often asks us to do very scary things. Loving ourselves enough to love someone else is one of them."

Helen took a drink from her cup and thought for a long moment. Then she looked up at the beautiful green-eyed flight attendant and asked, "Do you have a grandmother named Sylvia?"

Back home on New Year's Eve, Helen busied herself in the kitchen preparing shrimp scampi and Waldorf salad and baking cheese biscuits. Grace and Frankie were on the sofa in front of the fire, and the new mama was nursing her little baby. Jake was bringing in more firewood because it had started to snow again. It could be a long night. The plan was to eat and play Scattergories (although it would be weird with only three people) and watch old Jimmy Stewart movies until midnight, if they could make it that far, and then crash. Gracie looked over at her mother, who was very quiet as she prepared their meal of scampi and Waldorf salad.

"You never did really tell me, how was Wales?"

"Lovely. It's so beautiful over there. The countryside is glorious and the coastal route is spectacular. We went for a walk in a beautiful forest and ate fish and chips and drank buckets of tea and ate crumpets, and toured Dylan Thomas's house in Swansea," Helen expounded.

"I don't want the scenic tour, Mom," Grace sighed. "How was it with Gerard?"

"He's a very sweet man. I miss him, but it's probably just vacationitis." Helen said quietly, all the while tearing at the lettuce leaves with more force than was required. "No," Helen suddenly corrected herself. "I miss him. I really do."

"Are you sure? Are you sure it's not just wishful thinking or lust? It must have been beautiful over there. You were on vacation. Christmas. It must have seemed ideal." Gracie grilled her mom.

"What's the difference? He's there, and I'm here. No discussion. It's just, we had such a nice time. Oh well, at least I know I can be friends with a man without holding the thoughts of him hostage in my head. He helped me cry."

"What do you mean?" Grace asked, now suddenly alarmed. "Did he get physical with you?"

"Oh, no," Helen assured her. "Nothing like that. I was just able to open up in a way I never had before. Being with him let me take down my walls and have a good cry over my mom and my dad and even your father. I realized when I lost Gerard that I hurt so much because I had lost them before. He'll never know this of course, never know how much I care."

The room was quiet, the fire crackling, the baby snoring slightly as she slept. Suddenly, with a jangle of bells and an arm full of firewood, Jake tumbled through the door calling, "Hey, look what I found out here!" Helen looked up and in bounded Perdita, snow caked to her feet and shivering, whether with delight to see everyone again or the cold. It was hard to discern which.

"Oh, you little monster," Helen said, picking up the wet dog and immediately wrapping her feet in kitchen towels to melt the snow. "You were only out there for ten minutes." Perdita wriggled to get down, licking Helen's lips in the process, and then bounded off for the living room.

"Incoming," Helen called as Grace braced herself with the baby, and everyone laughed.

Dinner was delicious. They ate in front of the fire while the baby slept in her nursery and Perdita slept on the warm rug in front of the hearth. It was peaceful, so peaceful with the crackling wood and the gentle conversation, the sleepy parents and their contemplative host. They managed to get through three rounds of Scattergories and half of *It's a Wonderful Life* when Helen heard Grace snoring slightly. She looked over and Jake's head was dropping down and springing up again, as he attempted to be a polite guest. However, both had gone without much sleep for the past few weeks, and soon, no doubt, Frankie would be awake again and wanting to nurse. Helen nudged them gently toward the guest room, where they collapsed in a heap. Standing in the doorway and looking at the two, she was reminded of years gone by when Grace was just a baby and she and Frank had pulled together to handle the difficult nights. She said a quiet prayer that their marriage would be more successful than hers had been. She was certain it would, although, of course there were never any promises.

Because she was still a bit jet-lagged, her body thought that it was much farther along in the day, or night, than her clock told her. Consequently, she was not tired and could not sleep. It was 11:15 p.m. She could still watch the end of the movie, she reasoned, then she could pop a bottle of champagne, maybe drink it all, and go to bed. Why wait? Why not pop the bubbly now? She did. She sat in front of the dying fire watching the rest of *It's a Wonderful Life,* eating chocolate drizzled cheesecake and drinking champagne while she continuing to dissect her life and cry. She felt like one of those Hindu gods holding brass clappers in each of eight hands. She felt miserable, stupid, gluttonous, depressed, happy, nostalgic, hopeful, and serene all at once. Surely, she needed brain surgery, or at least several years of intense therapy.

But no amount of therapy would take away the awful feeling that she had of waste. She had wasted her life. She had wasted her time. And now she had wasted her love. As she sat on the sofa after the movie was done, looking into the quivering embers, she felt for a moment as if she were drowning. She thought that she had been doing so well, that she had come so far, as she gulped back new tears. Then she hiccupped. And she hiccupped again. Again and again and again. At first irritated, she started laughing. And hiccupping. She did the old trick of drinking out of a glass of water upside down, only this time it was champagne and the fizzles went into her nostrils, which made her laugh more. Suddenly life did not seem so grim. She gave herself a bit of room to be human and make mistakes. Not only that, she gave herself room to be adorable and to know that she was adored.

Her earlier self-pity melted away, and she found herself counting all the blessings in her life. Grace. Frankie. Jake, to start. Gerard, for opening her heart. Frank's loyalty for nineteen years as she pursued her career. Her career! New books and friends. Micah. Nicholas. Ron. Lou. Abi and Mike. Her house. Her dog. The firewood. Jack O'Toole. The snow. The sound and the moon on the sound, painting its creamy path. There was so much. And of course, Sylvia, who had really started this whole process and guided her along the way. All the regrets about parents and lovers suddenly left her. She was, in this moment, good with herself in a way she had never been before. Being so good, she was good with them all.

"Happy New Year!" she whispered. New Year's had arrived as she had hiccupped. Helen turned off the lights, checking in on Frankie one last time before she climbed the stairs to her bedroom. She took the stairs slowly, so as not to creak the floor and make too much noise, and she felt the cold wood of the banister very smooth under her hand. Then, as she reached the top step, she heard bells. Not her phone bells, but bells. It took her a minute to realize that they were the bells by the back door. Quickly, she went back down and to the door to stave off any further ringing lest it wake the sleeping child. She had no idea who it could be. Jack O'Toole? A neighbor? Kids playing a prank? She flipped on the light, but it was too dark outside to see. She opened the door, and in walked Gerard, this time, she hoped, for good. Perhaps, this time he'd stay forever.